MAYDAY

Grethe Bøe

MAYDAY

Translated from the Norwegian by
Charlotte Barslund

Copyright © Grethe Bøe 2024
Translation Copyright © Charlotte Barslund 2024

The right of Grethe Bøe to be identified as the
Author of the Work has been asserted by her in accordance with the
Copyright, Designs and Patents Act 1988

Charlotte Barslund asserts her right to be identified as the translator of the work

First published in Norway as *Mayday*
in 2021 by
Cappelen Damm

Published in Great Britain in 2024 by
Mountain Leopard Press
An imprint of HEADLINE PUBLISHING GROUP

1

Apart from any use permitted under UK copyright law, this publication may
only be reproduced, stored, or transmitted, in any form, or by any means,
with prior permission in writing of the publishers or, in the case of
reprographic production, in accordance with the terms of licences
issued by the Copyright Licensing Agency.

All characters in this publication are fictitious and any resemblance
to real persons, living or dead, is purely coincidental.

Cataloguing in Publication Data is available from the British Library

ISBN (TPB) 978-1-914495-34-2

Typeset in Sabon LT by CC Book Production

Printed and bound in Great Britain by Clays Ltd, Elcograf S.p.A.

This translation has been published with the financial support of NORLA.

Headline's policy is to use papers that are natural, renewable and recyclable
products and made from wood grown in well-managed forests and other
controlled sources. The logging and manufacturing processes are expected
to conform to the environmental regulations of the country of origin.

HEADLINE PUBLISHING GROUP
An Hachette UK Company
Carmelite House
50 Victoria Embankment
London EC4Y 0DZ

www.headline.co.uk
www.hachette.co.uk

In war, truth is the first casualty.

Aeschylus

Prologue

Over the wasteland of compacted ice the silence quivered. Sparkling snow crystals danced around the woman lying in the frozen expanse. She fought to remain conscious. When she was very young she would lie still on winter nights, and she lay like this now, listening intently. Can you really hear snowflakes fall?

She raised her hand with difficulty. The glass on her watch had been smashed and the hands had stopped at the moment when everything exploded. The compass, against all odds, had survived. She was going north, but she had to get home to Norway.

The cold cut her to the bone. All sensation in her fingers and toes was lost a long time ago and now she began to shake uncontrollably. Her face was frostbitten. At first it had itched like crazy, but now it felt numb, as if it was no longer hers.

Snowflakes melted on her eyelids, giving her some relief. The sleep she had been fighting for far too long gradually overpowered her. It was like a soft blanket and a mug of hot cocoa in front of the fire, it was like naked bodies, warmed by the sun, entwined on sun-drenched rocks. Saltwater in her hair, beads of sweat on her forehead, the smell of suntan lotion and the sea. Ylva smiled. Skin soaking up the sun, she could feel it now, the heat, it radiated from inside her and out, filling everywhere. Why not give in to it? Surrender to the luminous dream? She felt no pain.

Capitulate now and the nightmare would be over. She would be at peace. Her breathing slowed, the sense of warmth dissolved inside her, and she lay lifeless on the ice.

"Wake up!"

A sharp voice cut through the darkness. Ylva opened her eyes and stared across the frozen landscape. No-one was there.

"If you fall asleep now, you'll never wake up!"

It was her father's voice. But that was impossible, she had seen him die, he was dead, wasn't he?

Ylva looked about her. Nothing but white plains as far as the horizon.

She gritted her teeth and struggled to get up on her knees. A stabbing pain erupted in her eyes, and she wobbled as she felt the iron taste of blood in her mouth.

For pity's sake, she could take no more. Her eyes welled up and the landscape dissolved in blurred, blue watercolours. The tears burned the thin skin around her eyes. She ran a hand across her face and forced herself to keep her eyes open long enough to see the steaming blood be absorbed by tiny ice crystals on the ground. It looked pretty. She felt nauseous, the enticing emptiness beckoned her once more, it enveloped her, it was like drowning in an embrace.

Don't give up now, you have to get across the border, she told herself. With her last ounce of strength, she pulled herself upright. One step, two steps, the border was miles away, three steps . . .

Her body trembled and her legs buckled. She barely noticed the sharp cold against her cheek as her head hit the rough snow crust. She was losing the ability to register pain and she knew only too well what that meant. Pain was the most reliable sign of life, but Ylva could hardly feel anything. Dry needles of frost drifted over the plain, covering her with a fine icy blanket of rime.

In recurring glimpses she saw her father lying on the basement floor. He was reaching out to her, his arms like powerless tentacles. He struggled for breath in shallow, desperate gasps. She saw his lips move, but no sound came from them. The right corner of his mouth was contorted into a sickening grimace as he hoarsely whispered . . . something.

Ylva had never been able to work out what it was.

What were you trying to say, Dad?

Ylva looked across the glittering wasteland; it was like being inside the snow globe her father had given her that last Christmas. Now she was like a defenceless new-born baby inside the thin glass bubble just before someone shakes it.

Curled up in a foetal position and staring deliriously into the sky, Ylva became aware of a dark shadow. Gliding in ever lower circles and with its gaze fixed on her, she saw a huge golden eagle. The beauty of the bird was terrifying; its brown wings had pale flecks and its white tail a black stripe at the tip. Ylva smiled. Its wings cast a heavy shadow over her. She closed her eyes.

At that moment the eagle swooped and with its talons perforated her flight suit, her jumper and her skin. In one movement it sank its talons into Ylva's chest. She felt them scrape against her ribs and she threw herself onto her stomach. The eagle adjusted the angle of its wings to take off with its prey. She felt the air pressure from its wings, but she was too heavy for it. Even so the eagle did not relinquish its hold of her; it was hungry and needed to eat. With its wings extended into a two-metre-wide fan, it looked down at her. Ylva no longer had the strength to form her mouth into a scream, her face and lips were a frozen white mask. She looked up and met the eagle's amber stare.

Ylva had heard of eagles flying off with reindeer calves, and she had seen an eagle's curved, sharp beak tear lumps of meat from its writhing prey out on the plains. Now she felt its claws sink deeper into her. The eagle continued to watch her, she groaned in agony. Then it struck.

I

One week earlier

It was dead calm when Exercise Arctic Blizzard kicked off. Sixty thousand troops were N.A.T.O.'s biggest ever winter exercise and as it rolled across northernmost Norway the impact was enormous. Although the soldiers had been assigned to various bases in the region during the exercise itself, many had made the journey to Bodø to be present at the official opening, and the small town was buzzing with life.

The fighter pilots would be briefed at Bodø Main Air Station before the exercise exploded into life the next day, and Ylva Nordahl was due to report at 17:00 hours in the largest of the hangars. She was over the moon. She heard laughter echo between its concrete walls, old colleagues who were clearly delighted to see each other again. She paused at the entrance and looked at the thirty-seven pilots from the Euro-N.A.T.O. Joint Jet Pilot Training Program at Sheppard Air Force in Texas. It was weird to see the pilots in this very same hangar where she had played as a little girl. Saying that, being back in Bodø was weird, full stop. For the first time since getting her wings, she was once more where everything had started. Yet everything and nothing was as before.

The hangar seemed smaller now and time had taken its toll. Here Ylva's father and his fellow fighter pilots had discussed the world's constant upheavals while the television set on the wall flickered in the background. She knew that her father and his colleagues had watched the news on the day the Berlin Wall fell and Ylva was born, Thursday, November 9, 1989. It was a massive turning point for him and for the world.

Thereafter, leaders on either side of the Iron Curtain no longer had to shore up their legitimacy by uniting their people against a common enemy. Everyone was on the same side now. Democracy and the invisible hand of the free market seemed to be the true end of history . . . Until Russia invaded Ukraine. Luckily, Ylva's father never had to experience that. Witnessing another war break out in Europe would have broken his heart.

The hangar had been neglected since the end of the Cold War, she could see that, but despite the physical decay, the atmosphere, the smell and the sturdy grey walls were the same as when Ylva was growing up there.

The hangar fell silent the moment Major V. "Ajax" Armour came in. As the U.S.A.'s first black female fighter pilot, she set the bar high. Her lectures at Sheppard Air Force Base were always popular. She took her time and let everyone settle down.

"Welcome, pilots, welcome to Bodø and to Exercise Arctic Blizzard."

The pilots looked up at her.

"Many of you earned your wings at E.N.J.J.P.T. this fall, and you know one another well. But now you're out in the real world and after the Russian invasion of Ukraine we know that what we learn here might become vital sooner than we think."

The excitement and the gravity of the situation stirred among the pilots.

"Everyone will be allocated their own F.W.I.T.-approved instructor, and you'll all fly at least two sorties a day."

A surge of anticipation rippled through the hangar. Everyone was impatient to take to the skies.

At 17:43 hours Ylva headed back to the main building where she was meeting her instructor. She knew his name, everyone knew Major John "Stone Face" Evans, and to have him assigned as your mentor was every pilot's biggest dream and worst nightmare. He was one of N.A.T.O.'s legendary fighter pilots and he was revered. It was also common knowledge that he was a misanthropic bastard.

On her way across the apron, Ylva passed a collection of F-35 aircraft. Further away there were several F-16 planes, Eurofighters and A.W.A.C.S. She wanted to fly every single one of them and felt like a kid in a toy shop. But these were extremely expensive toys. The fifty-two new F-35 planes that Norway had bought from the U.S.A. had cost more than 70 billion Norwegian kroner – and that was but a drop in the ocean compared to the $1.6 trillion the world spent on defence every year. Ylva couldn't get her head around how much money that number represented. A calculation she had done, mostly for the fun of it, one summer night in Texas, showed that humanity could eradicate poverty and make inroads into many of the world's diseases for roughly the same amount of money as one year's defence expenditure.

He was waiting for her as Ylva entered the lobby. Her initial reaction was disappointment. The legend John Evans looked like any other middle-aged man. Short hair, maybe 1.85 metres tall, sinewy build, standard flight suit. She didn't know exactly what she had been expecting, but she was dismayed that he wasn't taller. Apart from his cold, ice-blue eyes, the only thing she noticed which might suggest the old man had something to offer after all, were his jaw muscles. They bulged like bones under the clean-shaven, tanned skin on his narrow, angular face. Close up, he resembled more than anything a reptile, a Komodo dragon.

Everyone called him Stone Face and she could see why. Her best hope was to get him to tolerate her. He greeted her curtly.

"I'm Major John Evans and I'll be your mentor during this exercise. We'll meet here tomorrow at 06:00 hours."

That was all. Enough talking.

Ylva watched his gaze closely. Was he one of those macho men who thought women diluted respect for the sacred brotherhood among the alpha males in the air force? Was that why he could barely be bothered to look at her as he reeled off his order? Impossible to say, he was impossible to read.

But so what? Ylva had no interest at all in Major Evans' inner life. The chance to fly with one of the U.S. Air Force's best fighter pilots outweighed his charm deficit. She wanted his knowledge; his respect she would have to earn. That much she knew. She was not her father's daughter for nothing.

2

Bodø Arts Centre was teeming with smartly dressed politicians, uniformed generals, highly paid representatives from the military-industrial complex, officers and civilian consultants. The media presence was relatively modest, but Ylva noticed that N.R.K., T.V.2 and a couple of heavyweight journalists had seated themselves close to the stage. Norway's Armani-clad Defence Minister, Margrethe Bøe, stepped onto the podium and, in her usual anecdotal style, announced N.A.T.O.'s rationale for this year's exercise.

"According to the doomsday clock, the time is less than one minute to midnight. Russia's war in Ukraine and their threats to use nuclear weapons have pushed the world closer to global catastrophe. We live in a time of unprecedented danger. We must stay vigilant. Escalation of the conflict – by accident, intention, or miscalculation – is a serious risk. We must be prepared."

Ylva had often heard politicians refer to the symbolic face of the doomsday clock when explaining security issues. The Bulletin of the Atomic Scientists had monitored humanity's self-destructive urge since 1947. Originally the research team had monitored only the risk of nuclear war, but as threats from climate change and discoveries within bioscience had escalated to a level where they risked eliminating all human life, the team had started to include these uniquely human activities for collective self-harm in its prognoses. And now, according to the Defence Minister, humanity was sixty seconds from Armageddon.

Ylva watched the audience. Everyone was bathed in the blue light from the stage as they listened in respectful silence. The Defence Minister's speech was information they already had, but it was good to have it reiterated. After all, this threat paid their bills. This threat paid Ylva's bills. The moment had arrived to introduce the enemy and define the mission.

"One third of the world's untapped oil and gas resources, as well as considerable quantities of valuable minerals, can be found in the Arctic seabed. These resources will become accessible as global warming melts the tundra and the sea ice. The global energy crisis following the invasion of Ukraine and the ensuing sanctions have proven beyond question that the world depends on safe and stable access to energy. In recent years Russia has invested several thousand billion dollars in military armament in the Arctic, and this year's N.A.T.O. exercise will give us valuable skills in managing our shared interests in the northern regions."

The Defence Minister paused, took a sip of water, then looked across her audience. They waited, like bright, silent children, for her to continue. She turned the page.

Ylva normally paid attention to the Defence Minister, but this speech was telling her nothing she did not already know.

She got up, left discreetly, and sat down in the foyer. It was the first time she had been inside Bodø's new prestige building. She took in the view of the port on one side and the mighty horizon where the sea met the mountains on the other and it made her sad. Leaving her hometown had been no accident, and her being stationed here now was not her choice either.

She looked through the window to where her gaze was met

by a ghostly figure, her own reflection. She looked away just as a shadow flitted across the windowpane.

"Ylva! Is that you?"

She recognised the voice immediately and turned. And there he was, the man whom Ylva's father had always thought of as his closest friend. He beamed a smile at her. The years had left their mark, but General George Rove was still the cheeky American officer who had let ten-year-old Ylva climb into the cockpit and pretend she was flying to Texas. His thick, short hair was grey and his face was lined, but the sonorous baritone possessed the same friendly authority. She sprang to her feet and saluted.

"Mr Rove, sir."

Was that the right way to greet him? As a girl she had called him Goggo, but using that name now when addressing General Rove was probably not appropriate. He nodded in approval.

"Fighter pilot in the Norwegian Air Force."

Ylva straightened up; she found it impossible to hide how proud she was and Rove smiled with warmth and a hint of melancholy.

"Geir would have been so proud."

Hearing her father's name still hurt all these years after his death. Rove studied her. He had the ability to devote his full attention to you.

"It has been almost twenty years."

Ylva nodded. "Yes, sir."

He smiled again and waved dismissively.

"George. Call me George."

It was more natural for Ylva to call him Goggo, sir, or General Rove. She had never known him as George.

"Are you still in the U.S. Air Force, sir?"

He smiled again.

"Well, after a brief spell pushing paper with the Carlisle Group, I missed being in the field. You know what it's like."

Ylva smiled, no-one who had been active in the field could settle for long into a desk job.

"I got out in time. I run my own security business now and I work as a strategic adviser to N.A.T.O."

If anyone could advise on security and military strategy, it was George Rove, this much Ylva knew. Seeing him again was painful and yet it was also a consolation, he reminded her of her father and his powerful presence. Chaos had trailed in the wake of his death. They had been like brothers, Rove and her father, and no-one had been prouder than Geir as his friend rose up through the ranks and made it to general, a three-star general at that. He had admired Rove, she knew, and she could see why. Rove was incredibly charismatic and possessed the ability to come across as jovial and authoritarian at the same time, a combination few people mastered.

Ylva and the highly decorated general looked at one another. Rove's gaze rested on her, it lingered as though he were looking for an answer, the way he had done when she last knew him.

"How is your mother?"

He would ask about her, wouldn't he? What should Ylva say? That she pretty much spent all her time on the sofa, popping pills and channel-hopping? That she was so lost in the pitch-black labyrinth of her mind, that she rarely left the house? That she, like Ylva herself, did not think that Ylva's father had died from a stroke, but that he had been murdered?

Ylva faked a carefree smile.

"She's fine."

Rove's gaze didn't flinch, he wanted to hear what she wasn't telling him.

"Mary's the kindest and most sensitive woman I ever met," he said.

He was right about that, Ylva thought, and that was precisely why her mother was condemned to a life as the prisoner of her own delicate mind. Ylva was doing her best to avoid turning into her mother because she did not want to share her miserable fate.

He noticed Ylva's reaction.

"She was pretty broken up after your father . . ."

Enough. She had had variations on this conversation with everyone who had known her father but who never showed up after his funeral. She knew they wanted to hear that her brave mother was grieving, but being a good woman and a loyal wife, she had pulled herself together eventually and got back on her feet.

Rallied for king and country.

"She's great."

Ylva smiled and kept her gaze steady. This was a talent of hers: she had learned from an early age to say what people wanted to hear and to control how she came across, right down to perspiration, breathing and heart rate. She could do what had to be done. After a brief and puzzled silence, followed by smiles and inscrutable glances, Rove rounded off:

"Good to see you, Ylva."

"Good to see you too, sir."

Ylva nodded and smiled. Smiled and nodded. As Rove left for the auditorium, she dropped her guard and let her heart beat as hard as it needed to.

Twenty years represented two thirds of her life, but suddenly it felt as if it were only yesterday that she had played with her father and Rove in the hangar at Bodø Air Station. Ylva followed Rove with her eyes as he met Major Evans and went into the auditorium with him. Two old U.S. Air Force heroes, supremely dedicated and ready to save the world yet again. But did the world want to be saved by them?

3

Ylva shivered as she made her way across the square. Out in Bodø Fjord white-crested waves swelled before collapsing into themselves. She wondered what her life would have been like if her father had still been alive. Who would she have been? She took after him and she wanted to be like him.

"Where are you going?"

Ylva stopped in her tracks. The voice came from the only person who could take her breath away. The rush and the butterflies in her stomach made her dizzy. Not even the dreary gloom of Bodø city centre could bring her down to earth. She turned and there he was, smiling, surrounded by whirling snowflakes that danced like sleepy moths below the streetlights. Storm knew that Ylva did not want to be seen with him in public, but he just stood there grinning as if it were all a game to him.

Storm behaved as if he had nothing to lose, and for all she knew, he didn't. After a single night between the sheets, she had accused him of having a disturbingly trusting nature, given that he worked for C.Y.F.O.R., the Norwegian Cyber Defence Force.

"Relax, I'm mega paranoid," he had reassured her.

He had used humour to duck the implied question. Storm always gave ambiguous answers, answers she could interpret in any way she liked.

Ylva continued across the square.

"I'm off to see my mum."

"I can give you a lift."

"You don't need to do that."

"No, I don't need to, but I want to."

She stopped and looked at him. He smiled gallantly at her.

"Your wish is my command, ma'am."

Would he have said that if Ylva's wishes had clashed with his own? She did not think so. As she marched on, she quipped:

"All work and no play makes Storm a dull boy." Storm ignored his dismissal blithely. "We need to play some more . . ."

Ylva stopped, turned and looked up at him again. He was the tallest man she knew. The anthropometric restrictions of the air force meant that no person taller than 1.93 metres could become a fighter pilot and consequently there were no men close to two metres tall where she worked. Then again, a man like Storm would never have fitted into the air force anyway. No fighter pilot would dream of turning up for work with three-day stubble and hair tumbling down his back. Nor would any fighter pilot play dumb to conceal an I.Q. at least as impressive as his body mass. He brushed aside a snowflake which had landed on her cheek before pulling her close. Ylva immediately picked up the clean scent and the heat from his body. He was so wonderful to be close to, and she hated it.

"O.K., I'll drive you to your mum's, then you can come back and play with me afterwards."

The heat from his hand radiated against the small of Ylva's back and released an intense tingling in the pit of her stomach. You could say many things about Storm Bure, but you would never think of him as a dull boy.

4

The mess, the darkness and the smell of decay told her all she needed to know: her mother was having another one of her bad spells. Ylva took a deep breath and entered the hallway.

Don't start overthinking it now. She wouldn't have the strength to go inside and be the daughter she wanted to be. But the stench and the appearance of the hallway assailed her, the memories impossible to ignore.

Ylva glanced at the stairs. She kept her guard up as she took in the house; she could hear noises from the living room while the silence from the first floor drifted down and coiled itself around her. Echoes of the noises that had woken her twenty years ago lingered between the walls.

She had been asleep with *The Brothers Lionheart* on her chest, when voices snatched her from her dreams. She had sat up in bed and listened, her heart pounding; was someone outside? She peered from the window; the silence was made deeper by the snow, which let itself be whirled up below the streetlights by the gusts of wind. The clock on her bedside table showed 0330.

Still sleepy, she was about to crawl back under the warm duvet, when she heard the faint sounds once more. They were coming from the basement. She held her breath and pricked up her ears. The noise grew more distinct now, someone was whispering. Then she heard an ominous rustling, the sound of someone who should not be there, someone who did not want to be heard.

She crept into the passage. The door to her parents' room was ajar. From their bedroom she could hear her mother's heavy breathing and, in the strip of light from the passage, she could see all the pill jars on the bedside table, a menagerie of lifeless silhouettes. Her mother was deep into a dreamless sleep, but her father was not in bed. Where was he?

The little girl's bare feet slapped against the cold linoleum as she made her way as quietly as she could down the stairs. The door to the basement was open, the light had not been turned on, but she could hear the whispering more clearly now. Ylva edged closer. She felt a raw gust of wind burst up from the darkness. Her father groaned heavily. Then there was silence.

Ylva scarcely had time to hide behind the door when a figure ran up the basement stairs. A draught lifted the kitchen curtains as the door to the street was opened and the figure slipped into the night and disappeared. All at once the silence changed, it became icy and unpredictable. As if the old wooden house was holding its breath.

The silence from the basement sent shivers down her spine. Bare feet. Blue pyjamas with planets printed on them. She crept down the stairs. There, in the yellow light falling through the basement window, she saw him. He was lying on the floor with his eyes wide open, but staring blindly into the air. His breath came in hard gasps and spasms contorted his body. Terrified, Ylva tiptoed closer and looked down at her father. He seemed like a stranger, like a sick animal. He whispered something and she bent down, leaning her ear near to his mouth.

His breath wafted warmly against her cheek, but only a

guttural rattle escaped from his throat. She started to feel the cold and the hairs at the back of her neck stood up. She wanted to run, but her father's hand grabbed her slim arm, his lips moved, but no sound came out. Ylva wriggled free and retreated, too horrified to scream. He reached up to her, his lips continued to form mute words. What was he trying to tell her? Colonel Geir Nordahl looked at his daughter. The wild little girl stared back at him, terrified, her eyes filling with tears and confusion.

The spasms of her father's body subsided as a pool of urine spread around his groin and death seeped into his muscles.

The police and paramedics arrived. Her father was lifted onto a stretcher and carried away while her mother sobbed hysterically.

Ylva shuddered. Then she took a deep breath, shook off the harrowing memories and went into the living room.

The T.V. was spouting vacuous infotainment with logos as gaudy as the jingles were tacky. Her mother was fast asleep on the sofa. In her midnight-blue silk kimono and with her long, grey hair loose, she looked like an ageing version of Persephone. An aesthetic illiterate like Ylva would not have known who Persephone was had it not been for the woman on the sofa, who had dragged her daughter to every art exhibition she could find throughout Ylva's childhood. Ylva hated the story of Hades, the god of the underworld, who had fallen in love with the beautiful Persephone. What a cliché – rather than ask the lady politely for her hand and give her a real choice, Hades had kidnapped the beautiful young woman and forced her to be his wife. Whether Hades lived happily ever after with the traumatised and browbeaten woman, who would recoil in loathing every time he came near her, Ylva did not know because she rarely listened to her mother's wearisome stories for long.

She had never been able to understand her mother and was frustrated that she had refused either to embrace life as a pilot's wife or to carve out her own identity independent of the life that came with her husband's job. Instead her mother had suppressed her true self – mostly with pills – and lived a passive existence in constant limbo between other people's expectations and her own nature. It was the worst of all outcomes, Ylva thought. Her mother had been reduced to living like Persephone trapped in the underworld.

The army bases around the world where Ylva had grown up were strangely similar. No matter where on the planet the family was sent, it was as if they lived in the same place. Issues such as war, peace and business were decided in the world of men, while the women were relegated to a role as decorative, inconsequential enablers.

Every morning Ylva had watched her mother as she dressed in the plainest clothes she could find before she put her hair up in a tight bun and went out into the world. She had had to suppress herself, hide her true nature and make herself look unattractive in order not to trigger the jealousy of other women, provoke the condemnation of the mediocre or attract the embarrassing desires of men.

In her misery, however, her mother had taught her daughter many valuable lessons. One was that she must be able to support herself. Her mother had always been financially dependent on Ylva's father, and as a result was completely at his mercy. She never had the courage to break free and do her own thing.

Now Ylva was standing in the doorway, watching her mother snoring heavily. The kimono was stained, the silk creased and dull. The light from the T.V. flickered and cast gaudy flashes across the room. Sergei Lavrov, the Russian Foreign Minister, was condemning the N.A.T.O. exercise, saying it was once more clear provocation. Norway's Defence Minister assured the reporters that the exercise had long been announced and was in accordance with established conventions.

Ylva had heard enough and went to the kitchen. In the fridge were all the Fjordland ready meals she had bought five days ago, still on the shelves where Ylva had left them. In front of each one, she had attached a Post-it saying Monday, Tuesday, Wednesday, etc.

Beside her mother, on the table, were several jars of pills.

Ylva shook her gently.

"Mum . . ."

Ylva shook her again, a little harder.

"Mum!"

The news programme got on Ylva's nerves and she hunted for the remote among books, clothes and scraps of food on the sofa. Then her mother woke up. There was a startled jingling of bracelets as she sat up, alarmed, and stared at Ylva as if she were a total stranger.

Ylva retrieved the remote from under her mother and turned off the T.V.

"Hi, Mum."

Ylva's mother seemed confused, almost scared.

"I'm just here to pick up a few things."

Her mother nodded, saying nothing, then she picked up the remote and turned the T.V. back on; the room was filled again with blue light and murmuring voices.

She sat like a scrawny, frazzled baby bird, staring apathetically into the blue light. Ylva went to the kitchen and heated a meal in the microwave. But Mary pushed the tray away.

"You need to eat, Mum."

Her mother nodded mutely, but continued to stare as if hypnotised into the television's flickering screen. Ylva let out a sigh of exasperation and looked around at the mess, the books, and all the filth. Her mother had turned the living room into a mirror of her inner chaos, and Ylva was overcome by irritation – no, by revulsion.

"Mum, I'll be away for a while on this exercise, but when I'm back, I promise I'll tidy up in here. O.K.?"

Her mother did not seem to hear. Ylva looked sadly at her mother's medication. How much psycho-pharma could an unhappy woman take?

Unlimited amounts, it seemed.

"Do you need anything?"

No reply.

Ylva left.

5

Evans shivered in the cold. Why anyone bothered living this far north was beyond him. The freezing temperatures made the chronic pain in his back pulse through him and though he had grown used to its latent murmuring, everything worsened with the cold. He knew that the exercise had been arranged in the much-hated dark season of the Arctic winter precisely because the soldiers needed to learn how to handle the almost constant night and the bone-numbing cold. He wondered whether snow-storms and permanent darkness were worse than the heat and the blood-red Ghibli winds of the Libyan deserts.

Meeting his new protégée, the ambitious Lieutenant Nordahl, had made him realise how exhausted he was. These damned youngsters were bursting with energy and confidence. What made a beautiful young woman like this Nordahl pick a life as a fighter pilot? It beggared belief. She could be protected and carried through life by men who would happily die for her. Men like him. Why the hell were men fighting if women believed they could fight better than the strongest, bravest and most disciplined men?

The military as an organisation wasn't made for women. It was made to turn aggressive alpha males, the planet's most blood-thirsty killing machines, into single-minded warriors serving the common good. Evans respected women, that wasn't the problem.

He loved women. As mothers, lovers, as friends and as the antidote to male aggression. If women really wanted to save the world, he thought, they should try to be a proper counterbalance to men's brutality. Women ought to cultivate their femininity . . .

He stayed where he was and squinted at the outline of Steigtind, the mountain northeast of the runway. The Northern Lights raced across the sky. A piece of eternity was lit up and, for a fraction of a second, it was all he could sense.

"Thanks for taking the time to meet me, John."

General Rove had approached noiselessly from behind him. He was on time as always.

Rove was one of the people who had fought hardest to get the U.S. Air Force and N.A.T.O. to take responsibility for rescuing Evans from Libya when he had been held hostage there. Although they had never met before now, Evans knew that Rove had risked everything to save him. He had read the report and knew of Rove's unswerving loyalty, one for all and all for one. Where politicians and bureaucrats had washed their hands, Rove had shown strength.

"How are you finding life mentoring new pilots?"

Evans made no reply, but continued to gaze at the Northern Lights dancing across the mountains.

"It's an important job, Evans."

General Rove knew that Evans had worked hard to keep his job in the air force after Libya. The role of mentoring new pilots was a clumsy attempt to cover up the fact that the great hero was damaged goods.

"Congratulations on the Distinguished Flying Cross. It was Libya, wasn't it?"

Evans' rusty voice was low and hard.

"Afghanistan."

"Of course. Well deserved."

Evans said nothing, he was pondering the darkness.

Astronomical darkness can only be truly experienced far away from human light pollution. He had longed for the liberating absence of light and had hoped to find it up here in the north. The dreaded dark season had proved to be anything but. For a few hours around noon, the sun, which hung just below the horizon, radiated a picturesque, almost magical winter light. He had heard colleagues talk about the Arctic light, but he could never have imagined the impact of the soft pastels which enveloped the landscape during these exquisite hours. It never grew fully bright during the day, but it was not wholly dark, either. Nor had he been able to imagine the effect of the mesmerising Northern Lights which lit up the night. He had seen them before, of course he had, everyone had, but never like this.

Rove glanced sideways at him.

"Evans, I know what happened . . . with your family. It's tough. I'm sorry."

Soon there would be no darkness left on earth, Evans thought. How far north would a man have to travel to find a place where humanity's artificial light did not pollute the night?

Where could the darkness truly defend itself against the light?

"Far too many of us have been through it. Civilians don't get it. It's hard."

General Rove inhaled, then leaned towards Evans in confidence.

"I know."

Evans looked at Rove without expression.

"You do?"

Rove nodded glumly.

"Unfortunately, yes. I handled it badly myself. When I was in combat, civilian life was all I ever dreamed about. A good job, decent pay, family time. It was everything I longed for. A predictable life among peaceful civilians, time for friends and hobbies." Rove flashed a wry smile. "I hated it."

Evans nodded in silent recognition.

"Honour and fine office jobs can never compensate for the loss of fraternity, for everything you have sacrificed."

Evans took a deep breath, his back hurt and he shifted restlessly.

"*We* know what you have sacrificed," Rove said.

The last thin tongues of Northern Lights darted across the Steigenfjellene mountain range, flickering like flames, like spirits, before they dissolved and disappeared.

"I was only doing my job."

Evans' voice sounded hollow and flat.

"You are one of our bravest, and your country should thank you for your service with so much more than medals."

Evans looked at the general with scepticism. What did he want? Why was he standing here in the icy winter night saying everything Evans had longed to hear?

And why had Rove asked Evans to meet him out here in the cold?

Rove followed his gaze towards the night sky left black by the Northern Lights.

"The Arctic is the new Middle East."

Evans glanced briefly at the general, but Rove had spoken without drama, as if he were simply stating a fact.

"If the Arctic is the new Middle East, I guess people like you will become very important," Evans grunted. "And rich."

Rove smiled. "Not if, but when. Trust me, this is where the big boys will be making their money in the future."

Evans looked at Rove without expression; he distrusted every three-star general who left the military fraternity for civilian top jobs. Civilians in general and big business ones in particular were opportunistic rats. That was just how it was.

Rove seemed to read Evans' mind because he smiled thoughtfully.

"We protect people and they reward us for it."

Evans gave a bitter laugh. "You're mercenaries, nothing more."

Rove tightened his coat around him. Evans could see that the proud general was freezing cold.

"Yes, you're right about that, but security firms like ours are hired to protect aid organisations, ambassadors and businesspeople where the military can't or daren't go in."

Evans knew the spiel. "Or where the army doesn't want to get involved for political reasons?"

Rove nodded.

"That's right. We protect civilians in lawless areas where no army dares or wants to get close." The general paused, then he laughed disarmingly and threw up his hands. "And we make an awful lot of money in the process, I have to admit it."

Evans could not help but smile. "Good pitch."

"We protect our clients. That's all."

"For money."

Rove responded with a friendly smile.

"Do you work for free, Major Evans?"

Evans' financial problems were well known and like most people, he also had bills to pay.

"Security is a mathematical equation based on the threat assessment versus the effect of various countermeasures. But safety, now that's a whole other ball game."

Evans looked quizzically at Rove.

"Go on?"

"Safety is a feeling. People's sense of being safe isn't based on probability and mathematical calculations, but on psychological belief. Giving people real security costs money, it takes commitment over time, specialist training, flexibility, equipment, as well as skills and vision. But politicians can't sell security to the voting public, they have neither the budgets nor the timeframe for it, so instead they sell safety. The feeling of being safe. People want feelings, not facts."

Evans took a deep breath in, the cold air stung his chest.

"People are far more scared of terrorism than of wasps, although many more are killed by wasps each year than by terrorists."

Evans smiled. Rove was an excellent salesman.

"Politicians sell people the feeling of being safe, while we grow rich selling security to politicians because the politicians aren't stupid."

Evans was aware that Rove knew better than anyone what he was talking about. After all, the man was a war hero who, after spending time as a top brass in Washington, had founded America's biggest security company. And now Rove had his eye on the north.

6

Ylva lay awake listening to Storm's rhythmic breathing. She preferred to sleep alone, it was more relaxing and more comfortable. She always slept alone, no matter who she was dating. She stared out into the room where the palest moonlight seeped through the big northeast-facing window. Apart from that, everything was black.

It was almost a month since their first night, and it really should have been just the one. Except that was not how it had turned out. When he lay like that, vulnerable and turned in on himself, she could sense the heat and the strength he exuded. She could feel his naked body wrapped around hers. She was cold. He was warm. They had reached a dangerous point.

With a smile Storm had accepted Ylva's refusal to stay over at his place, that under no circumstances would she want to wake up the next morning by his side and for them to have breakfast together. She did not want to make plans for the day, the week, the month, or a life together. She did not seek security, she did not need validation. On the contrary, she wanted to be independent, free. He said it was exactly what he liked best about her.

She reckoned it must have been the same qualities that had attracted her to Storm in the first place; he, too, seemed sufficiently independent and blessedly free of complications.

Ylva had zoomed in on him one Saturday night at 02:17 at

Nordlændingen pub in Bodø. He towered a head above the rest of the establishment's rather scruffy-looking clientele.

Storm's beard and his black T-shirt with a grinning skull stretched across his broad chest and the caption MC MANIAC in red and white capitals, had been the first indication. His raw muscles and the *Don't let your tongue get your teeth knocked out!* warning on the back of the T-shirt had convinced her. He had to be a member of Hells Angels or an equivalent pseudo-masculine biker gang. If she hadn't been so drunk, she would have noticed that his beard was carefully trimmed, the deodorant an expensive brand, and his big hands were neatly groomed and soft. But Ylva was fairly hammered and seeking a thrill which the two-metres-tall biker looked up to providing.

When Ylva had left Bodø four years earlier, she had nothing to lose and everything to prove. Returning to the dull backwater that now was Bodø as a fighter pilot about to take part in N.A.T.O.'s biggest ever winter exercise was her sweet revenge over the town that had killed her father and broken her mother. Ylva had been so eager and impatient to start the exercise that she needed an outlet for her excess energy. The guy standing with his legs apart, swaying and singing along to Metallica with his eyes closed, had seemed like a perfectly acceptable distraction before the adventure began.

Undeterred, Ylva had walked up and positioned herself right next to him; he had glanced down at her with a knowing smile. With a nod to his T-shirt, she shouted through the music:

"What club are you in?"

"Mensa," he shouted back.

She hadn't seen that coming.

He had bent down and asked Ylva what her name was, the

music was pounding so loudly that she had to lean even closer to him in order for him to hear.

"Ylva," she shouted.

He nodded and pointed to himself.

"Storm."

Ylva looked at him, he was still standing with his face leaning close to hers, and so she had to ask:

"Is that your name or a warning?"

His grin was inscrutable.

"That's up to you!"

Bring it on, Ylva thought, and there they stood while the deafening music tormented their eardrums. It was impossible to carry on with the conversation – not that there was much more to say.

Finally she cut through the noise:

"O.K., Storm, let's get out of here."

Three weeks and four nights later she could find her way to Storm's apartment with her eyes closed. And now she intended to make her way back to the barracks in order to get some sleep. Carefully she lifted his arm off her and slid out of his embrace. He let out a sharp intake of breath and Ylva stopped moving, scared of waking him. His profile was finely outlined against the light outside the window, his forehead was smooth and his mouth soft. Without the quick repartees, his laughter and the crazy hair, he seemed gentle, almost harmless.

His gaze, which always fixed her in the present, was closed. The warmth of his body and the rising and lowering of his chest with each breath almost persuaded her to go back to sleep.

Time stopped at night for Ylva, it was almost like falling, a sinking through black clouds and finding herself trapped in a void. She tended to focus on the one thing that lifted her back up: the feeling of sitting alone in the cockpit, hurtling down the runway as she engaged the afterburner and was airborne in a roar. High in the sky no-one could touch her.

Ylva sat up in bed and peered into the room, looking for her knickers which had ended up somewhere among their clothes on the floor.

"Don't you ever sleep?" His voice was smiling even when he was drowsy.

"I sleep better alone."

Ylva slipped quickly out of bed. Storm wiggled lazily to the side of the bed and began trailing his fingers over the snarling wolf tattooed on her neck.

"I thought wolves were pack animals."

Ylva rummaged among their clothes, his fingers stroked her softly.

"I'm a lone wolf!" she declared.

She fumbled her way through the parts of a computer he must have taken apart and a dozen books scattered around the bed.

"Lone wolves are the most vulnerable," he said.

She sensed his wry smile. He had a habit of pushing metaphors too far.

"And the most dangerous," Ylva retorted. His mess irritated her. "I thought you cyber defence lot needed a sense of order."

He bent forward, kissed the wolf on Ylva's neck and a strong desire sparked deep inside her. Damn. He knew that she would react like this. Storm whispered:

"Nope, we're fans of chaos theory."

His beard tickled her as he shimmied down and let his tongue play along the Gothic letters written where her knicker elastic would have been. *Marcet sine adversario virtus.* Ylva had it tattooed into her skin in order never to forget: Valour becomes feeble without an opponent. Seneca was there to remind her never to be afraid or avoid challenges, but to face and master them. Ylva also interpreted the quote as meaning that passion fades without challenge, hence its piquant location.

She located her bra.

"I like order," she snarled. "Chaos is overrated."

All that remained now was tracking down eight centimetres square of black lace, thrown somewhere on a twenty-five square metres floor.

"Chaos is only one of several possible systems, Ylva."

He ran the tips of his fingers down her spine, up along her side and around her breasts; she leaned towards him instinctively. He caressed her skilfully and her skin responded treacherously to his fingertips.

"For every action, there is an equal and opposite reaction," he whispered into her ear. Ylva moaned, his breath was hot.

He was aware of her reaction, he loved that he could so easily turn her on; she was impossible to tame, but easy to arouse.

"Chaos is attractive precisely because it's so extremely sensitive to context," he smiled. Ylva gasped as he brushed his fingers across her stomach.

"If you control the catalyst, you control the course of action, if you control the course of action, you control the chaos, and if you control the chaos, the world is yours."

Ylva trembled and sighed, she wanted him so badly. The light outside was inky black and cold, while in here it was warm. No-one was waiting for her.

Storm represented risk, vulnerability, and she had to get him out of her life. But it was too late to get up and go home now, wasn't it?

She slipped softly back under the duvet, back to his sensuous skin, his powerful body and the fervent, anarchic desire he aroused in her. She buried her fingers in his messy hair and ran her nails down his spine. He smiled and Ylva pulled him close, one last time.

7

Murmansk isn't just the biggest city in the Arctic, it's a state of mind shared by three hundred and twenty thousand long-suffering fatalists and hardened survivors who resign themselves to four months of punishing cold and total darkness every winter. The town's *raison d'être* is the grey, bleak and forever clanging port which, thanks to the Gulf Stream, stays ice-free even when hell freezes over, as it so often does. The enormous port area is the elbow in the fjord off the Barents Sea. Sixteen million tonnes of cargo pass through it every year, supplying roubles, dollars, arms and drugs to people who have few scruples.

Igor Serkin ran through the gloomy industrial town. Moist air and icy winds from the sea made sure that the biting −12°C felt particularly bone-chilling this morning. He passed humourless Soviet architecture and *nouveau riche* shopping malls thrown together in a vulgar, dystopian swamp, the reason Igor loved this town. The rusty steel structures, the crumbling concrete apartment blocks, the noise from the port and its shady gangsters gave Murmansk a charm as contagious as gonorrhoea.

"How can you tell if people from Prichaly lie?"

Igor remembered how his grandfather's steel-blue eyes would sparkle with merriment whenever he asked him the question.

"They open their mouth."

The joke set off his grandfather's hoarse, hawking laughter every time, and Igor had to smile although he had heard the joke a hundred times. His grandfather was a sailor who had come to love the hardiness and brutality that characterised young adventurers who earned their sea legs in the Barents Sea, and he had wanted to pass these qualities on to Igor, his only grandchild.

The time was 06:35 and Igor ran on as if in a trance. Pah ... pah ... pah ... Nikita Legostev's "Futurama" pounded in his headset. Running to the beat of Russia's Eminem, Igor passed warmly dressed but hunched early risers making their way to work as if walking to the gallows. His run also took him past Murmansk's fastest-growing demographic; the homeless who every hour of the day would stand like pillars of salt around the city's central station, waiting. And waiting. And waiting.

Pah ... pah ... pah ...

Igor ran up Vorovsky Street where he passed two men aiming a blowtorch at a frozen lock. The night had been cold, just as the day would be.

Igor kept up a good pace. He turned left into Chelyuskintsev Ulitsa, passed the memorial to military honour and continued past the church of the Saviour on the Waters. Then came the steep section where he veered off the road and headed up the open terrain. Igor maintained a steady pace through the snow on the stretch towards the Aloysha statue, all of thirty-five metres tall. A grandiose monument in armoured concrete to commemorate the patriotic sacrifice of the unknown soldier during the Second World War. The remains of the soldier were said to be buried under the eternal flame, which with heavy symbolism was placed right in front of the statue. Igor always stopped there to enjoy the vision of the city huddling below him. His pulse throbbed in his temple and his breath rose like a column of steam. He turned off the music to enjoy the sounds of the city that never sleeps.

The stone face of the Aloysha statue was turned west towards the Valley of Honour, bearing silent witness to the day when the German bastards had suffered the full force of Russian steel. A freezing cold winter's day in 1942. Igor felt as if he had been there himself and experienced every minute of the battle. His grandfather had told him countless stories from the Arctic war; especially the fatal bloodbath, which had sealed the Germans' fate, he would describe in graphic detail.

Igor's great-grandmother had sent four sons off to fight. She had watched, crying and praying, as her children, her great happiness and love in life, walked down the road, ready to do their duty. Four Russian brothers had gone to war that winter and only one came home.

Mankind's utter madness, the willingness to sacrifice, to perpetuate evil, all flourished during the battles against the Nazis in the Second World War, but it was the Siberian cold, darkness and winter which ultimately brought about Ragnarok. Of the more than three million German soldiers marching into the Soviet Union on June 22, 1941, sixty-seven thousand were sent north to take Murmansk. Few returned.

The Nazis had factored in considerable Russian resistance, but not the diabolical effect which months of darkness and weeks of non-stop howling snowstorms and severe cold would have on their own soldiers. Their supply lines faltered, communication lines failed, and neither their uniforms nor their equipment were designed to help the German soldiers combat the Arctic elements. Across the border in Norway, the Germans had succeeded in their invasion and more than sixty thousand Russians were interned in labour camps in Finnmark. The plan was for the German soldiers in Russia to take Murmansk and together with the German front in Finnmark to consolidate Germany's power in the north. It was a good plan. On paper.

Serkin's grandfather and his brothers had volunteered to join the Polar Army. The Russian leaders' strategy was a tried and tested one: first they waited for the winter cold, food shortages, boredom and homesickness to break the spirit of the young, ill-prepared German soldiers; then when the winter storms were at their fiercest, the Russians would attack the German quarters with merciless force. The German generals were unprepared and panicked. They ordered every man to brave the snowstorm and fight.

His grandfather remembered everything as a white nightmare. No-one could see a hand in front of them or hear anyone's voices. Soon they had no idea who was fighting who, and even on the first day of the battle many men froze to death on either side of the battle line.

Their baby brother, Aleksey, was ordered to defend the supply lines. Because he was the youngest and rather delicate, the brothers believed he was better off staying where the fighting would reach last. It was the safest place. It wasn't until several days after the battle that they found him and two German soldiers frozen to death. The young men had huddled together in order to keep warm. They lay clinging to one another like puppies – in a desperate attempt to survive the snowstorm.

In the frontline the three older brothers were fighting shoulder to shoulder, bullets screamed past them and detonating shells dyed the inferno coal black and orange. Shattering explosions, the chatter of machineguns and the howling winter gale mingled with the sound of men fighting and dying. Snow and ice penetrated every gap, it slipped up their sleeves, down their necks and into their boots. The cold stung and robbed everyone of their strength. The fighting men were dazed and confused. Who was friend? Who was foe? Where were the bullets coming from? How long had they been fighting?

All senses were numbed, you killed anyone you saw. His grandfather had confided in Igor that he had felt pain sear through his own body the moment his twin brother was killed, more than a hundred metres behind in the ranks. Panicking, he had run back to save his brother, knowing full well that he risked getting shot by one of his own or disgraced as a deserter. But in the midst of the chaos, none of that mattered. Suddenly he saw half his brother's face stare at him with one terrified eye and a yawning mouth, the other half shot off.

A viscous stream of blood and brain matter flowed from the split skull, while the surviving eye stared at him in lifeless terror. Every time his grandfather told him about the agonising choice between continuing to fight or running to his dead twin brother, the tears would come. And the rage. The strong man would fall silent, words were inadequate, but his fist was clenched so hard that his knuckles went white. His older brother had later died from septicaemia after a shell splinter pierced his left eye and lodged there.

After three days of atrocious weather and chaotic fighting, more than eight thousand Russian soldiers lay dead on the battlefield. Many more Germans died, but no-one took the trouble to count them. Only fatherless children, yearning lovers and heart-broken mothers knew the true toll of the German defeat.

The battle of the Arctic was over for now.

* * *

Igor could not stop for long, the high point of his daily run was yet to come. He ran down the hill to Semyonovskoye, the lake where he and other swimmers had sawn a hole measuring five by fifteen metres in the thick ice. When he reached the lake, Igor dumped the bag with his towel on the ground and pulled off his running clothes. The cold wind lashed Igor's naked skin before he took a deep breath and dived into the icy water.

As he broke through the surface and disappeared into the black void, the cold gripped him instantly and his brain exploded in pain. Every instinct told him to get out of the water, but Igor swam on. As his head broke the surface again, he breathed in through his nose with forced calm and then out through his mouth. If he panicked now, his body would seize up and he would drown. Igor did not panic. His face was soon numbed by the cold, it felt as though needles were piercing his every pore. Eventually his adrenaline kicked in, and Igor found the strength to execute another swimming stroke.

He swam four lengths, only about sixty metres, but it would have to do for today. He pulled himself up onto the ice, collected his towel and dried his body hard and thoroughly before he wrung out his running clothes and put them back on. He mustn't stop moving or the cold would get him. A faint light from the sun, which still had not managed to rise completely, painted a golden band across the horizon. Igor ran towards the light and the housing blocks which flanked the lake.

The home run. He sprinted up the path, through the entrance door, up the stairwell and into the flat where his family had just finished breakfast.

"Good morning, munchkins!" Igor took off his shoes before he entered the apartment and kissed his wife on the back of her neck. She shrieked.

"Your nose is ice cold."

Her mischievous blue eyes always made him smile.

"The rest of me is warm," he whispered.

Igor's father, Aleksey, was sitting in the narrow living room. He had fashioned a small zone for himself with books, newspapers and an old computer. As usual he was following the news on the Internet.

"Listen, they've lined up many thousands of N.A.T.O. soldiers right by the border. I reckon they've finished pillaging and plundering the Middle East and helping the Ukrainians and now they've come up here."

Natasha smiled calmly as she cleared the table. "Get dressed, kids."

The children ran from the table as Igor headed for the bathroom.

"N.A.T.O. is inching its way towards Russia. Take a look at this!" His father pointed angrily to a map of Russia which showed how the country was surrounded by N.A.T.O. bases. He had neatly marked every base with a blood-red circle.

"Relax, it's just an exercise," Natasha smiled.

"So they say, yes. You can get to the end of the world by lying, but you can't get back again," Aleksey barked. He had got that from his father, Igor thought, as he stepped into the shower. He remembered how his grandfather had always instilled this in him.

8

What is the origin of a myth? When did Major Evans go from being one of a great many ambitious fighter pilots to becoming the legend John Evans? During the inspection of the plane, Ylva wondered what Evans might have been like as a child. She could see him as a serious, intense boy who would watch the carefree play of other children with a guarded expression while making sure he never lost himself in the moment. When did he learn that in order to survive he must never show fear, mercy or weakness? When did he start to clench his teeth so hard that his taut jaw muscles would come to bear witness to a lifelong, embittered battle against the world? Can something like that be detected early? In the case of Evans, Ylva was tempted to believe that he had come into the world fully equipped with an irrepressible fighting spirit and steely control.

Whatever it was, he had become a skilled fighter pilot, just as cold, hard and as focused as a projectile fired with the single goal: to kill. There was no trace of the young Evans now, and the adult Evans was impossible to read, but the pilot Major Evans instilled total respect. That she recognised.

The Major checked his watch, a pilot's old and battered watch.

"Ready for take-off?" he said.

"I thought you'd never ask, sir," she quipped, unable to hide her excitement.

Evans looked at her without a glimmer of humour. Awkward.

She noticed that he wore his watch on his right wrist and wondered if he was lefthanded.

"My dad had one of those."

"A Benrus?"

"I don't know the make except that it was a similar, single-function instrument, worn around the wrist as an identity marker and a time indicator."

Evans looked at her without expression.

"How many functions do you need to tell the time?"

And with that, her grim-faced instructor went to the back of the hangar to get ready. Ylva made a mental note that humour was not going to be a successful social strategy. Fine, she could save herself the trouble. All that mattered was that she would be airborne very soon. In silence they donned their woollen underwear, an immersion suit, anti-G trousers and a combat jacket. What they were wearing was the product of high-tech engineering, and Ylva was still green enough to get a kick out of the multifunctional features of the uniform.

She tried acting casual as she pulled up the sturdy zip on the inside of her trouser leg, scared of looking clumsy at this early stage. Putting on the flight suit always did something for her; things fell into place. She liked the feeling she got from wearing it, becoming someone else. Becoming herself.

They walked to the now ready F-16. They slipped smoothly into their seats. Evans at the back. His task was to observe Ylva while she flew, and she was going to fly to impress. They put on their helmets and the Major's voice crackled over the intercom.

"So that you know, Benrus is a bifunctional instrument: it's fitted with an analogue compass."

Ylva had to smile, right? He did have a sense of humour after all. Cool.

"Not bad for an old watch," she said.

He said nothing.

Ylva started the engine and taxied out onto the runway while she thought about the many missions Evans had flown; impressing him would not be easy, this much was obvious. Ylva's goal in life was to stay in the air regardless of the battle situation, as Evans had always done. Save with one exception. It was too embarrassing for all concerned that the U.S. Air Force's very best pilot had been shot down in Libya, held captive and tortured for eight months by Gaddafi's opponents, who were the very people the U.S.A. and N.A.T.O. were fighting for. The situation on the ground is never anything like the one politicians and bureaucrats see from their reports and satellite images. On the ground alliances change more easily than people change their clothes. The group keeping Evans captive was not ideological; they were doing it for the money, only that. The problem, of course, was that the U.S.A. refused to pay ransoms to terrorists. "Leave no man behind" had proved to be a hollow slogan, one the elite liked to bandy about to raise morale and bolster the low opinion the public had of the military-industrial complex. The politicians were happy to hand out medals and honorary titles, but as for practical help on the ground when all hell broke loose, forget it.

To the politicians' enormous relief, media coverage of Evans' appalling fate evaporated in the news frenzy that followed the Benghazi attack. In the pandemonium caused by the collapse of Libya, one downed pilot was manageable collateral damage. When, eight months later, he surfaced in Tangier a free man, no-one asked any questions about what had happened. At least not officially.

* * *

On the runway Ylva could feel butterflies in her stomach, the wonderful anticipation before take-off. She took out her checklist.

"External lights – as required."

"Trim – centre."

"Pressure – check."

"Altimeter – set."

"Warning/Caution lights – check."

It was like music. Rhythmic, predictable, hypnotic. Where other pilots relied on talismans or favourite shirts, Ylva had her checklist. It was a mantra, a meditation. She would often repeat it at night where it would keep even the bloodiest nightmares at bay.

"Speed brakes – closed."

"Landing light – ON."

"Probe heat – ON."

"Injection seat – ARM."

The plane rolled slowly on and at the end of the runway she turned it up against the wind. Ylva contacted the control tower.

"Bodø TWR, Lion 35, ready for departure."

"Lion 35, runway 25, cleared for take-off, contact departure passing five thousand feet."

"Full throttle."

She opened the throttle and the plane responded with a roar as the jet engine kicked in. Ylva was slammed back by the g-force as sets of runway lights sped by – faster and faster.

At C.Y.F.O.R.'s headquarters Storm was chuckling as he followed the plane on the screen.

"Oh, I love it when my woman takes to the skies."

9

The President began the day with his usual regime, save for one exception: it was 07:15 when he got up. Being a night owl, he was usually sound asleep at this time. So, he was glad of the rare sight of rays of the sun which still hung below the horizon by the Moscow River. From the east-facing terrace he savoured the soft light as it replaced the darkness. He preferred the clarity of the moonlight, but he was moved by this peaceful moment where the innocence of the dawn dyed blood-red the six-metres-high walls of the Novo-Ogaryovo Palace.

He went through each stage of his morning regimen, unfazed by the din and bustle beyond the walls of the dacha. Everyone who knew the President was aware that self-mastery, discipline, and control had made him the man he was today. His staff were always ready for work at eight o'clock precisely, often only to wait for hours for him to rise and carry out his forty minutes of swimming, weightlifting and breakfasting before, in his own good time, he would agree to see his minions.

They knew that the Moscow night was a source of inspiration for him. The absence of others induced a sense of unresisted command that he required to focus clearly on his goals. Sometimes he would pause in his work and potter about the palace gardens or sit on the simple sofa in his office and watch the news on T.V. He welcomed isolation, even the extreme version his staff imposed during the pandemic. It suited his temperament. He seldom travelled to his office in the centre of Moscow. He preferred to be far from the clamour of bustling crowds and ceremonial . . . until he discovered that this was where his underlings preferred him to stay. The insight stung him. They all positioned themselves now, he could feel it, smell it. How they all colluded and scurried about in the shadows, anticipating his demise. The palace intrigues and infighting had begun years ago. The President knew what they whispered behind his back. He was an ageing leader of a corrupt totalitarian state, who had idiotically thrown Russia into a needless war with their kinfolk in Ukraine. Gleefully they discussed and dissected his miscalculations, how he let witless ass-licking oligarchs, psychopathic war-profiteers and fanatical Orthodox zealots lure him into an unwinnable war with a people whose only transgression was to pursue independence. They said he had lost his grip, that he was a madcap potentate of a failed state. He shuddered, the hairs on his neck stood on end. Although he could feel the ambition of his young, ambitious subjects, he was undeterred. The President was nobody's fool. He was a man who trusted no-one. Old age did not mellow him. He was not the satiated, warm-hearted patriarch who gracefully left the reins to his successors, basking in the gratitude and love of his tribe. No. Old age scorched him. He had risen from darkness and dissolution to rage against the well-versed and tempered "enlightened" man, the chattering clowns of the decadent global elites.

Ukraine. How could he have miscalculated so spectacularly their will for freedom?

The dacha came alive at sunrise. The rose-tinted light pouring from the east over the immaculate snow promised a glorious day.

Compared to his neighbours, the President lived modestly.

Outside the thick, steely fortification in which he was ensconced, Russia's nouveaux riches had barricaded themselves into their extravagant palaces behind massive walls, steel doors and platoons of security guards. That was the price they had to pay for their ill-acquired fortune. Private security companies were enjoying their heydays all over the world, including in Russia. The President had invested his money in several of them. Although he was not a great reader, the President was well versed in Russian history. And when he chose the Novo-Ogaryovo Palace as his home, its dramatic origins and background were a part of its appeal. He wanted to live in this exact spot precisely because of its bloody history, so that he would never forget the lessons harboured in its bricks and mortar. The dacha reminded him of how swiftly a mob could kill their leader as a sure sign of gratitude for the freedom he gives them. The plebs craved and detested freedom. They could never expect what courage it required, what strength. A mirthless grin flitted across the President's face as he scanned his opulent surroundings. The palace was built by Tsar Alexander II, otherwise known as Alexander the Liberator. A man of weak character, detached from reality and the empire over which he ruled. As the population grew and resources became scarcer, the clueless landowners could neither suppress nor feed their desperate serfs, forever on the brink of starvation. High on Western illusions of "liberalism", the downtrodden vassals demanded their freedom. How naive. The "liberator", intoxicated by *"Liberté, égalité, fraternité"*, by chilled Champagne and *fois gras* sprinkled with Rosseau, magnanimously freed all Russian serfs by decree. The President knew his story, embodied by this glorious dacha. Riots and mayhem broke loose, as the starving serfs now were free and unemployed. This was hidden from the glorious tsar, who thought himself deserving of a magnificent summer residence. And so the sumptuous dacha rose with its spiky turrets and Gothic arches; the emancipated peasants with no lords to serve and no land to till, had to look for paid work away from the farmlands in order to survive. People fled to the cities to seek their fortune there. They did not find it, quite the opposite. These dire, humiliating consequences of freedom were unimaginable to anyone ensconced in the Tsar's gilded halls. In 1881 the great liberator was murdered by his freed but disillusioned subjects. The President despised Alexander; the man was a cretin, also because he had sold Alaska to the U.S.A. in 1867 for $7.2 million! It beggared belief! Given today's geopolitical situation, it was possible that this was the most absurd decision ever made by a Russian leader.

The mustard-yellow neoclassical villa where the President now spent most of his time was built by Georgy Malenkov, Stalin's loyal lackey. Malenkov was a patient, hard-working civil servant, of that there was no doubt. Towards the end of 1940 he had eliminated nearly all the Soviet Union's generals and more than half its officer corps. This had become necessary when Stalin discovered that this particular social group had begun to ask questions about his leadership style. Malenkov's effective liquidation of Russia's excellent but restless military elite contributed to Hitler's decision to invade Mother Russia the following year. Certain of victory, the Führer announced that German soldiers would be back with their families in good time for Christmas. It was Hitler's crucial error of judgment. He didn't reckon with the Russian *rasputiosia*, when the vast expanses of Arctic tundra turn into miles and miles of metre-deep mud and slush.

The President admired Malenkov's pragmatic attitude to numbers. Apparently he did not lose any sleep over the twenty-seven million Russian lives that were forfeited to defeat the Germans.

Not at all. The will to sacrifice its own people was and still is the Russian leadership's great military advantage. And it worked. In spite of Germany losing only a fifth of what Russia lost in terms of soldiers on the Eastern front, the Soviet Union won the war. Briefly. But as so often in Russian history, Malenkov the war hero would be betrayed by those closest to him. Brimming with faith in the future and with a touch of post-war hubris, he set about modernising Communist Russia's antiquated agricultural system. This upset the paper-pushers in the Kremlin and before you knew it Comrade Malenkov was declared an enemy of the Russian people.

The Novo-Ogaryovo Palace, however, turned out to be pleasurable, but the President did not allow himself to take its grand parks for granted, nor its delicate avenues winding their way among the artificial lakes and richly ornamented villas. He was and would remain a scrapping street urchin from the roughest neighbourhoods in Leningrad. The extravagant luxury in which he wallowed now felt otherworldly compared to the din and squalor of the single room he and his parents had shared with two other families. The palace scent of fine leather and polished mahogany still seemed alien to him, although a lifetime separated it from the stench of fear, rot and decay. Rather than indulge in decadent hedonism, he had created the perfect working environment where his solipsistic routine was interrupted by brief ritualistic encounters with other humans. His only joy lay in working with total control and supreme calm. He had no need of close friends or anything so ridiculous as romantic love. Everyone in his circle knew that they would be abandoned at any time should they not live up to his demand of total loyalty. The President liked to say that his need for love was met by the people of Mother Russia – as if . . .

Halfway through his swim, the President felt an ache in his right shoulder. His joints felt stiff and sore, but he pushed on. The morning exercise was followed by a breakfast of cottage cheese, omelette and fruit juice. He ate alone.

Normally he would work at a calm and steady pace, but today there was a high level of activity in the corridors. His staff had been at work for hours already and the defence ministry had set up a second office in one of the villas. Everyone was there; it was a big day for which they had prepared for more than a year. There was a hush as the President entered the room. He was served a cup of black coffee, which he enjoyed unhurried in silence ... and then he announced the mobilisation of fourteen thousand military personnel, forty-seven ships, two submarines and twenty fighter planes to the Norwegian–Russian border in the Arctic.

10

Some moments capture everything you have ever dreamed of and worked for. Moments when happiness arrives with bubbling euphoria and you know you are doing what you were born to do. Leaning back comfortably at an angle of thirty degrees and cocooned by the U.S.A.F.'s hard, narrow pilot's seat, Ylva enjoyed a panoramic view of Lyngsalpene. The mountain peaks appeared to float as they towered over the low morning clouds, and the cold winter light dyed the snow magenta. The silence inside her helmet formed a stark contrast to the roar that filled the air outside the F-16. All Ylva could hear was her own breathing behind the mask. Her body trembled just as it used to do when, as a little girl, she would fly this route with her father. They might have been tootling along in an old Saab Safari aircraft doing a measly 110 knots, but Ylva had felt like the most badass top gun pilot even then.

Now she was cruising, relaxed but focused, at a speed of 400 knots, her left hand resting confidently on the throttle, her right hand guiding the joystick. The controls felt like an extension of her body and responded to her touch.

Ylva had grown up around this type of aircraft and she could still remember the pilots discussing why they believed it was the sensitive fly-by-wire system in particular that had ensured more

F-16 Fighting Falcons were built than any other fighter jet in the world.

A slight adjustment of her left hand and the jet engine tossed the seven-tonnes plane through the air like a hawk. Major Evans, behind her, was following her every move, keen to point out any mistakes. He had barely spoken since introducing himself, and that in itself was unnerving. Was he doing this to mess with her mind?

"Lieutenant Nordahl, are you watching your altitude?" Ylva glanced at the head-up display.

"Yes, sir."

Major Evans grunted over the intercom; he offered no positive feedback, only surly reminders of procedures. Ylva concluded that he was trying to rattle her and cause her to second-guess herself. She reckoned that he subscribed to the old-school method of breaking people down in order to rebuild them in his own image. Ylva had no intention now or ever of letting anyone break her down, but she was capable of reflecting the expectations of others and could act sufficiently subdued so that people eased up on the pressure and gave her less hassle. She was good at that.

Five hundred kilometres to the northeast, a Bristow supply helicopter was approaching the Hoop Viking oil platform in the newly opened Hoop field near the edge of the ice and close to the Russian border. The weather was fine and visibility was good. Apart from a coastguard helicopter operating around Bjørnøya, no other traffic had been reported in the area and the flight looked set to be routine. Captain Eriksen was relaxed. He had flown this trip frequently for two years and the predictability offered him a welcome oasis of peace. With three children under seven, time in the cockpit was his only real break.

He scanned the instruments. Everything glowed green, they were ready for landing and he commenced their descent. He looked across to his co-pilot.

"You can watch the view, Bjørn, I'll take control."

"Fine, you have control."

Eriksen took over and focused on the instruments. Then he started his descent.

The calm was brutally interrupted.

With a massive burst of noise, a fighter jet crossed right in front of them. Eriksen jumped in his seat before quickly banking the helicopter into a sudden left turn. The aircraft shook and the rotor blades rattled as they passed through the airwave trailing in the wake of the fighter.

"What the . . ."

Eriksen looked up from the dashboard to get his bearings. The two pilots watched the fighter disappear. They could see its afterburners glowing.

"That was a Russian. Where the hell did he come from?"

"Hoop ops, 204, we just had a near collision with a Russian fighter."

In the horizon he saw the fighter coming back; it seemed to grow alarmingly in size as it approached.

"What the hell . . . Commence descent."

Eriksen pushed the collective down and the helicopter dropped towards the water. With another roar the fighter passed, this time only metres above them.

Serkin flew so close to the supply helicopter that he could enjoy the looks on the pilots' horrified faces as he passed. He leaned back and deftly turned the Fullback yet again. The supply helicopter was flying close to the Russian border and, in the light of the tense situation created by the N.A.T.O. exercise, Serkin's orders were to frighten it as far away from the border as he could.

Ylva was enjoying the silence and the majestic landscape below her. Although she had flown this route towards Lyngsalpene countless times, she still got a thrill every time she crossed Storfjord and saw the mountains plunge 1,883 metres straight down into the foaming sea.

During her training she had displayed exceptional self-discipline and stamina. The instructors on the base were impressed. Major Evans, however, was not convinced. She was cognitively fast and every test showed that she had maximum spatial awareness – not usually a female genetic quality, he reckoned. All the evidence indicated that she was fearless, had above-average situational awareness and could prioritise with the speed of light. She was as aggressive, confident and decisive as the male pilots were. But she surpassed the men easily when it came to endurance and motivation. Who the hell has such dogged, infernal willpower? What was she compensating for? Evans had asked to fly with her during the N.A.T.O. exercise and, to his irritation, Major Armour had sung the girl's praises.

Ylva had passed her training with distinction and had already been given her wings, but Evans had a feeling that something did not add up. Something jarred.

Ylva steered the F-16 right towards the highest peak at the centre of the mountain chain. Seeing the mountains approach, Evans muttered predictably:

"Nordahl, mind the terrain."

She did not flinch; she knew what she was doing. She accelerated and the fighter zoomed towards the looming mountain. A collision seemed inevitable, but Evans did not intervene. Cool, she thought, he was just as hardcore as she had hoped.

At the last second Ylva made an abrupt ninety-degrees manoeuvre which took the F-16 right up the mountainside and, as they shot across the peaks, she flipped the plane 180 degrees so they ended up flying along the other side facing the rock. As they hurtled towards the ground, it was now a matter of accelerating, something which felt so obviously counterintuitive, but the red-hot gases from the engines had to spark off with maximum power in order to propel the plane up along the side of the next mountain. If she chickened out now, it was over. Ylva did not chicken out, she opened the throttle wide. As the craft plunged downwards, their speed made Evans' stomach lurch and he smiled.

She was not too bad after all.

There were no more negative comments from Major Evans, and Ylva decided that that was the highest compliment he could give her.

"Tiger 13!"

A voice from Sørreisa radar control hailed them.

"A civilian helicopter is being buzzed by a Russian fighter. It needs escorting from Hoop field back to the mainland A.S.A.P. You're the nearest craft."

Ylva expected Evans to respond, but he remained silent, thereby giving Ylva the authority to act as commanding officer.

"When is it departing Hoop?"

"The slot time is 08:30."

A swift glance at the fuel gauge confirmed that they had enough for the escort trip.

"Copy, mission accepted."

Ylva steered the plane in a wide, rising curve back across the sea, turning its nose northeast.

11

Major Ivana Khodrokovska was still at work at Monchegorsk Air Base. Despite the snap exercise, things there were calm, even a mass mobilisation like this one had become routine for the Russian armed forces. She studied the radar screen, which showed that traffic in the international airspace between Norway and Russia was normal. A red dot next to the Hoop field on the Norwegian side had attracted her attention. Its coordinates combined with its speed made it likely that it was a Norwegian service helicopter on its way from the oil rig. She checked the time. Yes, it matched the fuel times they had registered previously. It was the same helicopter they had buzzed earlier. A sharp ringing on the internal line shook her out of her reverie. The Major straightened up instinctively when she saw that the call was from a direct line at the Defence Ministry in Moscow. She cleared her throat and answered it.

"Major Khodrokovska."

She heard a deep voice on the other end.

"Khodrokovska, you have orders from the top to intervene at 75.26°N 39.32°W."

Ivana looked at the screen again where she saw that Serkin's Fullback was on its way back to Monchegorsk.

"SU-34 is leaving the area as we speak."

"Tell him to return immediately."

Major Khodrokovska was taken aback. She wondered how much fuel Serkin had left, adding a detour at this stage might prove dangerous.

"SU-34 Serkin doesn't have enough fuel and is heading back to base. I'll scramble Artyom for this mission."

"Negative. SU-34 Serkin will return to the area. That's an order."

Ivana baulked instantly.

"This is outside protocol. We should—"

The caller hung up. Astonished, Khodrokovska stared at the handset. What was the name of the man who had given the order? Had he even given his name?

Khodrokovska felt her mouth go dry, she loathed contravening protocol. Was there something about this helicopter that she ought to know? Why were they willing to risk the loss of an aircraft and a pilot just to buzz a helicopter?

She got up and headed to the lavatory. It was rare for her to hesitate before following orders, but she had a bad feeling from the moment she heard the voice on the other end of the line. On her way through the office she asked her second-in-command to check who it was who had called her from Moscow. The strange message was probably a part of the snap exercise. Monchegorsk Air Base was in a dilapidated state, so much so that in the lavatory she could smell the rot that was eating away at the walls. Ivana had a pee, then washed her hands and decided that the order was likely to be a test of the team's ability to react. She had to give Lieutenant Serkin the order without further delay.

12

At 08:54 the Defence Minister issued a press release stating that Russia was responding to N.A.T.O.'s aggression by carrying out a military exercise alongside its border with Norway. The exercise would commence at 09:00 Moscow time, and in less than twenty-four hours it would demonstrate Russia's determination to defend herself against any and every security threat in the Arctic region.

Mayhem ensued. Western leaders were acutely aware that Russia's attacks on Chechnya, Georgia and Ukraine as well as the annexation of Crimea began under the guise of "snap exercises". This rapid deployment was a familiar overture to disaster. The next step in the exercise was to unleash a cyclone of disinformation. The realm of war was no longer purely kinaesthetic, a true military "exercise" had to involve reality-distorting hybrid attacks. Faced with a barrage of conflicting claims, people do nothing, or better, turn on each other.

As the press release exploded in the news, the West's most useful idiots, the media, hastened to serve the purposes of the Kremlin. Within minutes, headlines declared that Russia was once more prepared to deploy the country's nuclear capability to counter N.A.T.O.'s presence in the Arctic.

The President leaned back and observed. His calm expression hid a sense of foreboding. His aching shoulder made him grimace, but aware of his staff's ever-observing eyes the President recovered his composure. After all, *maskirovka,* the art of deception, was his *métier.* He was a master in this most Russian of military doctrines: treachery and cunning. To him it was a straightforward operational art. Observing the sure-fire sequence of cause and effect in narrative-warfare normally gave him a deep satisfaction. Today however, he had a sense of unease. Perhaps he was just tired. Or ... The President did not complete the thought. He dreaded to recognise what was obvious to the world; he was getting too old for this.

Wearily, he watched his staff as they went about their work. They had honed their skills through many conflicts. Russia's weaponised disinformation was a force to be reckoned with. The information campaign they now disseminated was visceral and emotionally charged. Alertness to danger was a prerequisite for survival. The coddled and entitled creatures of comfort he saw populating the West were up for a rude awakening. By sending out the most divisive narratives, by creating a sound and fury of claims and counter claims, it would very soon become difficult to distinguish fact from fiction.

The President exchanged a glance with General Svetla, his most trusted adviser. They both grew up in the post-war streets of Leningrad and shared the bond of vicious blood-brothers. Preferably other people's blood. The old general looked calm and focused. He had planned this exercise well. The President prided himself on trusting no-one, but Svetla was different. They were of the same mind, and were mutually dependent on each other.

The President watched the Western media mayhem play out on the television in his office. He muted the volume and looked down at Connie, the black Labrador enjoying an untroubled sleep under his massive mahogany desk. The Labrador, named after former

U.S. foreign minister Condoleezza Rice, yawned and stretched. "Connie, you're starting to get lazy," the President mumbled. The dog pricked up her ears. He scratched her tummy.

While tranquillity reigned in the palace by the Moscow River, the beginnings of bedlam stirred in busy offices and on news desks. The Kremlin staff communicated in a controlled manner. Over the years the President had carried out many snap exercises and each time N.A.T.O. denounced the manoeuvres as a violation of the Vienna Document. They would point to the 2011 agreement in which all signatories promised full transparency on their military manoeuvres in Europe. As if he did not know the resolution very well. He had, after all, signed it!

But he knew that if he ever loosened his grip, if he showed so much as a hint of fear or fatigue, his house of cards would come tumbling down. He grimaced at the thought. Were that to happen, he could at best hope to be killed by those "close and loyal friends" who had advanced in his retinue and enriched themselves on his journey to the pinnacle of power, and who all envied him the view.

He got up and Connie was immediately by his side. They went out into the gardens. The sunlight crashed and shattered into billions of glittering reflections from the snow. He breathed in deeply.

13

Three hours from the mainland, glowing fiercely in the middle of a sea of howling gales and biting cold, lay the Norwegian oil platform, Hoop Viking. Captain Eriksen had just taken off from the helipad and was heading southwest. Sleet lashed the windscreen and Eriksen could feel the wind taking hold. The mood in the cockpit was nowhere near as relaxed as earlier.

At Monchegorsk Air Base, Major Khodrokovska was following the helicopter on her screen. She could now see two dots move south close to the Russian border, one dot moving noticeably faster than the other.

"We have a fast mover."

Major Khodrokovska looked at Oleg, the young sergeant who had seen what she had seen.

"An escort?" he wondered out loud.

She nodded. Of course the Norwegians had dispatched a fighter to guide the helicopter safely back to the mainland, they must have anticipated that the helicopter would be buzzed again on its return trip. Major Khodrokovska sighed, it would give Serkin a chance to prove how light and elegant the Fullback was compared to the old workhorse, the F-16. He would like that, she thought, and shook her head. She was fond of Serkin even though he was just a big kid.

*   *   *

Ylva looked at the surreal and beautiful sky as she gently circled Eriksen's helicopter. The deep blue merged with the huge dark clouds that rolled along in slow motion. They looked like black ink spilling over a vast canvas. She was lucky to experience the world from God's perspective; it filled her with awe and reminded her how tiny and vulnerable human beings were.

In front of her the sluggish little chopper pottered along at a snail's pace. Major Evans was still silent, he let her stay in control and she was pleased about that, but the mood in the cockpit was strained. She was starting to wonder if he had fallen asleep, but she soon discovered that he was monitoring her every move when he grunted with disapproval over the intercom. He seemed anxious almost, as if something was in the offing. Was the famous Major Evans nervous at the prospect of a possible Russian interception? The tension rose steadily and although Ylva loved flying interceptions during exercises, she, too, could sense the pressure. However, she had better not get her hopes up. After all, they had not seen any Russian planes yet, nor was it likely that one would turn up.

To relieve the tense atmosphere Ylva made a last-ditch attempt at conversation.

"Sir, I've been wondering, when did you start flying?"

"Since before you were born."

"Oh boy."

"Not so very long ago."

Ylva said nothing more, how old was he really?

Evans studied the clouds gathering on the horizon. Below them the waves surged ever higher. Out here a storm could form in a few minutes. Ylva had been given a weather report before they took off, a severe storm had been forecast. All she wanted to do was to escort the old bumblebee back to Kirkenes so they could head to Lakselv airport to refuel. It was a shame that the going was so incredibly slow, God Almighty, how was it even possible to stay airborne at that speed? Ylva had barely finished that thought before she saw a Russian Fullback creep up behind them.

"Sir, we have company."

Serkin's Fullback passed them with a deafening roar. Ylva breathed steadily, watched the Russian make an abrupt U-turn and fly back below them. She felt a quiet exhilaration, O.K., it's about to kick off. Mentally she had flown this kind of mock interception countless times, and now she was going to show Evans and that Russian who was boss.

"Sir, requesting permission to respond."

"Negative. We're in international airspace, he has as much right to be here as we do."

"But . . ."

The Russian pilot let the Fullback glide over the N.A.T.O. plane. Ylva looked up through the glass in the roof and met the pilot's gaze as he raised his mobile to take a picture of her. The idiot was clearly there to test their nerve. Serkin dropped his plane in front of them and with expert skill reduced his speed and flipped from side to side as if waving. Ylva felt herself go cold with rage, but she rapidly regained her equilibrium. She needed to be in control before she responded.

Then Serkin turned on the afterburner in front of them and the jet wash caused the F-16 violently to shake.

"Nordahl, do not lose control!"

Evans' mechanical voice over the intercom irritated her extremely. Who was the one losing control here? Hello, she never lost control. She found peace in situations like this. She accelerated, flew very precisely up alongside the Russian and settled close to him. She could see the Russian pilot's worried expression and with ice-cold calm produced her own mobile phone to photograph him. The gloves were off, the battle had begun.

Ylva gave it full throttle, the F-16 shot forwards and as she pulled up the nose of the plane, g-forces pressed her so hard into her seat that it hurt to breathe. Adrenaline at once flooded her body and instinctively she tensed her leg and stomach muscles to counteract gravity pushing the blood from her upper body and brain into her legs. At the same time, the inflatable air pockets in her g-trousers responded and added to the pressure so that the blood was forced back up into her brain. Which was where she needed it. The adrenaline rush subsided and was followed by the trickling sensation of an endorphin rush. Oh, this was seriously the greatest feeling in the world, it was almost better than sex. Her breathing settled and she smiled blissfully, oh yes, definitely better than sex.

The buzzing quickly escalated into a duel where both planes flew aggressively to force the other to give way. They provoked each other to take ever greater chances. Evans watched, it was what he had been expecting.

"Nordahl! Calm down!"

Ylva passed the Fullback with full afterburner. The Fullback keeled, now he was the one being buzzed. She could taste his fear like cold iron in her mouth. Behind her Major Evans was staring at the fuel gauge. In a dogfight with full afterburner, the F-16 had a high fuel consumption. Evans quickly did the maths and let Ylva carry on.

Furious, Serkin positioned himself once more behind the N.A.T.O. plane. Ylva responded by accelerating aggressively before making a hard right. Evans and Ylva could barely move because of the g-forces generated by the manoeuvre, and again

Evans felt gravity force the blood from his brain and upper body into his feet, buttocks, arms and elbows. If Ylva pushed the F-16 to the max, it would pull up to nine times gravity, and then his modest 85 kilos would weigh 765 kilos. Of course she was going full throttle. The speed had a considerable impact on both his body and his head, even his eyelids grew heavy and closed. His skin burned and stung, and he knew that he would have blood effusions where the tiny capillaries in the skin had burst due to the enormous pressure.

The pain was familiar, it made him clear and focused. Without blinking, he registered that Ylva pulled the joystick harder to rid herself of the Russian flea, but of course the Russian only accelerated and appeared behind them again.

Evans felt his pulse rise. He had a choice to make now, he could let Nordahl show off a little more, mark her territory before shaking off the Russian and flying home, feeling pretty good about herself. That would have been the smart choice and she was handling the plane with great skill.

Serkin moved closer. Evans could read the way a plane flew as parents can read their children's faces. This Russian pilot was immature and Evans was not surprised when Serkin activated the afterburner. He sensed that the Russian was caught up in the battle.

Evans gritted his teeth, drops of sweat ran down his back. It was tempting to do nothing, but that wasn't why he was here. His job was not to sit there like an old woman and hope for the best. He looked behind him, the Russian had flown in a big circle and was coming at them again; if he was to intervene, now was his chance. The fatal moment had come and he was ready.

"Nordahl, I'm taking control."

"Eh?"

Before Ylva had time to respond, Evans took control of the F-16. Serkin failed to anticipate the change in pace as Evans reduced the speed with the brakes and had less than a second to react. As quick as a flash, he swerved to avoid the N.A.T.O. jet, but not fast enough. The Fullback jolted as its wing clipped the underside of the left wing of the N.A.T.O. craft. The sound was shrill and intense, and Evans felt it like a cold claw to his guts. This very spot, below the F-16 craft's left wing, was its Achilles heel, the only vulnerable point in an otherwise near-perfect armour. What were the odds?

A loud bang erupted from the craft's central nervous system. The computer which controlled the fly-by-wire system short-circuited. That was it, their fate was sealed. Evans knew that whatever happened from now on would turn out to be a nightmare far worse than the one he had survived in Libya. There was no going back now.

The avionics in the cockpit short-circuited as well and all G.P.S. and electronics in the control panel went black. Evans looked out, flames were coming from the tear under the wing, and black smoke flew backwards as the electricals burned out. The plane rolled severely. He fought to keep control, but the operating system did not respond. The plane shook hard and veered. As they lost altitude and the frothing ocean grew ever closer, he considered yet again letting go and simply waiting for the plane to smash itself to pieces against the wild waves and sink to the bottom. It would be over in seconds, an end to all the pain. He held his breath. A few seconds of hesitation and then nothing, but he did not hesitate, his survival instinct took over, and he regained control.

Serkin trembled with shock as he positioned himself behind the F-16 to study the extent of the damage he had caused. A cold shiver went down his spine when he realised what he had done. His order had been to buzz, not to damage the N.A.T.O. craft. The consequences of damaging, possibly crashing a N.A.T.O. plane on a peaceful escort mission in international airspace would ruin his career and humiliate Russia. He could feel his panic rise, but he could not undo what he had done; he turned off the afterburner and fled the scene.

It took Ylva several seconds to recover from the shock. She looked out. Sections of the underside of the wing had fallen off and plunged into the sea below them. The left wing had been cut up, the fuel tank perforated and it was leaking badly. Her thoughts were spinning: had the Russian actually tried to make them crash? Why? They were on the Norwegian side of the border, carrying out a normal escort flight. Her heart raced as she watched the Fullback leave them behind.

She felt paralysed by panic, but registered that Evans had managed to put the plane on a slow turn to the left. With the fly-by-wire system damaged, the F-16 was almost impossible to steer. Ylva had to get a grip of herself, she felt as if everything was happening outside her, as if she were watching events play out in slow motion. Take a deep breath now, don't panic. I need to focus. She breathed more calmly. *That's right. Go through the checklists, we need to get the avionics to work*, Ylva told herself as her training kicked in. She had imagined this scenario during her many visualisations of what to do if she were ever shot down. She knew that she had only a matter of seconds, so she checked the fuses in the cockpit and tried to get the avionics working again. No response, everything was dead.

With the electronic system down, they could not communicate or summon help. Nevertheless she tried, at first calm and insistent, then increasingly desperate.

"Mayday, mayday, mayday. Tiger 13, mid-air collision. Aircraft difficult to control. Severe fuel leak. Mayday, mayday, mayday."

In Monchegorsk Major Khodrokovska looked on with a growing sense of unease. The N.A.T.O. jet zigzagged through the international airspace before crossing over to the Russian side of the border. What on earth did they think they were doing? It looked as if they were chasing Serkin's Fullback into Russia! Had they lost their minds?

Horrified, Major Khodrokovska continued to watch the screen. It looked as if the N.A.T.O. craft was heading straight for the nuclear base. This she had never anticipated. Was it a test? A part of the Russian exercise? She took a deep breath, she needed to think straight. The procedure was unequivocal.

"N.A.T.O. fighter F-16, identify yourself and your mission or you will be shot down. Over."

She listened to the silence on the net. No response.

The seconds passed, the N.A.T.O. plane could attack the nuclear base at any time and wipe out all life in a radius of more than 700 kilometres. She contacted Lieutenant Serkin, who would be flying over Murmansk soon.

"SU-34, this is Monchegorsk calling. A N.A.T.O. fighter has crossed the border and penetrated Russian airspace. Stay close to him and be ready to engage."

Serkin went cold with fear. What? Were they coming after him?

He gritted his teeth, armed his weapons and watched the radar as he turned the aircraft around. Ready and prepared to shoot down the intruder, Serkin's finger rested on the trigger.

Ylva went on calling for help on the emergency frequency, but she knew there would be no response. Her thoughts were racing. If they could reach the Varanger peninsula, they could eject there. She peered at the horizon in the hope of seeing land, but visibility was too poor, it was snowing and the wind was gaining strength. The storm had arrived and Ylva could barely see the wings in the snowstorm.

Evans was only just able to keep the plane airborne. Through the snow he could make out the contours on the ground and could only navigate by what he could see. The snowstorm might just as well be a sandstorm. The abnormal sounds of the plane keeling and losing speed were etched into his nervous system. The standby compass in the cockpit showed that they were slightly east of the course they ought to be on, but where exactly were they? How far east had they flown?

A mechanical grating from the engine told them that the plane had run out of fuel. As Evans steered it into a shallow dive, the engine stopped completely. The plane sank into the clouds and was swallowed up by a grey mass of hailstones and ice.

Ylva was watching the altimeter and the standby compass. The ground below them was difficult to see in the appalling weather, but in a glimpse she spotted a horseshoe-shaped mountain range she knew well. She had been there several times.

But that was impossible, how had they ended up so far southeast? They must have flown beyond Murmansk and the Monchegorsk Air Base.

"Sir, we're over Lovozero, there are mountains here. We ought to bail."

Ylva looked over her shoulder to see if Evans had heard her, and he gave her a thumbs-up. Out of the corner of his eye, he registered a grey stripe of condensation right behind him, a missile was fast approaching them. Lightning quick, he yanked the joystick to the right and the fighter jet dodged the missile at the last second. Ylva saw it pass half a metre from the cockpit.

"Evans! Bail!"

Ylva pulled the lever between her legs hard and with a tenth of a second interval they were ejected from the plane and into a dense grey storm cloud of compacted hailstone and sleet.

The air pressure hit Ylva like a wall and knocked the breath out of her. She gasped desperately for air as she hurtled to the ground at more than 200 kilometres an hour.

Instinctively she got herself into a box, a neutral freefall position with her stomach down and her arms and legs extended. Her fear sent waves of nausea through her as she was tossed around in wild somersaults. Powerless, she plunged through the air like a human projectile, not knowing what was up or down.

In order to recover her composure, she carried on talking to herself.

"I have vertigo, I need to count. One thousand and one, one thousand and two . . ."

She calculated their altitude at the time of ejection. They must have been at a height of three thousand metres or thereabouts when they ejected. She would need to release her parachute after fifty seconds of freefall.

Gusts of wind bounced her about like a rag doll, she spun round and round at an insane speed. Her stomach lurched and she threw up.

Serkin flew back to put himself in the wake of the N.A.T.O. plane which disappeared between the snowdrifts. Furious at having missed it the first time, he fired another missile. The pressure from the explosion as the missile hit the F-16 seconds later knocked the wind out of Ylva and she was thrown horizontally through the air. One hundred metres further down Evans caught a glimpse of the burning wreckage of the plane coming towards him. He tried to move out of the way, but a sharp pain engulfed him as a fragment hit his calf and got lodged. Evans howled and curled up, the pain was all-consuming, but his screams were drowned in the blast from the F-16 as it exploded on the ground.

Surrounded by an unreal inferno of flames, wreckage, clouds, smoke and snow, Ylva tried to regain her composure before releasing her parachute. It opened with a crack above her and everything suddenly grew eerily quiet. The pilot's seat to which her body had been strapped until the parachute unfolded, disengaged automatically and plummeted away beneath her.

Her body felt lighter now and she focused on gaining control of the parachute despite the strong gusts of wind as her descent turned into a surreal floating through fluffy clouds.

Serkin watched the explosion with remarkable composure. The burning fragments of the N.A.T.O. plane fell as if in slow motion towards the snow-covered ground below him, and there they stayed, glowing hot. The heat from the explosion created an opening in the snowstorm and he could see that the F-16 had crashed on the outskirts of a town. He was horrified when he realised that the town was Apatity. He had family there.

His heart pounded as he contacted Monchegorsk. He heard himself deliver his report, his voice was steady, he was in control.

"Confirmed kill, N.A.T.O. F-16."

14

The conditions made it impossible to calculate the distance to the ground and Evans was totally unprepared when he crashed into a deep snowdrift. The metal fragment in his calf was rammed in more deeply by the impact and he cried aloud from pain. He lay motionless for a minute, trying to get his breath back. Above him the snow was blowing just like the sandstorms in Ghibli, but the cold burned him more than the 45°C desert. Dazed, he took off his helmet, but the moment he struggled to his feet to get his bearings, the wind took hold of his parachute which billowed like a sail behind him. Evans was pulled off his feet and hauled across the hard, frozen tundra.

Two hundred metres away, Ylva landed deep in a pile of snow with her parachute flapping across the ground. She gathered it underneath her and bundled it up as best she could. It wasn't until she had secured the parachute, taken off her helmet and put on a balaclava that she straightened up and looked about her.

Where was Major Evans?

The gale was still blowing and she could not see him anywhere.

"Major Evans!"

She turned her back to the wind and cupped her hands round her ears to be able to hear the Major's voice in the storm. There was no response. Whichever way she turned, all she could hear was the howling gale.

She stood for a moment, confused and despondent. Searching for him in this weather was pointless. He could have landed anywhere. She straightened up. The wind was from the northwest, the same direction as they had come from. Evans had ejected a fraction of a second before her so he must have landed in the direction of the wind. Ylva freed the emergency raft, which was still connected to the rucksack after the pilot's seat itself had disengaged. She decided to take it with her, and started to walk into the wind. It was her only hope. Panting, she reached the top of a steep ridge and from up there she saw a figure lying further down on the other side of the slope. Ylva called out as she ran.

"Major Evans!"

He did not reply. She waded through deep snow to reach the motionless figure.

"Major Evans, sir, are you O.K.?"

It was not until she reached him that she could hear him groan with pain.

"Do I look as if I'm O.K.?"

The ground where he was lying was uneven and rocks protruded underneath him. Evans tried to get up, but collapsed. Ylva could see that he was bleeding from a cut to the back of his head and that a singed bit of metal was sticking out from his calf.

"Sir, let me . . ."

She squatted down and carefully touched the metal fragment. Evans yanked back his foot so hard that Ylva was knocked over. She looked at him. Evans was pale and beads of sweat had formed on his forehead.

Ylva got up.

"Sir, I need to examine the cut on your head and then remove a metal splinter from your calf."

Evans was trembling, his lips were blue from cold, but he nodded briefly.

"But first we have to minimise the loss of heat."

She looked about her. Close to them was a big snowdrift which on its western side would shield them against the wind. Rapidly she scooped out a trench deep enough to hold Evans, then she gathered up his parachute. The fabric chute, ten metres in diameter, would offer some insulation against the cold. She helped Evans to a standing position and then walked him to the trench. He collapsed heavily, but being sheltered from the wind helped.

Ylva checked to make sure that no ice or sleet had got between the skin and the clothes around Evans' neck or the gaps by his wrists or boots. Ylva knew that although they were wearing specialist underwear, Gore-Tex survival suits and g-trousers, the Arctic cold would prove fatal if they got wet. When she had made sure that no snow had entered between gaps in his clothing, she examined the cut to the back of his head. Fortunately it was little more than a graze which had already stopped bleeding.

"You can put on your balaclava, sir, it's just a scratch."

She found the balaclava in his rucksack and helped him put it on. The Major seemed embarrassed, then irritated at having to accept help.

She cast a worried look at the metal splinter sticking out of his leg.

"Sir, I recognised the mountain range where we ejected, we're close to Lovozero in Russia."

Evans stared at her.

"Where?"

"Lovozero . . . Russia."

And that was when reality hit home. They had been forced to fly too far east and now found themselves behind enemy lines. It was a nightmarish *déjà vu* and he needed a moment to process it.

"Sir, did you hear what I said?"

Evans nodded grimly. He felt an intense pain in his leg and for a moment he panicked. He did not want to go on, he could not go through this again, his heart was racing and he struggled to hide his emotions. He stared up at Ylva standing over him. Her gaze was focused, she was thinking. Her composure was infectious. He felt his panic abate and he consciously switched to survival mode.

"Don't stand there chatting. Get on with it," he grunted.

Ylva squatted next to him. She inspected the wound. The metal was approximately ten centimetres long and shaped like an arrow which disappeared into Evans' calf. Blood trickled from the wound, staining both his trousers and the parachute.

"The challenge is to get your leg well enough for you to manage the trip back."

Evans twisted and growled at her:

"Our challenge is not getting caught by Russian special forces. No question but that Spetsnaz are hunting us right now. This is their backyard. We're in deep shit."

Ylva sat down, sheltered from the wind, took off her combat vest and opened her flight suit before unlacing Evans' boot and placing his foot against her naked stomach. Evans flinched when he felt the heat from Ylva's skin against the sole of his foot. It radiated into his body. It felt strangely intimate and soothing.

Evans let himself sink back and stared feebly at the snow whirling above him. He had been in this situation before, wounded behind enemy lines. That time he had stared into a sandstorm that blocked out the merciless North African sun. Evans had been a different man then, a man whose idealism, pugnacity and courage knew no limits. Now he felt the cold, the despondency. No-one ventured out on the Arctic tundra apart from Russian special forces, not in the middle of the winter. What the Russians would do when they captured the pilots who had flown towards Russia's biggest military nuclear air base, he could only imagine. But this was part of the deal, he reminded himself, as the consequences of what he had done began to dawn on him.

Ylva had managed to ease Evans' trouser leg over the shard without having to cut the fabric. She studied the surface of the wound. She twisted the metal very carefully. Only a little more blood trickled out. Good.

"Sir, I think it missed any arteries."

Evans did not have the strength to respond. Ylva got out the lighter and the knife from her survival kit, and set them on the ground in front of her. It was not until then that she took off her gloves and cupped her hands around Evans' ankle. They looked at one another, Evans nodded, he knew what she had to do. She tried very gently to wiggle the metal shard loose. The pain ripped through him and he cried out, flinging his arms up and arching his back. Ylva deftly avoided the blows, she saw them come and let the pain subside before carrying on. But it was no use; the fragment was too embedded in his calf to be easily extracted.

"Steady now, sir."

Evans glared wildly at Ylva, then he pulled himself together. The wind made it tricky to light the lighter, but eventually she succeeded. With her back to the wind, she shielded the flame as she held it against the sharp blade of the knife to sterilise it. She looked down at Evans.

"Ready?"

He clenched his teeth and nodded.

Ylva placed the knife parallel with the metal and wedged the blade between the metal and the flesh. She tried to gauge how deeply she would need to push it in to reach the tip. The blade sank approximately four centimetres into Evans' calf muscle before she felt the point where the hard metal ended and soft tissue met the knife. Ylva noticed how Evans tensed his jaw, then without hesitating, she flipped the blade and the metal shard was lifted towards her. With stiff, frozen fingers she tried to pinch the fragment and pull it out completely, but it was covered in blood and too slippery. Evans writhed in pain.

"Sir, I need to ease the shard out further in order to get a proper hold of it."

Evans nodded. Yet again Ylva held the gas flame to the knife; the smell and the sound of Evans' roasting blood made her well up with nausea. She wanted to turn away, but managed to steady herself. When the knife had cooled a little, she drove it further into Evans' calf to wedge it once more under the fragment. Through the gusts of wind she could hear the gurgling sound of flesh and blood being compressed. She had to bear down heavily on the knife to raise the shard far enough for her to get a proper grip. She clasped it with frozen fingers and with one hard tug she managed to pull it out. Evans' cries drowned out the howling gale. Then he fell quiet and lay still and all they could hear was the mournful whisper of snowflakes that chased each other restlessly across the tundra.

As the shard left the flesh, Ylva saw fresh blood run from the wound and was relieved. That told her that she had got the whole piece of metal out.

With trembling fingers, Ylva put pressure on the gaping wound, but the blood now spurted in heavy gulps. Her fingers were frozen stiff and she was not able to apply sufficient pressure to stem the blood and bandage the wound. Evans was now deathly pale and spasms racked his body.

"I need to cauterise the wound, sir."

He knew what that meant. Exposing flesh and blood to extreme heat would bond the proteins the way protein in an egg is hardened when it is fried. He knew that it would stop the bleeding. The problem was that burn injuries to the surrounding tissue would increase his risk of sepsis. Cauterising the wound would buy Evans some days in which to get to a doctor before the infection became fatal. He also knew he had no choice.

"Do it, Nordahl, get it over with."

Again she let the lighter flame lick the blade of the knife and this time without letting it cool down, she plunged the knife into the open wound . . . fizzzz . . .

Evans stared up at Ylva in desperate agony. He gripped her hand and tried to wrestle the knife from her. Ylva braced herself, she could not let go now. She pinned him down with a firm gaze while the glowing hot knife scorched the damaged tissue and sealed the wound. It hissed as flesh and blood were burned to a thin, charred crust. Evans' rage of pain subsided and as his adrenaline level dropped, he lost consciousness.

Ylva pulled out the bloody blade, wiped it clean in the snow. The wind had eased off, and she noticed that they were surrounded by a clear white light. She cut a strip off his parachute and bandaged the wound.

Evans lay very pale and still and made not a sound. Except for a few reflex twitches, he seemed lifeless. On the ground next to him was the bloody metal fragment and Ylva studied it before sniffing it. The nauseating stench of blood and fuel was impossible to mistake. Just to be sure she lit the lighter and held the flame against the metal. It started burning with an intense blue flame. It had come from the fuel tank. Evans opened his eyes and squinted feebly at the eerie flame; they both knew what it meant. It wasn't a question of if he would get septicaemia, but when.

Once his wound was bandaged by Ylva, Evans struggled to get to his feet. This was worse than Ghibli, he began to realise, far worse. There was no point in fighting it, he had only himself to blame for the situation in which he found himself. Now he had to think of a way out. He glanced at Ylva, who had stood up beside him and was looking about her.

"Sir, our plane must have gone down some kilometres southeast of where we are now. The Russians will start searching there. That gives us a head start." He nodded. Ylva looked up at the light seeping through the snow-laden clouds. The sun was to the north. The time must be about ten in the morning. That gave them some idea of which direction was west. Evans looked at his watch. The glass had been cracked and the hands bent, but the compass was still working. The arrow pointed north.

15

The President was furious. This was no accident. A N.A.T.O. fighter jet did not by chance fly straight at a Russian nuclear base. Stone-faced, he listened to his staff's report from Monchegorsk. The incident must have been staged by somebody who would benefit from dragging the Arctic into a shadow war. But who, other than himself, would want to unleash turmoil in the Barents region?

The West's media frenzy was flickering across the television screens behind him. A babel of news anchors, rapidly compiled graphics and hyperbolic conspiracy theories. "N.A.T.O. plane shot down by Russia during N.A.T.O. exercise", "Russian attack on N.A.T.O. demands firm response!", "Is Finnmark the new Crimea or the new Donbas?" Political fortune-tellers were getting themselves very hot under the collar. This was just one more blitz in Russia's war on the West, they proclaimed. The experts explained to the world that the F-16 incident was obviously staged by the Kremlin to legitimise a long-planned attack on N.A.T.O.'s border in the north.

True enough, he had had his share of fun toying with the Western media circus, but he found it repugnant nonetheless. He realised that the Western "freedom of speech" was little more than a cleverly staged spectacle of fake news, vacuous infotainment and clickbait. He learned this the painful way during the collapse of the Soviet Union, when all unifying narratives were shattered and the Russian state descended into chaos. At first he was bewildered, but then he saw his country's humiliation and breakdown as a golden opportunity. He had invited media strategists and spin doctors from the West, so that he could learn how to use the chaos to his advantage. And by this means, he rose to power.

The most valuable lesson his Western spin doctors taught him, was that the common people craved sincerity, and a hero's journey wrapped in exciting visuals. It did not feel natural to him. As the nihilistic former K.G.B. agent that he was, he had a clear leaning towards irony, understatements and covert threats. Like all of his countrymen he was jaded and embittered, his expectations of leadership and heroism were below zero. The Russian people were demoralised by their own heroes. Just another grey-faced, shifty-eyed Polit-bureau would not be the answer. Nobody believed in those types anymore. He had to reinvent himself, and with the help of spin doctors he rose like a phoenix from the fuming ashes of Mother Russia's cremation. Shiny and new, he introduced himself as a fresh-faced, Chechnya-pounding super-hero. A uniquely Russian version of the hero's myth emerged with images of him as a bare-breasted, macho leader on horse-back replete with sanctimonious, traditional orthodox values and moral superiority. Might, sex appeal and religious fervour. He had it all for a while.

He who controls the narrative, wins the war.

So, what was the narrative here? The President forced his attention back from musings of the past to the clear and present danger. The report from a Major Khodrokovska stated that everything proceeded as normal until the N.A.T.O. aircraft started chasing the Russian Fullback. The F-16 had not responded when the Major hailed it as it crossed the Russian border, instead it carried on heading straight for Monchegorsk before it was heroically shot down over the town of Apatity. The number of casualties was thirty-seven and still counting. Images from the town were shown on all T.V. screens: burning wreckage set fire to a hospital and an apartment block. Pictures of civilians with burn injuries and charred patients were causing tempers to fray. The army had already located the remains of the pilot seats, so the pilots themselves could not have gone far. Spetsnaz units were on their way.

The situation was too unstable for the President's liking. The pilots had to be captured. He would not let them go unless they gave him every bit of information about who was behind this, how the operation had been planned and why. Then he would let them go, through death. After all, he was not completely heartless.

The President had been ambushed by how this had happened, but he was not astonished that something potentially catastrophic had occurred. He knew that the relatively high level of international peace, cooperation and rule of law that had been the norm for the last seventy years was, historically speaking, the exception. In reality, chaos was the norm. That was nature's way; everything had to be destroyed in order to be reborn. Over and over and over again.

The President ignored the debate on what had happened and who was to blame and went to the window. He stood there in the now pale grey winter light and gazed at the number of foreign policy specialists making for the administration building. A black Mercedes pulled up in front of the entrance and out stepped Norway's stately and jovial ambassador, Tom Erik Gran. The President watched him closely. The ambassador's hair was ruffled and his suit jacket unbuttoned, he seemed stressed. This suggested to the President that the Norwegians were equally unprepared for the N.A.T.O. plane's journey to Monchegorsk. So the Americans alone had to be behind this, but which internal faction in Washington was at the helm now? Who would have been able to issue such an order?

It was most unlikely that the exercise he had announced only a few hours earlier could have triggered this response. For a N.A.T.O. fighter jet to set its course for a Russian nuclear base would have to have been planned and cleared at every level and that would have taken weeks. Where did his intelligence fail him? The President cursed himself for not having anticipated all the variables that set in motion this train of events.

The pain in his shoulder had spread to his head and neck and brought him back into his body. His rapidly decaying body. Well, he would just have to reshuffle his cards. General Svetla was already on it, the old general's response to the shocking development was as expressionless, cool and unfazed as always. Mayhem was his preferred theatre of war. They did not make generals like that anymore.

16

Every time Evans put weight on his wounded leg, Ylva heard him breathe in short, angry gasps. The storm had eased off, and she was relieved to see that her calculations had been correct; she knew where they were. She had been here before.

Trudging across the frozen Lake Seydozero was a beautiful nightmare. The lake faced south and the north wind had left behind deep snowdrifts with an icy crust that cracked and gave way with every step. Ylva could almost feel the pain that seared through Major Evans every time his injured foot went through the crust and hit compacted ice. His face gave no sign of emotion save his straining jaw muscles, the beads of sweat on his upper lip and his pale grey face. It was all she needed to know.

They kept a good pace and despite the deep snow and a vicious headwind, they managed to cross the lake in a couple of hours.

"Sir, if we can keep going for another three to four hours, we'll reach the caves in the mountains. We can rest there." Evans stared at Ylva, tiny icicles hung from his eyebrows and eyelashes. He had already developed itching sores along the edge of one eyelid. He raised a hand to his face.

"Don't touch it!"

"What?"

"You'll irritate your tear ducts, you've already got frostbite around your eyes. Don't touch it."

Evans made no reply, but carried on walking, grim and silent. His expression was furious. Ylva heaved a sigh of irritation; she could not see the point of this antagonism. A failure of team spirit, she thought. As the senior officer he was responsible for morale, for setting the tone. Major Evans was an unprofessional, selfish loner; fine, she could take care of herself and she would simply ignore this grumpy old man.

The north wind lashed them with sharp ice needles and though they walked as fast as they could, the cold soon extended its grip to their faces, fingers and toes. Eventually the silence began to get on Ylva's nerves; her physical discomfort and her exasperation were both growing. What was the point of not talking? Was this a battle of wills? She had been wondering what had really happened during the collision, but had been unable to form a clear picture. What had she done wrong? She could not understand it. The situation was unreal and she dreaded to think what was going on in the outside world right now.

"Sir, do you think the Russian pilot will say what happened? That we . . . that this . . ."

What was she really asking? Did she think the Russian pilot would admit that his buzzing them had gone wrong, that he had first crashed into the N.A.T.O. plane in international airspace and later shot it down over Murmansk? Or had the Russians staged the incident, was that possible?

"The hawks have been provoked. We won't get a Powers deal."

Major Evans sounded bitter. Francis Powers, the American U2 pilot who was shot down over the Soviet Union in 1960 on his way to Bodø from a N.A.T.O. base in Pakistan, had been captured and sentenced to ten years in prison for espionage. The so-called "U2 affair" led to Khrushchev cancelling his attendance at a peace summit in Paris. He threatened to drop a nuclear bomb on Bodø. Thanks to diplomacy on both sides, the Americans eventually managed to persuade Russia to return Powers to the U.S.A. and a long political or military crisis was averted. Evans did not think that today's political operators had the sense or the will to handle a situation such as this one so astutely.

They walked on in silence with the light fading. They both knew that not far away a substantial N.A.T.O. force was close to the border, and that the Russians, for their part, had mobilised a significant force of their own. Ylva and Evans were like matches in a powder keg.

Evans came to a halt and looked about him. The landscape was bathed in a cold, milky fog which erased the horizon between the sky and the earth. If it had not been so bitterly cold, it would have been serene.

"Where are we?"

Ylva followed his gaze across the frozen lake. In the summer its water would ripple like liquid lead and reflect the mountains.

"This is Lake Seydozero."

Major Evans looked grimly at the steep massif.

"Could you be more specific, Nordahl?"

"Sir, we're approximately one hundred and eighty-nine metres above sea level, 67.49°N and 34.51°E, at the foot of Lake Seydozero and the Khibiny massif. And that's Angvundaschorr over there." She pointed to the peaks looming over them.

"The highest point is approximately twelve hundred metres above sea level, but we can walk around it lower down. On the other side it's mainly rough scrub and tundra until the town of Rayakoski, and that's close to the Norwegian border."

Evans nodded briefly, then he resumed marching.

* * *

Though they were shielded from the north wind once they reached the foothills, it also grew colder. Ylva studied the blue light and calculated the time to be somewhere between three and four in the afternoon. The light would disappear soon and the terrain would become impossible to navigate. The lake was surrounded by dramatic rock faces and ravines. They would have to cross steep gorges and dangerous, stony mountain passes to get to the other side of the massif. The mountains, however, also provided them with shelter and places to hide, and they would need those because Russian soldiers would be combing the landscape in their hunt for the missing pilots as soon as they had failed to find their bodies among the wreckage.

Some way further up the incline Ylva stopped, looked at the cliff face looming above them, and smiled. Major Evans stopped as well, then he gave her a puzzled look.

"Nordahl?"

"Sir, do you know what that is?"

He followed Ylva's gaze and his eyes widened. In the deep blue late afternoon light he saw the outline of a giant tower above them, nearly eighty metres tall.

The light was perfect and the enormous, anthropomorphic creature looked as if it was coming out of the mountain, as if it were walking towards them.

"This is Kuiva."

"Kuiva?"

"According to Sámi mythology, this is Kuiva the Giant. They believed he lived in this mountain."

Evans looked at Ylva sceptically.

"This area is one of the holiest places for the Sámi people."

"How do you know this?"

"I lived not far from here as a child."

"Don't tell me you're a damned Russian?" Ylva ignored the accusation.

"My mother's family is from this region and we lived with them for several months after my father died."

The look Evans gave Ylva was inscrutable; his narrow blue eyes peered through the ice that had formed on his eyelashes.

"It's said that the Hyperboreans came from here," Ylva said.

His gaze rested on her until he took another look at the figure above them. It seemed frozen in time. Then he passed a weary hand across his face.

"Go on."

"There is much superstition and many legends associated with this region. In the last ten years alone more than a hundred people have disappeared up here. No-one knows how or why."

Major Evans sighed impatiently.

"I meant go on walking, Nordahl!"

She kept her mouth shut and started walking.

The darkness descended heavily over the landscape as they scrambled up the mountainside. Although he never said a word, Ylva could feel that Major Evans was utterly exhausted.

No-one knew better than he how pain could consume your thoughts. Seconds blurred, every shrill, agonising minute becoming an eternity. But he could take it. Among the smouldering ruins of Fezzan, the experienced doctor working with his torturers could hardly believe his eyes. Evans had gritted his teeth and endured the sack over his head and the water which was poured over him relentlessly. Then there was sleep deprivation, his injuries from the plane crash, infections, hunger, thirst. Evans had won the respect of the Mujahedeen, hardened and deadly mercenaries from the worst wars in Afghanistan, now hired to fight in Libya. But apart from a sizeable ransom provided by an unknown benefactor after eight months of captivity, the Libyan rebels got nothing out of John Evans. He had endured the unendurable and survived the impossible.

But this was worse. Not because of the throbbing pain in his leg or his constantly aching back, no, it was the cold. Icicles had formed on his eyebrows and eyelashes, and every intake of breath stung his lungs. He had lost feeling in his toes and fingers. He looked at the slip of a girl fighting her way up the mountainside ahead of him. Was she Russian? There had been nothing about that in her file, it had just said that she spoke some Russian and he had not paid enough attention. Who was she? Evans struggled to keep up with her. He decided to find out as much as he could about her and make the best use of her until he was picked up.

17

N.A.T.O.'s Secretary General was a rational man who had ample experience of complex crises before now. He thrived on the pressure, his emotions rarely got the better of him. Now he sat very still as he listened to his experts.

"What's the status of the search and rescue mission?"

Norway's permanent representative at N.A.T.O.'s Security Council cleared her throat:

"Secretary General, the search and rescue operation is in progress in the Hoop area, and an S.A.R. Queen helicopter from the 330 Squadron at Banak is in the same location searching for wreckage. We have also despatched a frigate from Mehamn and K.V. *Senja* has set out from Bjørnøya, both are bound for Hoop. Exercise Arctic Blizzard has been put on hold, of course, but all personnel will remain in the region prepared for active duty."

"And the Russians?"

He looked across to the head of N.A.T.O.'s Defence Committee, who shook his head.

"We're still trying to contact the President, so far without success. The contacts we have report they have no idea what caused this."

The Secretary General hid his impatience and listened attentively while his team offered well-argued opinions about what N.A.T.O. ought to do next.

Should they show willingness to act, mobilise their ground forces and strike back? Or be flexible and adopt a wait-and-see policy? Was it better to be transparent and enter into a dialogue? Or be strategic and keep your cards close to your chest?

The Secretary General's face was inscrutable as he studied the faces staring at him from the screens on the wall and around the meeting table. Situation reports, analyses, facts and intelligence: everyone produced intelligent, reasonable assessments. Of course they did. They were all intelligent and reasonable people.

The Secretary General's thoughts wandered to an old country house he had recently found with his retirement in mind. He liked its rustic character and he was fond of authenticity and simplicity – or at least he liked to think so. After a career in the world's uppermost corridors of power, he had grown used to living with exceptional quality. Everything ran like clockwork. Occasionally he still felt like an outsider in the midst of this cosmopolitan elegance and he told himself that he missed the simple life. But did he? He had decided to give himself time, plenty of time, to find out what he really liked once he was ready to retire and move to the old wooden house. It was cruel, really, that you were not granted time for reflection until the end of your life.

"What are you thinking, sir?"

The question came from General Grant, N.A.T.O.'s Head of Operations. The Secretary General looked up, what was he thinking? Those who knew the Secretary General's leadership style knew that he never first set out his own thoughts, but would listen to everyone's contribution and have the situation illuminated from as many angles as possible. He did not like the question and now, with everyone looking at him, he could feel the tension in the room.

The Secretary General glanced at his strategic military adviser, a young man with great potential. The adviser knew that his boss would want to know more before he answered that question and said:

"The most important thing right now is to exhibit calm and gain a complete picture . . ."

The answer was so obvious that hardly anyone in the meeting noticed the tone the young man permitted himself towards a decorated general.

Who doesn't want calm and a complete picture? the Secretary General thought. But a complete picture had so far been conspicuous by its absence and a rising unease – or was it more than unease, was it a growing fear? – pervaded the meeting.

Grant, the ageing general whose potential was definitely behind him, puffed himself up.

"With respect, sir, this act of war may be in effect a declaration of war, not a theoretical strategy conference. If there is any prospect of there being a war, we must be on the offensive. We must seize the initiative."

"If this is a declaration of war from the Russians, they already have the initiative," the young adviser said.

The Secretary General smiled, yes, he liked the young man. But now everyone's eyes were on him again, they wanted to hear the Secretary General's opinion. He sighed and looked around at the agitated participants with some concern, but he said nothing. He waited. A female cyber defence expert cleared her throat discreetly on one of the screens; he saw glimpses of the New York skyline behind her. The Secretary General nodded and said:

"Go on, please."

"Sir, if we react as the Russians expect, they will most likely resort to a predictable response pattern towards us. We must not trigger or provoke unpredictable reactions from the enemy, but rather start by identifying the motives and needs of the other side."

"Right, and what's the Russian motive in this instance?"

"To dominate the Arctic," General Grant said.

The Secretary General's young adviser smiled politely. He interrupted the general again. "They already do, General. By virtue of being the world's biggest Arctic power, they are in full control up there. The question is rather: why would they want to destabilise a situation that already works in their favour?"

This was the key question. Why were the Russians doing this now? General Grant slammed his hand on the table and got everyone's attention. He looked firmly at the Secretary General.

"Sir, the Russians are busy mobilising what we believe to be a force of fifteen thousand soldiers on the Norwegian border, we can't wait for them to finish mobilising before we respond!"

He let his words sink in before he went on, calmer and more professorial now: "If the Russians are behind this, they're certainly well prepared. We must be on the offensive and put as much pressure on them as we can in order to provoke a reaction, we must force them to show us their hand and what they're willing to sacrifice."

The Secretary General listened. It made sense, he didn't want to come across as weak, not towards the Russians.

"What do you suggest, General?"

General Grant said, "We must attack when they least expect it." There was murmuring around the table. "The Russians are busy mobilising their albeit somewhat limited resources at the Norwegian border, that's their focus, so we should put our N.A.T.O. bases to the southwest on alert."

Renewed murmuring around the table... what did N.A.T.O.'s bases in the southwest have to do with this?

"The art is knowing when to fight and when not to fight," the young adviser said.

The general smiled sarcastically.

"Do you have any other platitudes to offer?"

"How much time would we need to prepare an attack?" the Secretary General wondered out loud.

Muffled discussions across the group.

"That depends on what kind of offensive we have in mind. Conventional assaults take time. Psychological operations, air and cyber-attacks are easier to mobilise. Strictly speaking, we ought to prepare a hybrid attack with contributions from P.S.Y.O.P.S., cyber, air, sea and ground forces," the general said.

The Secretary General nodded.

"Thank you, thank you for your contributions, we will put all our forces on alert, prepare a strategy to be implemented across the board, and in the meantime with all possible expedition and on every front, most especially from the Russian forces on the Ukrainian border, we will collect more information."

In other words, yes, please, to both. More mumbling and run-ups to discussions, but the Secretary General indicated that the meeting was over, and everyone went their separate ways.

Everyone was happy to agree to disagree. This was N.A.T.O. after all.

The Secretary General had a break of thirteen minutes before his next meeting. He checked his mobile, no messages.

Ever since he received the news that the Russians had shot down the N.A.T.O. plane, he had expected to hear from his good friend Tom Erik Gran. The Norwegian Prime Minister had dispatched the experienced ambassador to meet with the Russian Foreign Office as soon as he knew that the F16 had been shot down; if anyone could pour oil on troubled waters, then it was Tom Erik Gran.

He would swiftly determine whether the fate of the N.A.T.O. plane was the result of deliberate Russian aggression. Politics, however, was a game, and the Secretary General knew that anything said during the meeting would be hard to believe, and for that reason what he was really waiting to hear was Gran's personal impression of the Russian mood. Much could be gleaned from nervous glances or unusual reticence among the Russian civil servants, but most of all he wanted to know how Lavrov had come across. Was he direct and informal or was he evasive? But how to interpret these behaviours? Direct and informal could be a tactical diversion. Likewise, evasive might mean that the Russians, too, had been ambushed and that they were scared, just as N.A.T.O. was. The ambassador was a particularly good judge of character and the Secretary General would trust his opinion. Meanwhile they would have to wait while they prepared for every possible scenario, even the worst. Especially the worst.

His back ached after having sat in meetings and video conferences for hours. He stood up stiffly and tried a few stretches, which only made things worse. What had the N.A.T.O. plane been doing so far into Russian airspace? And why did no-one on the western side have any information as to what was going on?

That in itself was suspicious; somebody always knew something, but who?

He stayed to watch the simulations, computer programs that worked out possible scenarios. He liked this approach; the capacity of artificial intelligence to process vast quantities of data and variables was exhilarating. The downside was that although the simulations produced various outcomes, these were limited by the explicit parameters that fallible human beings had programmed into them.

So this was nothing more than fancy guesswork. The disadvantage of artificial intelligence was precisely that: it was artificial.

His telephone rang. The Secretary General checked the number, but decided to let the call go to voicemail. It was N.A.T.O.'s press secretary, she would need more information. The pressure was increasing by the hour, people wanted answers, they wanted to know what the next step would be. N.A.T.O. had to respond, he agreed with that, N.A.T.O. would have to give as good as it had got, of course. But the as-yet unanswered question was, what were they responding to?

The Secretary General had instinctively thought that he needed a rational solution to the incident, but then it struck him that this was precisely what all the computer simulations and analysts were working on. The rational aspects were being thoroughly explored, but what about the irrational elements at play? How would he gain an understanding of them?

He rubbed his aching back. There was no shortage of theories and analyses, but what he needed to access now were his emotions, his intuition. That was always more challenging. But never mind, he had a few minutes to spare and decided to give it a go: what did the Russian president feel right now? Which impulses and deeper motives drove him? What were his hopes? What were his fears?

They had met each other several times over the years and their interactions had been for the most part professional and courteous. The President came across as cunning, composed and rational, and the Secretary General had formed the impression that he was afraid of appearing emotional and irrational. Thus it followed that he cared about his image, about what people thought of him. He spent a great deal of time and resources presenting himself as an alpha male and he would never do anything that made him look foolish. That was a good starting point. They must not do anything that might humiliate him.

The memory of their first meeting came back to him. It had been a warm September day in 2000. As soft sunlight poured through the tall windows in the U.N. building, he had attended the General Assembly for the first time by virtue of being Norway's newly-elected Prime Minister. He remembered the tension; as a head of government in the General Assembly he wielded considerable power, and with it came the corresponding responsibility. He was also aware that in the U.N. he would be surrounded by the most hawkish operators he would ever meet. But he loved the challenges and the game. And so did his counterpart, the Russian president.

They had both come to power through the capitulation of others, and both were tactical and patient opportunists; neither of them was ultimately revolutionary or inclined to maximise crises. When they had first met, twenty years ago, the mood had been characterised by Glasnost and was the most relaxed relationship between Russia and the West for more than a century. But now the situation was, if anything, more complex and tense than during the coldest decade of the Cold War.

Keeping your cool in such circumstances had proved invaluable.

The Secretary General was reminded of Stanislav Petrov, the Russian Lieutenant Colonel who had prevented a possible nuclear war in 1983. The tension level between Russia and the West was at its height when Petrov, the duty officer at the command centre for the Soviet Union's warning system for potential American nuclear weapons attacks, received an alert from a surveillance satellite that the U.S. had launched five nuclear missiles at the Soviet Union. His orders were that if he identified a nuclear attack, he was to launch a counterattack with all of the Soviet Union's nuclear weapons. Petrov had to make a decision that would decide humanity's fate. Rather than obey his orders, Petrov decided first to investigate if any Soviet surveillance radars had registered the rockets. They had not. Should he trust the land-based radars or the satellite surveillance? Petrov concluded that they could not risk starting a nuclear war based on the alert from the surveillance satellite, and he held off. The fifteen minutes in which the Russians waited without knowing if they were about to be subjected to a nuclear attack must have seemed endless, but when no nuclear missiles appeared, they concluded it must have been a false alarm. Later it was established that a Soviet satellite had interpreted reflections of sunlight in the state of Montana as a missile being launched.

In 1983 they had about thirty minutes in which to respond in the event of a nuclear attack; today they had five minutes at the most. The Secretary General thought that if anyone had deserved a Nobel Peace Prize it was Lieutenant Colonel Petrov.

18

The only sound was the crisp crunching with every step they took of the frozen snow crust. It was after her father had died that Ylva had often roamed this area with her more adventurous cousins. The mountains and the lake were steeped in myths, and her cousins made a few roubles showing U.F.O. fanatics and Hyperborean tourists the way to the top of the mountain. Now she was trying to work out what would be the quickest route around the peak and down the massif on the western side, an area she had never hiked before.

The period immediately after the death of her father was the worst, but in some ways also the best, in Ylva's life. She had little memory of what had happened in the immediate aftermath of having found her father dying on the basement floor. Everything was chaos. Her mother had, bizarrely, exhibited considerable composure. When Ylva told her about the shadow she saw seconds before her father died, her mother had believed her. The police, however, found no evidence. No D.N.A., nothing to suggest that her father had been the victim of a crime. On the other hand, because pilots are subjected to extremes of pressure and g-forces, they are at increased risk of medical complications such as blood clots to the brain. Thus it was, according to the autopsy report, that this was recorded as the cause of his death. The snow around their house had not a single mark on it. It was clear that no-one had entered other than through the front door, and the only people to have come in that way were the emergency crew. Nevertheless, Ylva's mother was convinced that Ylva had spoken the truth.

Their family worried about how Ylva and her mother would manage the tough time after Geir's death. They were aware of Mary's sensitive mind, and when Ylva's cousins invited them to stay with them in Lovozero to grieve their loss, Mary accepted the invitation. It gave her something new to explore and learn. Her niece had married a Russian reindeer-herding Sámi, and thanks to Glasnost and open borders between Norway and Russia, they were at last able to visit one another. Mary soon took an interest in the history and rights of the Sámi people in Russia.

She found peace in the company of her relatives and, for a time, she seemed almost normal. After long days with the reindeer herd on the plains, she would sleep through the night with very little in the way of drugs. She grew more pensive and introspective, but she smiled more often, albeit inscrutably. She would also, for once, listen more than she talked, which made a welcome change as far as Ylva was concerned.

But soon after they returned to Bodø, Mary's condition deteriorated and eventually she lost her grip altogether. She began to talk incessantly. She rambled about Ylva's father being the victim of a geopolitical conspiracy, claiming that he had known something that had got him killed. In time her conspiracy theories became so fanciful and her accusations so outrageous that the police stopped returning her calls. She was prescribed stronger medication and, like so many other people who refused to conform, she was chemically cudgelled and then, not until then . . . did she fall silent.

Her silence got on Ylva's nerves. She began to miss her mother's babbling about myths, spirituality, spirits, etymology, literature, politics, metaphysics, epigenetics, music, culture, rituals, psychology, paintings, movies and history, spiced up with various scientific facts about ... well, about everything ... In particular Ylva missed her "quasi-scientific" lectures on quantum physics and entanglement. Because when Ylva bothered to do her own research and read up on the science behind the various subjects her mother had talked about, it turned out often that she was right. She knew the hard facts and was au fait with much of the recent research in a variety of fields.

During the day Mary would read or watch the news non-stop, at night she would read books or surf the Internet for the most progressive scientific and political lectures. But what was the point of all this learning? After all, she had no-one with whom she could share it. It was precisely because she saw everything from multiple angles, because she immersed herself so thoroughly in every subject, and because she was looking for connections and conspiracies where there were none, that she lost herself in these endless streams of research to the point at which she was declared insane. It was no wonder she lost the plot, Ylva thought, no mind could handle such quantities of information.

As she battled her way through the cold, Ylva caught herself yearning for her mother's bright, animated voice, which with scattergun speed described the world in an unedited stream of consciousness of colourful stories, humorous observations, scientific explanations and epic conspiracy theories.

With a pang of sadness Ylva thought that if her mother had been here now rather than the grim, sullen major, she would have held forth about the components of permafrost and the ancient Arctic Yakut horses that could survive −50°C – she had obviously ridden one. Most of all, she loved to lecture on *sastrugi*, the long wave-shaped ice ridges which the wind carved out of the snow-covered landscape. Walking on *sastrugi* was a nightmare, Ylva thought, but her mother loved how they undulated like silky sand dunes along the direction of the prevailing wind. *Sastrugi* combined all of her mother's interests, the aesthetic patterns in the ice crust were sculptural guides that also revealed local weather patterns. A grasp of knowledge of this could mean the difference between life and death out on the tundra.

Then her mother would segue for no apparent reason into something as random as ... the Hyperboreans, the giants from the land north of the northern wind – as described by Herodotus, no less, long before the birth of Christ and Cleopatra's liaison with Julius Caesar. Her mother preferred Greek mythology to theology and Roman history. She would probably have described Herodotus' accounts of the mythic Hyperboreans with intense animation and drama, something being old and surrounded by myths always made it especially meaningful to her. And if Ylva knew her mother, such a lecture would soon lead to a prolonged philosophical discourse about how the Sámi people came originally from the Iberian peninsula. Genetically speaking, we descend from the North African Berbers, she would declare. And yes, of course her mother had lived in a tent in the desert with the Berbers for several months, not once, but twice. She liked the Berbers. Though the Berbers did not refer to themselves as such, they called themselves "Imazighen", which meant something like "free men", and that was probably what she liked about them. Free men – who doesn't like free men? Ylva thought. And once more she missed Storm. She smiled to herself and thought about his eyes, his hands, his lips.

Evans watched Ylva smile as she walked. What the hell was the girl laughing about? Had she lost her wits? He would have to keep a close watch on her mental state. He depended utterly on her judgment to get out of here alive. And the judgment of somebody chuckling to themselves given the mess they were in was decidedly precarious.

They walked through an icy, clear and moonless night. The outline of the mountains was gradually erased against the dark sky. Evans could feel a cold, eerie sensation starting to grip him. Finally he would get to experience the absolute darkness he had dreamed about. The darkness was exactly as all-encompassing and as impenetrable as he had feared and hoped. Evans had many regrets in life, as an executioner for the most aggressive and mighty power in world history there were countless reasons to have regrets, but right now as the darkness was about to swallow him up, he felt a dawning certainty that he was ultimately doing the right thing. Those he wanted to protect, those he had to protect, would be alright now. Thanks to him. He had done the only right thing he could.

He tried to think back to the moment when he should have brought his army career to an end. Of the fifty or so armed conflicts in which the U.S.A. had been involved since the Second World War – the majority having been relatively unknown shadow wars that no-one cared about – Evans had taken part in six. Starting with Afghanistan, then Iraq and Somalia; after a brief spell back in the States, he was deployed to Uganda before he was redeployed first to Syria and then to Libya. Evans had travelled the world. But later the doubts had set in. Had it been worth it? Had he really been making the U.S.A. safer? Was he truly protecting his country and his people with all these military interventions in other parts of the world? Once upon a time Evans' intentions had been good, but the road to hell is, as is well known, paved with good intentions.

The silence was broken when Evans heard a faint hum in the distance; he recognised the sound and heaved a sigh.

"They're here."

"Who?"

"Russian surveillance planes."

Ylva reacted immediately. They slipped under a large limestone outcrop. Seconds later the spy plane passed over them. The limestone canopy prevented them from being detected by the heat-sensitive camera. The plane flew on.

Evans looked at Ylva.

"They've worked out that we didn't go down with the F-16."

Ylva nodded.

The hunt had begun. They were the prey.

19

When Igor Serkin left for work eighteen hours earlier, he had been a nobody. By the time he came home, he was the great Russian hero. He was devastated.

The day had been a total catastrophe. The promising start with a run, breakfast with his family and a mission that was to have been nothing more than a simple buzzing, had turned into a disaster Serkin could never in his worst nightmares have imagined. The adrenaline rush that had surged through him as he shot down the N.A.T.O. plane had ended abruptly when he saw it plunge to the ground and explode into the middle of Apatity. Serkin did not know how many thousands of souls lived in the mining town to the west of the Khibiny mountains. He had watched the explosion as the body of the plane hit the snowdrifts in one violent flash. Then followed the huge fireball that rose towards the sky. The heat from the explosion and the subsequent fire created a clearing in the snow. Serkin watched the fire as it began to spread.

The moment he landed he was summoned for a debriefing and he had told them everything, including the part where he had clipped the N.A.T.O. plane and possibly damaged it during the buzzing. He had been expecting a reprimand followed by a thorough investigation, but his superiors seemed to be in charge of the narrative even before Serkin had given his statement. He did not know whether to feel relieved or intimidated when he was ordered not to talk to anyone about what had happened during the buzzing; he was permitted only to confirm that he had followed an order to shoot down the N.A.T.O. plane, which was heading for the nuclear base in Murmansk. That was the official story, the end.

His superiors had not expressed any surprise at the incident, and that was what troubled Serkin the most.

He had an almost surreal sense that everything was unfolding according to a plan unknown to him, a feeling that only intensified. It was as if he were nothing but a pawn in a much bigger game. But what was the game? What indeed was his part? And who was in control?

The debriefing did not take long and when he returned to the hangar, he was greeted with applause. Having changed out of his uniform, he went to face the reporters who were gathered outside the air base. Serkin followed orders and said only what he had been told to say. Feeling relieved and frightened, he registered that the media swallowed the story whole.

At home his family was on the sofa watching television, the news of the N.A.T.O. attack dominated every channel, and his brief statement was shown over and over. He was presented as a hero, Igor Serkin had saved the nation. By shooting down the N.A.T.O. plane, he had quite possibly prevented an attack on the nuclear base, it was said, a handful of fatalities in Apatity was a small price to pay for something that could have been Russia's biggest nuclear calamity since Chernobyl.

It turned out that the N.A.T.O. plane had crashed into a fertiliser plant on the outskirts of the town, and footage of charred bodies lying scattered like torn rag dolls flickered across the screen. Injured children and adults were tended to by volunteers and healthcare workers while terrified eyewitnesses described how the explosion had rocked them like an earthquake. Emergency vehicles had been unable to reach the scene because whole sections of the road had been demolished. They saw footage of farm animals running free where fences and barns had been destroyed, and apartment blocks with gaping holes where the walls had been peeled off so that people's ruined homes were displayed like doll's houses. The numbers of fatalities and injured had yet to be confirmed. The evacuation of the area was being delayed by the authorities still worried about dangerous gases in the air around the fertiliser plant. A hospital and several apartment blocks had collapsed and only skeletons of some buildings remained – like warnings of what was to come.

The Russian authorities assumed that the N.A.T.O. flight had failed to reach its ultimate target, Monchegorsk Air Base, and aimed instead for the Polyarnye Zori nuclear power station, one hundred and sixty kilometres south of Monchegorsk. It was a blessing that Lieutenant Igor Serkin had managed to shoot down the N.A.T.O. plane before it reached its target.

Serkin felt a strange chill creep under his skin. The narrative of the N.A.T.O. plane being here to bomb the nuclear base in Monchegorsk was taken as read, presented as fact. But it could not be true. How could they know anything about the mission of the N.A.T.O. plane until they had interviewed the pilots? Before N.A.T.O. confirmed it? It was guesswork presented as a fact. Serkin listened to the interview with the President, which was repeated on a dizzying loop. Russia would respond to this attempted attack, N.A.T.O. could be sure of it, he said. So was Serkin. It was the only thing he really was sure of.

At the air base Major Khodrokovska had, to her relief, avoided all the commotion and was fortunately also spared from having to deal with the reporters and their questions. A more ambitious and publicity-craving superior made sure he became the public face of the success. While the media circus was going on outside, Major Khodrokovska remained alone in the hangar, looking at Lieutenant Serkin's plane. She studied it and soon discovered a scratch on its right wing. On closer inspection, she noticed traces of khaki paint. A dent indicated a severe collision. Major Khodrokovska fetched a sharp knife and a test tube, then she scraped off flakes of the khaki paint. She would get them tested.

20

Ylva made sure they walked in a westward direction on the northern side of the mountains. She was aware that Major Evans was battling against the pain in his leg, and she knew that exhaustion was starting to get the upper hand. As it was for her too. She glanced over her shoulder, saw the contours of Major Evans' grim face, and stopped. Night had crept up on them and covered the landscape.

"Sir, do you need a break?"

The reply came promptly: "No!"

Ylva looked at his leg, a dark red blotch could be seen above the top of his boot where blood was seeping through his uniform trousers. Walking in deep snow in −30°C in a nasty headwind took its toll on your strength and Ylva knew that she would struggle to navigate in the darkness. Besides, she needed a rest.

"We're better off stopping now, so that we . . ."

Evans ignored her. He refused to stop and, staring stiffly ahead of him, he continued to drag himself across the ridge. Ylva bit her tongue. The stubborn old bastard really did not know what was good for him, carrying on now was unbelievably stupid. She stopped.

"Sir, I'm not sure of the route and I can't navigate in the dark. We risk doing more harm than good if we keep going."

Evans heard Ylva perfectly, but he carried on walking

nevertheless. She straightened up and looked about her; dense clouds were covering the moon, making it difficult to see anything at all. The contours of the snow-clad mountains stood out only faintly against the night-black sky to the east. She heard Evans stop and was expecting a harsh order, but he said nothing, he just stood there, staring at her.

"Sir, I think . . ."

She broke off; a big shelf stuck out from the rock face right behind him.

It was perfect. With leaden legs she trudged over to it and without saying a word, she started digging out the snow from beneath it.

Evans watched her. He had been wondering ever since they walked past the stone giant on the eastern side of the mountain: who was she? Should he be worried? Could she be a threat? Why hadn't there been any information about the girl having lived in Russia. Surely that was relevant? Was this a set-up?

Evans had grown accustomed to this state of constant vigilance and smouldering aggression; the enemy could be anywhere, could be anyone. Was Ylva an enemy? He didn't have the energy to think about it now, he just wanted to focus on the one person he had always been able to trust, he wanted to think about her. No-one else.

Everyone knew that Evans loved his wife Kathryn, their daughter Leah, and the home they had built together in Willow Springs, Texas. He was stationed near their home for several months after he and Kathryn had married and their daughter was born. It was the happiest time of his life. But eventually he had to return to active duty, and Evans accepted a fairly standard operational role in Syria. He felt it the moment he left, something had changed, life on active duty had lost its appeal. Now that he had a family of his own, he started to see the local population through different eyes. Keeping the necessary emotional distance became more difficult, and he was increasingly asking himself: why are we doing this? Why are we bombing countries thousands of miles from America?

Such thoughts were not new; every soldier has them from time to time, but for Evans they began to dominate. He started to change. When he was out in the field, he was homesick and missed his family, when he was back home with his family, he missed the energy and the sense of camaraderie in the field. It turned into a kind of routine, commuting between his quiet home life in Texas and his intense life in various conflict zones abroad.

By the time Evans was sent to Libya in 2011, he had accepted that his role in life was to provide for his family and to serve his country – except that that was all about to change. After eight agonising months of being held hostage by Libyan rebels, his life would never be the same. When he was rescued and safely returned to Texas, the nightmares had started. His war would never end, the torture continued inside him, every day and every night.

He tried alcohol and it only made things worse; he tried antidepressants and they made him impotent, fat, lethargic and suicidal. His rage abated, but hopelessness and apathy set in. His memory failed him, he could scarcely remember his own name when he was at his worst. For Evans the goal became emotional numbness. Days where he could not feel a damn thing were the best.

He had pretty much made up his mind to end it all. He did not have the strength anymore to be on his guard all the time. He did not have the energy for his degrading, self-destructive behaviour, his guilt, his inability to have a single night's unbroken sleep. He was well-armed and well-prepared, all he had to do was find the right time.

Except he kept putting it off, he hesitated. He was not frightened of dying, but something was unresolved, he still had not done his reckoning. Time passed and he was in freefall with a brain that felt like tar when suddenly he was offered the job of instructor during a forthcoming N.A.T.O. exercise. He had not heard from the air force in a long time, perhaps this job could be a fresh start for him? His last chance to escape the degradation and return to service? Except that deep down he knew better. The job was only a postponement of the inevitable end.

He forced his thoughts aside and glowered suspiciously at Ylva who, with heavy arms, was carving out a snow cave in which they could sleep. He needed her now and she would eventually have to give him the answers he needed. But first they had to rest, he accepted that. He limped over to her. Without a word, he knelt down and started to dig.

21

"Will there be a war, Daddy?"

Young Sergey curled up under his duvet and looked anxiously at his father. Serkin smiled stiffly and tucked the duvet around his son's cold little toes. What could he say? Should he try to explain? Or say that he didn't know and that he, too, was scared?

"Don't worry about it, son," he said.

It was a stupid answer, as if Sergey would be able to stop thinking about it when they had talked of little else all evening.

"Will they bomb us?"

Serkin heaved a weary sigh. He dreaded the answer.

"We won't let anyone bomb us, son. We're safe. I promise you. Now go to sleep."

He could see that the boy was not convinced, his little feet fretted anxiously under the duvet. He put his small hand lightly on top of his father's strong fist.

"But they said on the telly that America might bomb us."

Serkin ruffled his son's hair. The boy's open gaze sought security and assurance that the enemy, whoever it was, would never hurt them.

"Do you know something, I think the best thing we can do right now is to take care of each other and trust our leaders. They'll sort it out, I'm very sure of it."

Young Sergey, however, refused to be reassured; the fear had taken hold.

"You'll protect us, won't you, Daddy?"

Serkin's eyes filled with tears and he looked away. Could he make that promise? He knew that the chaos that had erupted had a dynamic of its own.

What could he have done differently? It had happened so fast, he had not been able to think about anything except his duty to execute an order. It was what he was trained for, it was his job. And then there was the adrenaline rush, he had always loved that rush, but you don't think long-term in the fog of an attack.

After ten years in the valley of the shadows under Gorbachev's glasnost and Yeltsin's chaotic liberalism, Russia had stabilised and the military regained its rightful place in society; the workers' wages and people's pensions were paid on time; the sums might not be anything to cheer about, but it was enough for food on the table and a roof over your head.

Outside Russia everything was falling apart. Serkin had travelled extensively as a young man and had seen for himself the rat race in the West, the unceasing struggle for money and attention. Everyone vying to get ahead no matter the price. He had friends who would give an arm and a leg to move to the U.S.A., convinced that they could make it big there. But what was the point? Serkin wanted to have clear rules and solid ground under his feet. To him that was real freedom. Nor did he fancy the gold-diggers desperate to marry upwards for status. No, he wanted to be married to a real woman like Natasha, wake up to her smile and hear all the noises she made around the house as she got ready to go to bed. It was irritating, but he liked it, they were good noises and he had grown used to them.

Serkin had been given everything he could ever want: a cosy flat, two children he loved, a father who irritated the hell out of him, but who was there when the children came home from school, and who could do all sorts of useful things. And Natasha, of course, he adored his strong and sassy wife who was far smarter than he was, and who truly loved him. As he truly loved her. On top of everything he also had a fighter plane in which he could take off at regular intervals. And of which, once on board, he was king.

"Daddy, answer me, what . . ."

Serkin looked down at his son. He was so trusting and innocent. His soft, chubby cheeks, his delicate little body in the slightly too-big pyjamas, handed down from his cousin, and his hand resting on his own made Serkin's heart ache with sadness. This stage in life would soon be over; his son's childhood would end so fast. Serkin was not able to grasp all the consequences now, but his son's fear spread to him as well.

"You'll look after us, won't you, Daddy?"

He pulled himself together and with a reassuring and steady voice, he answered: "Yes, son, I'll look after you. Always. Like Grandad looked after me, and Great-grandad looked after Grandad. There's nothing to worry about, Mummy and Daddy are here, and we'll take care of you."

And he meant it.

Young Sergey smiled with relief. His eyelids grew heavier and his breathing slowed as his father's voice settled around him.

"They say you're a hero, Daddy. That you saved us."

Serkin's heart sank as he looked at his son, who despite his attempts to stay awake, was falling asleep.

"Daddy, when I grow up I want to be a pilot and I'll bomb all the bad people and protect the good ones. Just like you do."

He had to smile. He could well imagine little Sergey as a proud young man in uniform.

"That's right, son, we'll protect the good ones."

That had also been his dream when he was very young, he was going to protect people and straighten things out, people would be able to count on him. Young Sergey yawned and curled up on his side.

The little boy often dreamed of becoming like his father. He imagined it so clearly: him and his daddy flying above the earth and scaring off the bad guys. He had noticed how everyone at school was scared of the bullies, how no-one ever dared to intervene when they beat up some hapless victim. Everyone looked the other way, they acted as if nothing was happening and made sure not to catch the bullies' evil eyes themselves. It hadn't taken Sergey long to work that out because he was one of those who got beaten up and dumped in the snow. He didn't want to tell anyone about it, it was humiliating. But perhaps the bullies might leave him alone now that his daddy was a hero and had been on T.V.?

"Good night, son."

Then he tiptoed outside.

In the living room Serkin's father was transfixed by the television, Natasha was in the kitchen doing the washing-up. He picked up his mobile, Major Khodrokovska was calling him. Why was she ringing him now?

He had strict orders from his superiors not to talk to outsiders. Not a word, not to his colleagues, his family, friends, least of all to any journalists. He felt Natasha's anxious gaze on him as he put on his coat and stepped out onto the balcony to talk.

"Serkin."

"Good evening, Lieutenant, it's Khodrokovska."

"Good evening."

Major Khodrokovska never wasted time on small talk.

"Did you leave anything out of your report to me?"

Serkin was immediately on his guard; he lit a cigarette and took a deep drag to gain time before he replied.

"Are you referring to anything in particular?"

"Was there physical contact between the Fullback and the N.A.T.O. plane during the buzzing?"

Serkin said nothing, he was not sure if he was permitted to answer.

"Serkin, did you hear the question?"

He had heard the question and he could also hear Major Khodrokovska's irritation at his failure to respond. She knows about the collision, he thought, but she's clearly not a part of the inner circle seeing as she's asking me about the crash. He said nothing.

"Did you cause the accident while buzzing the plane?"

Serkin took another drag on his cigarette. She was definitely not one of those in the know. He said in a mild but firm voice: "I followed orders."

"This must be reported."

He saw his own reflection in the window, there were two of him. His family was inside where it was warm, he was out in the cold.

"I've given a detailed report to our superiors in Moscow, you'll have to ask them if anything is unclear."

"But they never said anything about—"

Major Khodrokovska stopped herself, she didn't want to say more or make it clear that she had not been briefed. Serkin realised that she must suspect what had happened between the Fullback and the N.A.T.O. plane and instinctively he wanted to discuss his dilemma with her, but obviously he could not, he had been given explicit instructions to keep his mouth shut. Besides, if the major was not already in the loop, there was bound to be a good reason.

"Was there anything else, Major Khodrokovska?"

He adopted a tone as neutral and professional as he could, hoping his voice would not betray his extreme discomfort. Major Khodrokovska understood that she was not going to get anywhere, and ended the conversation politely and formally.

Serkin stayed out in the cold, looking at the lights from the apartment blocks around him, and listening to the noise from the town in the distance. She has worked out that I clipped their plane, he thought, but she has not been told so officially. Should he alert the team from Moscow?

If she started investigating the incident on her own, the possibility of keeping it a secret would be undermined, and he would be left to take the blame. He shuddered, his discomfort eating away at him. No, she would have to form her own view and possibly take it to the relevant authority. He wasn't getting involved.

Besides, he did not want to say anything that might get Major Khodrokovska into trouble. The people in Moscow were not a bear you wanted to poke, everybody knew that. He took a final drag on his cigarette, then he stubbed it out and put the butt in his pocket before returning to the warmth.

22

General Rove could not imagine why anyone would choose to live so far north. Wet sleet was blown in from the sea. It was barely four o'clock in the afternoon and it was practically pitch dark. After almost a day and night of intense crisis management, he had gone back to his hotel for a few hours of badly needed sleep. It was a particular talent of his, he could sleep anytime, anywhere, regardless of the circumstances. A soldier sleeps whenever he can, and the next few days and nights would be long ones.

The stakes were very high and Rove was feeling the pressure, he could not afford to make any mistakes now. His priority was to make sure that Russia did not attack Norway and thereby trigger Article 5, the cornerstone of N.A.T.O.'s defence strategy. An attack on one country was an attack on all of its thirty member states, and it would bring about a war that on top of their involvement in Ukraine, Russia would never survive . . . unless she deployed nuclear weapons. Or rather . . . she could not hope to survive a global war against N.A.T.O., but as a nuclear power, Russia could drag the rest of the world with her down into the abyss.

Rove reminded himself that strictly speaking, the U.S.A. never fought for anyone unless her own interests were also threatened, and for that reason N.A.T.O.'s collective defence had only ever been activated once in its history – to defend the U.S.A. in response to the 9/11 attacks in 2001. The havoc that had followed in the wake of that decision still loomed over the Middle East. N.A.T.O.'s formidable forces might be able to bring any country to its knees, but it was very unlikely to wage an all-out war, not on top of its responsibilities in the wings of the war in Ukraine.

He observed the bleak winter weather as he was driven out of Bodø city centre, knowing that a little to the northeast military forces were gathering on both sides of the border, prepared to fight.

The Norwegian–Russian border might be one of the world's oldest and most peaceful land borders, but how strong was the trust between the Norwegian and the Russian peoples should ultimately a military conflict arise between them?

He had detected a noticeably more pro-Russian attitude in the border regions to the north than among the government class and the technocrats in Oslo.

East Finnmark had a special relationship with its neighbours; the area was liberated by Russian forces towards the end of the Second World War. The strangest war story that Rove knew was about what happened after the Russians had driven the Germans out of northern Norway. Rather than the Russians claiming the areas they had conquered for themselves, they retreated gallantly and handed back the land to the Norwegians. Who does that? He knew of no similar gesture from one country to another.

The Norwegian Joint Headquarters was teeming with activity when he reached there. On his way to his meeting, Rove noticed that the oddball from C.Y.F.O.R. was still at work. He stopped behind him. With hunched shoulders, the big guy was staring at the screens in front of him. There were six cans of Red Bull and half a baguette next to him.

Storm was somewhere in cyberspace. Rove said nothing, but he noticed that Storm had hacked the central nervous system of several Russian satellites and was right now following a satellite at 67.49°N and 34.51°E, high above Lake Seydozero in Russia. Rove frowned, what was going on there? The N.A.T.O. plane had crashed over Apatity and his team had concluded that the pilots must have ejected further to the northeast. Was Lieutenant Bure aware of something he did not know about?

Rove cleared his throat, Storm was startled and jumped to his feet when he realised who was behind him. He saluted the general.

Rove nodded in return and gestured for Storm to sit.

"What's the status?"

There was a dry crackle as Storm's fingers flew across the keyboard. He logged out of the Russian satellite and on to General Dynamics schematics for the F-16's main frame.

"Well, sir, this section controls the F-16," he pointed to a spot under the plane's left wing. "They could have strayed too far east due to a fault in the navigation system."

Rove nodded. Storm continued:

"However, the plane had just passed a comprehensive technical check-up and everything was in very good order. Besides, a technical fault in the navigation system would not explain why we could not contact the plane." Rove watched the swiftly moving 3-D simulations of various scenarios that Storm had contrived.

"Could anyone have hacked their system?"

Storm frowned, then shook his head. "It's impossible to hack and knock out the communication and the navigation functions in an F-16 craft. They're on separate circuits."

Rove looked at the map. "Why are you searching the area west of Lake Seydozero?"

Storm shrugged. "The logical choice would be to eject as close to the Koashva massif as possible."

Rove was taken aback.

"Logical? Surely there's nothing logical about this mess."

Storm carried on typing.

"Everything is logical if you know the causes that triggered it, the relevant variables and the inherent orderliness at play."

Rove hummed to himself, he liked these mad cyberneticists, they had a can-do attitude to most things.

Rove pulled out a vacant chair and sat down next to Storm.

"O.K., explain the logic to me."

Storm stretched out and Rove concluded that the man's neck and back hurt and that his eyes were red due to lack of sleep.

"Given that N.A.T.O. did not order our F-16 to fly into Russia . . ."

Storm glanced up, but Rove only waited for him to continue without expression.

". . . then the trigger must be unintentional from the N.A.T.O. plane's point of view."

"That much we've worked out."

Storm shrugged, he was thinking out loud.

"So they were on escort duty from the Hoop area to Kirkenes when the Fullback engaged them. Something must have happened while they were being buzzed." He scratched his beard. "Something that knocked out the central computer under the left wing. It's the plane's Achilles heel, all the electronics must have been knocked out. All the electronics in the plane."

Rove listened in silence as Storm carried on expanding his theory.

"If they lost control of the plane and tried to steer southwest with an analogue compass, there's a high possibility that they veered too far east due to the direction of the wind. There was a full gale blowing from the northwest. In theory they could have crossed into Russian airspace by accident. And if they did that and realised where they were by identifying landmarks on the ground while the Russians were coming after them, the only logical move would be to try to follow the wind and get as close to the Koashva massif as possible." He pointed to the town of Apatity. "That's why the plane crashed there. If they ejected ten to twenty seconds before the plane was shot down, the wind direction in the area and the wind force of 32 knots would carry their parachutes southwest. Lieutenant Nordahl is 1.74 metres tall and weighs 55 kilos, she has a B.M.I. of 18.2, Major Evans is 1.85 metres and weighs 84 kilos, his B.M.I. is 24.5."

Rove interrupted him.

"How do you know that?"

Storm squirmed in his seat, embarrassed.

"Well, sir, I hacked Major Evans' medical records, and I've lifted Lieutenant Nordahl up a few times, but I hacked hers too. Just to be sure."

Rove grinned and Storm said, "Anyway, I calculated the trajectory of two bodies ejecting at an altitude of ten thousand metres, the last altitude I have for them."

Storm showed Rove his calculations and Rove leaned forward to take a closer look.

"Two bodies at the altitude, weight and B.M.I. I just mentioned in the given wind direction and wind force would, if they were lucky, manage to land in this area, near the Khibiny massif."

Rove studied the information on the screen and on the map of the Russian mountain range that Storm had printed out. It made sense, Rove was impressed.

"But why would they try to land in a mountainous area?"

"Because it's harder to search. The mountains are full of caves where they can hide, and the area surrounding it is an Arctic wasteland. They may be hoping to cross the Khibiny massif and head westwards along this route."

Storm pointed to the map. Rove looked at Storm with disbelief.

"But surely the pilots didn't have access to such detailed local knowledge?"

Storm stared into the blue glow from the computer monitor. He let out a sad sigh.

"Lieutenant Nordahl does, sir, she used to live there."

23

Ylva and Evans put all their surviving strength into hollowing out the densely packed snow, and Ylva could feel the sweat trickle like raw moisture around her neck, under her arms and down her back. She stopped digging, opened her pilot suit and calmly took off the clothes covering her upper body. Evans looked at her aghast.

"What are you doing, Nordahl?"

"Sir, working in damp clothing will increase our risk of freezing to death."

Evans let out a heavy sigh. He had to concede that her survival instincts were exceptional. Then he too opened his pilot suit and took off his clothes. They stood in the cold, their upper bodies naked as they brusquely dried themselves and each other. The friction increased their circulation and the stinging sensation woke them up a little. Ylva looked at Evans, he had hideous scars all over his body. She knew how he had got them and said nothing, but he was aware of her gaze. Evans, for his part, registered Ylva's tattoos. He disliked tattooed women.

When they had dried off all moisture and sweat, Ylva turned her clothes inside out and put them on again. Evans did the same. Then they stood there for a moment, shivering.

Evans experienced a sudden sadness as Ylva crawled into the cave to dig it out further from the inside; she reminded him of his daughter, Leah, on one of their many camping trips to the Michigan Lakes. Everything was exciting and everything was great. The seriousness and the situational awareness he had tried to teach her the hard way was probably just an adventure for her. She was blithely confident that her daddy knew what he was doing, and that everything would turn out for the best.

Except that she was not safe. The worst, the definitively worst moment in his life was when he saw in his daughter's eyes that her trust in him had died. Her horrified expression as her safe world disintegrated and her daddy turned into a monster would haunt him for ever. High on prescription drugs, marijuana, LSD and alcohol, he had come home and attacked her mother, the love of his life, the woman for whom he would gladly go to his death . . .

He had struck her, she fell, he threw himself at her and before she had time to react, he hit her over and over and over. She screamed: Get out, you'll kill us! Her gentle face which he had loved and fought for, the beautiful young woman he saw in his mind's eye every night, her playful lips and sparkling, mischievous eyes . . . could no longer reach him. He saw only the liars, the sycophants, the torturers, the politicians, the bureaucrats . . . he saw a mocking enemy and he lashed out. He heard bones break, he saw blood spurt, he felt adrenaline and rage, a nauseating metallic taste in his mouth. And he kept on hitting. His eyes saw nothing, he hit, she disappeared and he hit. He hit with all his strength and fists like steel. He hit her over and over until she lay still, her gaze turned inwards. He had won, he hit first and he hit last. He was the stronger, she didn't stand a chance, she agreed with him on everything and there were no more questions. She was completely soft. He was the stronger. She lay still.

It was not until then that he came to. It was not until then that he realised that it was her, not the enemy, who lay bleeding and lifeless in his arms. In the doorway he saw his daughter stare at him, her eyes wild and terrified. The child slumped to the floor, her mouth gaping in silent screams: Mummy! Mummy! Mummy!

It was the last time he saw either of them.

Evans forced his thoughts aside and bent down towards the entrance. The cave was so small that there was barely enough room for both of them, but it would have to do. Ylva said nothing as he laid down as far from her as possible, which suited her just fine. The darkness and the cold walls of snow were claustrophobic, it felt as if they were buried in an ice coffin.

"I apologise for the facilities, sir," she mumbled.

Evans said nothing, he curled up in a foetal position facing the wall, his muscles ached and he was shivering with cold.

Ylva, too, could feel the cold take hold of her; now that they were no longer moving, they were cooling down rapidly. She wriggled out of the cave and into the moonless night.

"Sir, it's snowing heavily, we could light a small fire in the cave, the smoke will hardly be visible in the darkness."

Evans mumbled something she did not catch, but she interpreted it as agreement. Shivering, she went off to dig up dry sticks and some moss.

Some sticks and a spark later they managed to start a small fire, and it provided them with instant relief. As Evans raised his frozen hands to the flames, they began to tingle as if thousands of ants were crawling through his veins. Slowly the blood returned to his fingers. It hurt, but in a welcome way. Ylva sat down near the opening to the cave and examined her own numb fingers and toes in the glow from the fire. As her extremities warmed up, the skin grew red and she began to feel them again. Then she turned her attention to Evans and started checking him as well. His fingers were O.K., the toes on his left foot too, but when she saw his right leg, she grew alarmed. The skin was light grey in colour, cold and stiff. She gently prodded the skin to see if it moved compared to the underlying tissue. Evans winced from pain.

"Sir, in cases of frostbite ice crystals are formed in the skin, they burst the cells and the blood veins, causing cell death. I have to check."

"So what if I have frostbite? It's not like there's anything I can do about it," Evans grunted. Ylva said nothing, but continued to press on his skin, which just about sprung back.

"You have developed frostbite, but I don't think the tissue is dead."

Again she opened her pilot suit and pressed his feet against the naked skin on her stomach. Evans stared at her, the warmth from her skin was welcome and his breathing settled immediately and grew deeper.

"We have to make sure you don't get permanent frost injuries, sir."

He nodded. His leg began to tingle as it warmed up, the sensation was both ticklish and stinging as the blood was able to flow freely into his toes once more. He leaned back. Ylva sat still, letting his feet warm themselves greedily on her skin.

She had also noticed that blood was trickling from the wound to Evans' calf, and that was another problem. Any moisture increased the damaging impact of the cold considerably, and she knew for sure that Evans would soon develop gangrene from the fuel traces on the metal that had penetrated his calf. She also realised that the injury to his calf would increase the risk of frost damage to his foot and she was only too aware of what that meant.

Evans took out a protein bar from his backpack and they ate in silence. The small fire inside the cave glowed warmly; smoke drifted out into the night and mingled with the snow that was falling in heavy drifts. Evans' body was starting to warm up and he felt better. He looked at Ylva; her face took on a contemplative expression as absentmindedly she ran her hand over the green tattoos on her forearm. He smiled wryly.

"You're a walking encyclopaedia of clichés."

Ylva frowned.

"Sir?"

Evans straightened up a little.

"*Marcet sine adversario virtus* . . . What does that mean?"

He had read the wording on her lower belly as they took their clothes off to wipe away the sweat. Ylva did not respond immediately because what could she say? She looked down at her fingers, the tingling was easing off and her hands felt heavy and burning hot.

"No honour without resistance," she mumbled.

Evans' eyes widened.

"Jesus!"

"No pain, no gain." She flashed a crooked smile in the darkness.

He had to laugh, it felt weird. He laughed again. He had had no cause to do so in ages, and given the context there was really no reason to do so now.

"Hello, you're thirty years old, why all the melodrama?"

Ylva gave Evans an irritated look. She knew quite a lot about him, Storm had helped her with information which, strictly speaking, was not intended for the general public, and she had read up on her mentor. Evans had once been like her, he had believed in heroic myths and dreamed of great deeds, but that was before he fell from his throne in the air force's pantheon. She knew that he knew, but didn't have the energy to challenge him and changed the subject.

"My feet are cold."

Evans looked at her quizzically, she wriggled her feet and he got the hint. He opened his pilot suit with numb fingers, and Ylva pulled off her boots and socks, then slipped her frozen toes under his thermal shirt and warmed them on Evans' stomach. Her cold toes made him flinch, and Ylva grinned. She savoured the heat from his body and Evans began to relax. The situation was strangely intimate. They lay head to toe, the soles of their feet on each other's stomachs; naked feet, skin to skin. Evans thought to himself that it was a long time since he had last had skin contact with a woman. It was a long time since he had had any kind of contact with anyone at all.

"What other clever proverbs are you hiding on your body?"

Ylva thought about it, then she smiled.

"Live free or die!"

Evans whistled and raised his eyebrows, then without being aware of it, he started to stroke her feet. It was a reflex, he used to massage his wife's feet when they were watching T.V. series. Usually he found them boring, her taste was painfully sentimental, but Evans had enjoyed massaging her feet. No, he had loved massaging her feet.

"Death is not the greatest evil. General Stark after the Battle of Bennington," he nodded. Ylva shook her head, feigning indignation at Evans' ignorance.

"Nope, Stark nicked it, typical American. *Vivre libre ou mourir* is the original. The French Revolution."

Evans chortled, clenched his fist and raised it as if encouraging battle.

"*Vive la révolution.*"

"Yes, sir, live free or die, *vive la révolution!*"

Evans' smile was extinguished as swiftly as it had flared up. He stared into the faint flames from the fire.

"But that's easier said than done," he muttered.

"What is?"

"To live free."

Ylva scoffed, as far as she was concerned freedom was her sole goal. Her need to be free was irreducible, the faintest suggestion that someone wanted to control her or tie her down felt like a straightjacket and her entire nature rebelled.

"I'm willing to die for my freedom," she said. And she meant it.

Evans snorted mirthlessly.

"You really don't have a clue, do you? You're just a scared little kid living out a romantic fantasy."

Ylva made no reply, she could see that the fire was burning out, but she was too tired to go outside and hunt for more wood.

"When I was held captive by Libyan rebels, they took away my freedom and they would happily have taken my life away as well. It was purely the prospect of making a few dollars out of me that motivated them to keep me alive. And I've never wanted to live as fiercely as I did then, not ever. Even if it meant living in captivity."

"Is that where you got your scars?"

It was a stupid question, she knew the answer. Evans nodded.

"Let's just put it this way: their hospitality was influenced by the fact that I had just bombed their village back to the Stone Age."

"That must have been absolutely awful."

Evans did not reply, but continued to look at Ylva. In the dim light from the remnants of the fire she suddenly looked older. She had a face that held deep grief, he thought, she was an old woman in a young woman's body.

Evans closed his eyes.

"It was pure hell, Lieutenant, but coming home to freedom was so much worse."

Ylva wanted to know more, but his eyes remained closed and she heard his deep breathing. The conversation was over.

24

"I'm not saying our special operation in Ukraine is a failure, but we have to admit we could have done better! And in spite of the reverses we have suffered in the conflict we are not in a position to put more than fifteen thousand troops on the Norwegian border."

The President glared up at General Svetla, who loomed over him. He listened impatiently to his old colleague's unsentimental advice. "This is, however, a blessing in disguise," the general said, and the President perked up. This was what? He peered into the general's steel-grey eyes, they were burning with intensity.

"How?" he said.

"We are not getting any younger, my friend," the general said. The President's eyes grew colder. This was not an issue. Not at all.

"Russia is, we know, an ageing country, and the brain drain and exodus of youth after our special military operation in Ukraine, has weakened us. Soon we'll be a country of weeping grandmothers without sons and grandchildren to fight for anything," the general concluded. The President recoiled. Although the general was telling him nothing he did not know, he felt his palms sweat, and his face turn red. "What does that have to do with our present crisis?" he said. General Svetla leaned forward, his tone ominous. "Russia has been invaded fifty times throughout history and as we well know, N.A.T.O.'s encroachment on our borders is accelerating. If nothing is done now to plug invasion corridors and protect our boundaries, we will not have enough young soldiers to stop them if someone were to choose to invade us in the future." The President knew that General Svetla was right.

"Showing weakness now, will only encourage our enemies. We might not yet have succeeded as anticipated in Ukraine, but our special military operation there has diminished both the West's resolve and their resources to fight yet another war. It is certain that the war in Ukraine will have weakened the West's appetite for another conflict in the high north. Our backyard. This is a unique opportunity, Mr President. You can regain the initiative." General Svetla's words made sense. Even better, they felt like hope. Mother Russia was holding her breath; her embittered people waiting for a sign, a sign that would seal their fate as so many times before. Maybe this really was it?

The President got up and paced back and forth. "How can I trust that we have the manpower and the resources to see off N.A.T.O. this time?"

General Svetla said, "Ukraine is a flat swamp, populated by death-defying Ukrainians, as relentless as any Russian. We had no tactical advantages there, but the Arctic is different. It is one of the toughest battlegrounds on the planet. No foreign mercenary will go there, no Western government will send their dwindling military resources to lose that fight. Because Arctic nature is so merciless, the entire region is sparsely populated by only a few Norwegians, who prefer their welfare state and privileges to combat. They have disarmed their northern borders for decennia. Russia is the world's greatest Arctic state. That's where our true power lies!"

The President nodded. He felt curiously revived. "Thank you for your advice," he mumbled. "I'll prepare my response." The

President sat back down behind his desk, took up his pen and started to shuffle his papers. General Svetla stepped back. "We trust you to do the right thing, Mr President," he said and bowed before he left the room. The door closed behind him with a soft click. Perhaps General Svetla was right? Perhaps this really was his moment to resurrect his image as saviour of the Russian empire.

He may have grown up among the wreckage of war and in dehumanising poverty, and it pained him to see his parents suffer. All he could do was to suffer with them, because a child is powerless. But not for ever. His parents' anguish and Russia's humiliation became his calling and their pain his purpose.

Now he had his back to the wall yet once more, the unintended consequence of the debacle in Ukraine was that N.A.T.O. had encroached yet further, he had to defend himself and his country. They were one. The President tried to boost his own morale.

He walked calmly out of his office, the corridors fell silent. Like anxious children the staff look down as he walked by. He preferred it that way. General Svetla was on the beat and had gathered his team in the stately meeting room in the lower ground floor. They too waited for him in sombre silence. The President knew that they would follow him through thick and thin because they did not want freedom, it was too onerous. They wanted a father figure, the state, to take responsibility.

"My fellow Russians," he said, suppressing a slight quiver in his voice. "Russia is ready," he declared. "We have mobilised fifteen thousand combat-ready soldiers on the border of Norway. If they want a war, then they shall have a war."

The gauntlet had been thrown down; the next very few days would prove if his adversary would pick it up. In the back of the room General Svetla listened intently. He caught the President's eyes and nodded encouragingly. They needed three days to get ready for war, he had said, three. "Russia will give N.A.T.O. three days to prove beyond all doubt its innocence in the F-16 incident. After that the consequences are theirs to reap. We are here and we are ready!" The initial gasp of surprise was followed by stunned silence.

General Svetla was the first to react to the President's defiant speech, he clapped his hands firmly, igniting a clamour of thunderous applause. A momentary expression of relief crossed the President's tense face. People rose to their feet and cheered, hiding General Svetla from the President's view. The general took out his telephone and sent an encrypted message to George Rove: "He's on board. In three days we have our war!"

25

They could not just hide the evidence and keep silent. Major Khodrokovska shivered in the cold and looked down. Lieutenant Serkin was lying, but she did not know why. Dry, fine-grained snow had settled on a hard layer of densely packed ice.

Something was in the offing; the unease she had experienced since she had had the fateful telephone call from Moscow had mutated into sheer fear.

Cold wind swept around the corners of the buildings, filling the air with haunting howls. Major Khodrokovska was freezing, but she continued to gaze at the sky. The location of Monchegorsk Air Base was perfect, high above the Arctic Circle where the Northern Lights tore across the sky with almost unnatural force. They looked like neon lights.

Major Khodrokovska liked to watch the stars and the Northern Lights. When she was a little girl, she had believed that the lights were ghosts, spirits doomed to haunt the sky, eternally chasing release and forgiveness. It was how her grandmother had explained it to her, and she had loved the entertaining ghost stories with which she had filled the Arctic night. You needed to respect the Northern Lights, her grandmother had said. If you do not honour the lost souls, you will end up becoming one of them.

The green tongues of light pulsating over the Arctic sky filled her with awe, even on a disastrous night like tonight.

She thought that her grandmother's nightmare vision of her ending up as a haunted soul, condemned to flee through the night sky for ever, sounded attractive. And when she closed her eyes, she could still imagine taking off from the tundra and floating, as light as a frost cloud, upwards to eternity. She smiled to herself as she imagined the tiny houses and the River Litsa that wound its way down the valley before it merged with the Barents Sea below her. She wanted to travel up and far away from here, but she remained earthbound, shifting her weight from one foot to the other, being both cold and in two minds. It was not wise to ignore your gut instinct and blindly follow orders; she should have waited until she had checked from whom the order had been issued. She should not have allowed herself to become so stressed or to trivialise her misgivings. At worst the consequences of her weakness and lack of professionalism could lead to huge sufferings for people on both sides of the border. She shuddered at the thought. It made her sick. But there was little she could do now because the report had been compiled by her superiors and it had been approved by Moscow without objections. She was absolved of all guilt. Or not all, she was reproaching herself.

A door squeaked behind her and Major Khodrokovska was startled. She turned around. Through the glass door she could see that yet another delegation from Moscow had arrived, evidently tired after their long journey. The evening shift on the base was already at their posts, captured by the light from their computer monitors. They looked like zombies. Khodrokovska smoothed her hair where the winter wind had blown strands out of the tight bun at the nape of her neck. She adopted an unemotional and professional expression and, as she entered, she knew that to her colleagues she looked the epitome of the predictable, deferential and dogmatic head of the base. That had become her role in life.

She walked through the office landscape and fifteen minutes later she was sitting in the khaki meeting room to discuss the incident once again. She was too tired for any more formalities and got straight to the point:

"I've been to the lab."

General Svetla and the President's team of advisers looked up at her in surprise.

"Aha?"

Major Khodrokovska remained as professional and as neutral as she was able.

"I submitted samples of paint traces I found on Lieutenant Serkin's Fullback."

"Paint traces?"

Khodrokovska nodded.

"There may have been a collision. The planes could have clipped one another."

General Svetla looked hard at Major Khodrokovska, who continued:

"Damage to Lieutenant Serkin's Fullback is inconsistent with his report."

She registered immediately how General Svetla's eyes narrowed. A plump man from the Moscow team piped up:

"But Lieutenant Serkin never said anything about a collision to us. Are you saying that he misinformed us?"

Major Khodrokovska could feel the mood in the room change, she sensed an increasing hostility and realised immediately that she would have to tread carefully.

"Well, I found dents and paint traces on the left wing of the Fullback, and thought that the damage might indicate that—"

"And why was the N.A.T.O. plane in Russian airspace and heading towards the nuclear base?" An irritated General Svetla interrupted the major's reasoning.

Khodrokovska did not know the answer, she said, but she had a theory. It seemed unlikely, far-fetched even, but she had mulled it over all night and there was no other explanation.

"It's possible that the navigation system of the F-16 was disabled as a result of the collision."

General Svetla seemed agitated at the major's hypothesis, it contradicted their assumptions. He gathered up his papers, signalling very clearly that the meeting was over.

"Thank you for your report, Major Khodrokovska. I'll follow this up myself."

"But shouldn't this information be made available to N.A.T.O.?" she said.

The general and the team of advisers exchanged glances.

"We'll leave that to our leaders to decide."

Major Khodrokovska could feel her hackles rise, she understood that it was in the general's interests to cover up potentially erroneous conclusions on the Russian side.

"All we have to do is take a look at the plane. This could change the whole situation," she said.

The man in the suit looked enquiringly at General Svetla rather than at her.

"No-one has told me that the engineers discovered any damage," he muttered.

Major Khodrokovska rose.

"I can show you."

General Svetla looked at her with a sigh; he had worked with Major Khodrokovska for seven years and knew that she was pedantic and insistent. Once she had made up her mind, you might as well let her go the whole hog.

Ten minutes later Major Khodrokovska, General Svetla and the President's advisers were standing in the hangar. Major Khodrokovska strode purposefully towards Serkin's plane.

"Look, here it . . . "

Major Khodrokovska stopped in her tracks and stared at the wing. It was whole and intact, there was no sign of any dent or scratch.

26

Ylva woke up with a start. It was several seconds before she remembered where she was and that what had happened was not just a really bad dream. She and Evans had slept tangled up like new-born kittens inside the cave. The fire had burned itself out and the only heat they could hope to find was in being close to one another. She crawled out into the dawn light and calculated that it must be close to nine o'clock. They had been asleep for a long time. She shivered; for the first time she was able to clearly see the landscape through which they had struggled to make headway the night before.

The early hours of the morning had seen a change in the weather and now the landscape lay swaddled in soft duvets of white powder snow. Shades of deep blue, purple and magenta Arctic light flooded the tundra and there was not a single cloud in the sky. Behind them the mountains were outlined against the light coming from the northeast. In front of them, to the southwest, Ylva could see the craggy landscape tumbling towards the plains that separated them from Norway. She walked towards the edge of the precipice along which they had come and was relieved to see that yesterday's march had taken them further than she had dared to hope. They could cover the remaining distance in five to six days, unless Evans collapsed.

Her sleep had been blessedly free from dreams and deep until she was woken by Evans' groaning and writhing. At first she thought that he must be awake, but when he continued to mutter to himself, she realised that he was having a nightmare. Ylva knew exactly what that was like so she had moved closer to him, embraced him and stroked his hair gently. He had freed himself brusquely, frightened and furious like a wounded animal. It was not until she started singing lullabies in a whispering, soft voice that he calmed down. She lulled him into a merciful and dreamless sleep as a mother soothes an anxious child. His permanently grim facial expression softened, his jaw relaxed and that furrow between his eyebrows smoothed, he seemed simultaneously older and younger. The aggressive mask dissolved into a milder, more disillusioned expression, beyond help. Soon he began to snore, and it was not until then that she could sleep.

Evans woke right after Ylva and without saying very much, they packed up and set out on their journey towards the Norway border.

One step and then another . . . and another. With his gaze fixed on Ylva's back, Evans trudged through the deep snow, wading, scrambling and climbing down the left side of the mountain. Ylva had never been in this area before and wished she had a memory of the route through the pass between Angvundaschorr and Kedykvampakhk. She did not ask Evans how he was doing, she did not have to, she knew that he was in difficulty.

As they reached the most precipitous point, Ylva stopped and looked across the deep, narrow valley that unfolded below them. To their left they could hear the sound of running water, and Ylva knew that they had reached the waterfall that tumbles into the valley and ends up in the Tavajok River. Surrounded by tall mountains, the water had – over many thousands of years – carved a gorge through the valley. The river flowed westwards and wound its way into the lush taiga whose dense forest would provide them with shelter. They could gather firewood there and light a fire; a faint plume of smoke would be concealed by the trees and be difficult to detect in the night. If they could get as far as that the worst part of their journey would be over, but it would be an extremely challenging hike. First she had to find a route that would get them as quickly as possible down into the valley.

Ylva looked about her. The mountainous terrain to her right was steep and she could see scree between the chunks of ice. Their best option was to carry on down the less steep slope to the south. She began walking, and Evans followed her without a word although he was having a tough time walking on the uneven ground and rocks without aggravating his injury.

Suddenly they heard a strange rumbling. Ylva stopped in her tracks and listened, Evans looked at her quizzically.

"Nordahl?"

She raised her hand to silence him and looked back at the mountains with a frown. She could hear gusts of wind tear across the mountain ridges and the faint crackle of ice-covered branches and windswept trees, but the mountains themselves were silent.

Ylva squatted on her haunches and examined the snow. It was porous, light and downy. With her knife she cut out a cross section and studied its layers. An approximately 50-centimetres-deep layer of powder snow rested on a thick crust of compacted ice. It was what she had expected since it had snowed heavily in the night. She poked her knife at the transition between the layers in order to assess the texture of the snow. Then she turned her attention back to the mountainside.

"I'm guessing the wind force last night was between fifteen to twenty metres per second. Possibly more."

Evans nodded to agree that the wind speed had indeed been high, but he sensed that Ylva was worried about more than just last night's weather. She sat very still and listened with total concentration. Without taking her eyes off the white mountainside, she mumbled to herself.

". . . An incline of thirty-five to forty-five degrees."

"Nordahl, what are you doing?"

"It would have been ideal to try to get down here, but . . ."

Again she paused and looked up and along the side of the mountain.

"The wind shifted the virgin snow away from there and deposited it in the sheltered areas to the northeast." She pointed up to a large, windswept section of the southwestern side of the mountain. "It adds pressure on the snow right above us – where it hasn't had enough time yet to attach itself."

Again they heard deep rumbling. Ylva jumped. Now she was seriously worried, but then she straightened up slowly. Evans followed her gaze towards the soft, barely visible waves of white powder snow lying on the precipice. He registered that there were narrow horizontal cracks along the cliff above them and several vertical cracks along the mountain ridge.

"There could be an avalanche here," Ylva said.

A shiver went down Evans' spine.

"What do you suggest?"

Ylva carefully eased the parachute out of her rucksack and cut off a long piece. Her movements were guarded, she never took her eyes off the mountain and the snowdrifts hanging above them. Still taking great care, she walked to a tall, lonely tree a short distance from them. She stretched out the piece of parachute material between the tree on the one side and a boulder on the other. Next she made sure to both cover the fabric and erase her footsteps in the snow. Then she straightened up and looked at Evans.

"We need to follow our own footsteps back towards the precipice."

"O.K."

"Spetsnaz is most likely on our trail."

Evans nodded, it was a reasonable assumption.

"And if they follow our footprints out here . . ."

She nodded towards the parachute fabric, which she had stretched like a sail across the path their boot prints had made, and hummed. Evans got the idea and he, too, grinned. He could imagine the Spetsnaz soldiers on powerful snow scooters, following their boot prints to the edge of the mountain. They would crash right into Ylva's device, which in turn would dislodge the boulder above them. Then it would roll down the mountainside. Or alternatively, the tree would bend and snap or swing back with great force when the fabric ripped. If their pursuers maintained their speed, they would be thrown off while their scooters continued down the side of the mountain. The vibrations would trigger an avalanche.

"It's going to cause one hell of a racket," she grinned as she walked back and away, retracing her steps. Evans followed her, and felt his anxiety slowly loosening its hold on him the closer they got to the leeside of the broad slope.

It took them quite a while and they were both out of breath when at last they reached the place from which they had first set out. So they were back to square one. Ylva went to have a look at the steep canyon with the half-frozen river, which flung itself over the edge of the craggy rock.

Her gaze followed the ridge; it was even steeper further along and ended in a sheer drop covered with ice and scree. She heaved a sigh. Walking to the end of the ridge and hiking down into the canyon would take too long; besides, the scree was potentially lethal, there might be a rockslide at any moment. The swiftest route was to climb down near the icy river, it would take them about an hour. It was a no-brainer.

She took a step closer to the edge of the void and looked down. A wall of vertical ice plunged towards the bottom of the valley below them. The ice was lumpy and heavy rocks protruded in several places, giving them the chance of a foothold.

"Are you able to climb, sir?"

Evans stared at her in disbelief.

"Nordahl, you're not seriously suggesting that we . . .?"

He did not get to the end of his question. He already knew the answer and Ylva had begun to make her way over the edge.

27

Ali had gone off for one more shot of caffeine, leaving Storm alone in the computer room. He was watching the recordings from security cameras on Bodø Air Base itself and on other Exercise Arctic Blizzard locations. He strangled a yawn, he was so tired that he could barely see straight. He searched meticulously for something, a situation or a person who aroused his suspicion, something not right, something that deviated from the norm. It was exactly like looking for the proverbial needle in a haystack, but he had to start somewhere. He rested his eyes for a moment. They stung and itched from exhaustion. The short break, however, only made him feel dizzy, it was better to keep going. As he twisted and stretched his stiff neck, he went back to typing on the keyboard as he dived into the infinity of cyberspace.

Images flickered across the screen, people, soldiers and politicians crowding together and dispersing like ants. They talked, laughed, argued, came, stood, sat and ran. There were so many of them. Suddenly his eyes widened and he sat up straight. There, on a recording from the foyer of Bodø Arts Centre, she was. The camera by the entrance was showing images of General Rove and Ylva talking. They appeared to know one another; he would need to look into that. She looked small and guarded for some reason. Storm watched the recording closely. As the conversation ended, Rove made for the auditorium and Ylva was left on her own. The time was 18:37 – he had met her on the square only one minute before. Storm froze the image of Ylva and pondered. How well did he know the woman he realised that he probably, against his better judgment, loved? She had so many facets, so many secrets. He missed her, and watching her standing there all alone, looking in Rove's direction, provoked a feeling of despair he could not afford to indulge in right now.

Storm pressed play again. As General Rove headed for the auditorium, Ylva clearly slumped and her proud, friendly expression changed. She looked lonely, sad almost. Was that her? Was that the real Ylva? She looked around the lobby, gazed through the big windows at the Barents Sea outside, then she straightened up and headed for the exit.

Storm also noticed Major John Evans entering from the lobby to the right. He met Rove at the door to the auditorium. Storm straightened up and was surprised again to see them greet one another before they went through the large doors together to the auditorium.

28

"Listen to each other! Feel one another!"

Aleksey Galba gestured, rapt, as he called out in a mixture of Norwegian and Russian.

"Don't think, feel! Don't do, be!"

The musicians in the Norwegian–Russian ensemble concentrated on playing. The traditional friendship concert between Norway and Russia during the Riddu Riđđu Festival was only four months away, and every rehearsal with the master composer from Russia was a crucial opportunity.

"Don't perform, give! Enjoy!"

Mette Wang gazed across the ensemble: two spotty techno-guys, one from Murmansk and one from Tromsø, two throat singers from Tuva, a violinist and a cellist from Harstad, two Sámi drummers, a Sámi *joik* singer ... and where the woman with the bells, cymbals and Tibetan bowls came from, she could not remember. She might even be Tibetan? Or Mongolian, she looked as if she might be.

Galba's music was a state of mind, it was like meditation or prayer. The monotonous rhythms created a vortex of dreams; she had experienced many times how the music drew the audience into a symphony of hearts beating as one.

"Yes, now we're getting there ... now ..."

His round face crinkled with concentration into a thousand

wrinkles and his eyes sparkled. It was the fifth time Galba had come to rehearse and conduct his work with the ensemble in Finnmark, and although he was a sophisticated and cosmopolitan artist from Moscow, he felt very much at home in the small Arctic town.

The people of northern Norway were excited by his music and he was invited back again and again. Meeting the audience in Kirkenes had been liberating and so unlike the more reserved and cerebral recognition he encountered in Moscow and elsewhere in the world. He had been met with particular warmth and interest by Mette Wang, a local journalist. She had interviewed him the first time he visited, and they struck up a close friendship. Very close indeed. Mette was a strong contributing factor to his commitment to the orchestra and the festival. The financial and artistic rewards were quite modest.

The first time they met, she was obviously nervous. Not from star-struck awe of his genius, but rather because she had agreed to take on the job at short notice when the journalist scheduled to do the interview had broken his foot in a skiing accident. She had no idea who the internationally recognised composer Aleksey Alekseyevich Galba was or what his music sounded like, and that had never happened to the maestro before.

Following the death of her husband from cancer, Mette had lived alone with two arrogant cats in Tromsø. From time to time she would write an arts article for the local paper although she had long ago retired. It was especially niche arts events, which no-one else at the paper could be bothered to cover, which came her way. That was fine with her, she did not have the energy to write about pop stars and talent show winners or yet another Melgaard exhibition. She was done with that.

* * *

Aleksey was surprised when he visited Kirkenes for the first time; the small town was like a little piece of Russia in Norway. Cyrillic lettering on the street signs and the Russian-language local radio and newspaper were evidence that the sister nation to the east was important to the people at Western Europe's most northeastern border. He had been amazed to learn that there was a Russian library service and a Russian seaman's church, and that all shop signs were in both languages. As a Russian you could live in Kirkenes without ever learning Norwegian, not that that was his goal. Aleksey had taught himself quite a lot of Norwegian over the five years he had visited the town. He wanted to understand this country – and the lovely Mette – much better.

Neither of them had expected to find such a love at the autumn of their lives. But they did, and they knew how to enjoy it. Falling in love is wasted on the young, he thought, they didn't know what a miracle it was to meet your soulmate. But Mette and Aleksey knew, they were old, and they treasured the remarkable gift they had been given.

After the rehearsal everyone dressed up warm to go out for a meal. The musicians and sound technicians and Mette and Aleksey, who walked arm in arm, carefully navigated the icy street to a fish restaurant.

A random passer-by filmed what happened next, and the footage went viral. Three drunken Norwegians suddenly appeared from an alleyway and pointed to the Russians in the group before they started yelling at them:

"Fuck off back to Russia. Russian bastards!"

The thugs shoved and hit out at the Russian members of the ensemble, and when several Norwegians tried to come to the aid of Aleksey Galba and his countrymen, the situation escalated. The brawling Norwegians pulled knives and started stabbing their victims. A few agonising minutes later Aleksey Galba and his three fellow Russians lay bleeding in the snow. Russia had lost one of its most famous contemporary composers and Mette Wang had lost the love of her life.

The footage of the three Norwegians pointing at and murdering the composer was shared across the world's screens. In Brussels, N.A.T.O.'s Secretary General and his staff watched the dreadful images.

The Secretary General knew instantly how this would go down in Moscow and feared that it would encourage the Russian President's often-stated right to protect Russians anywhere in the world. Various forms of reprisals were presumably already in progress because the satellite system controlling all of Norway's air traffic was hacked and disabled for more than an hour very soon after the amateur video from Kirkenes was uploaded to the Internet.

The footage of the deadly attack also hit the Internet shortly before N.A.T.O. representatives and the Norwegian and Russian border commissioners were due to meet and unsurprisingly, it gave rise to outrage among the Russian delegation. The meeting was not a success. The Russians refused to let Norway or N.A.T.O. participate in the search for the N.A.T.O. pilots on Russian territory, and in the light of the murder, they took more seriously the view that the incident with the N.A.T.O. plane was a hostile action.

The Secretary General went over to the large window and looked out, grey daylight hung dully over the city. Brussels was not a beautiful capital in the winter. The video link to the Norwegian Joint Headquarters in Bodø was open and there, too, the mood was subdued.

Norway's Defence Minister looked into the camera.

"Secretary General, what are N.A.T.O.'s options?"

Before anyone managed to come up with an answer, there was a knock on the door behind her and General Rove entered. The Defence Minister frowned, she had not invited Rove to the meeting.

General Bale, the American head of Exercise Arctic Blizzard, smiled at her amicably.

"We took the liberty of inviting one of our key strategic advisers. I think you know Rove."

The Defence Minister greeted the general curtly.

"I don't believe a representative of a private company can be permitted to participate in this briefing. Norway has ratified the U.N.'s Mercenary Convention."

She glanced at the Secretary General on the large screen and registered that he too seemed taken aback at Rove's appearance, but since he knew George Rove well, he chose to wait. Rove, who had anticipated the Minister's objection, nodded politely and made for the door, but neither did he seem surprised in the slightest when General Bale spoke up.

"The U.S.A. never ratified that convention and General Rove has been an integral part of the U.S.A.'s and N.A.T.O.'s strategy team since 2016. It's in that capacity that I suggested that he be here now."

The Defence Minister glanced up at the screen, hoping once again that the Secretary General would intervene, but when no objections came from Brussels, she began to doubt herself. What was the protocol here? General Rove's reputation was established, he had a distinguished military career behind him and after some years in Washington, he had joined one of America's biggest private security firms. Under his leadership the company had grown and now boasted an impressive cadre of elite soldiers. In parts of Afghanistan and Somalia only Titans Security could operate because national military organisations were too unwieldy, too bureaucratic.

His presence at the meeting might even be to their advantage. Rove understood paramilitary strategies and asymmetrical warfare as well as anyone, and he could possibly be a valuable resource in the light of the frenzy that followed the murder of the Russian composer in Kirkenes. She hesitated, why didn't the Secretary General in Brussels say something? Or maybe there was nothing strange about it? If N.A.T.O. were to implement Article 5 and the entire alliance come to Norway's rescue, N.A.T.O. would take the lead, which meant that ultimately there was no getting round the Americans. She looked up at Rove who flashed a disarming smile at her. She held him in high regard. A few years ago she had heard him give a well-argued lecture at a N.A.T.O. summit in Brussels, and she liked the way he had provoked the military top brass. His subject was: "Why have the U.S.A. and the West lost every single war they have fought since the Second World War?"

The question was directed at the smug leaders in the auditorium, and the silence that followed was all the answer you needed. Although N.A.T.O., led by the U.S.A., was undoubtedly the world's strongest military power, with almost 3.5 million combat-ready personnel and an annual budget close to a thousand billion dollars, the alliance's war efforts had not been impressive. The power and the arrogance of its leaders were in proportion to the alliance's military capacity and the budget at their disposal rather than the results they could show for it.

Rove had shamed them with his lecture, which had been more like a dressing-down.

"N.A.T.O. suffers from strategic atrophy," he had said. "Large standing armies and expensive fighter jets are useless when today's wars are fought in the media, in cyberspace, in murky backstreets and desert landscapes. Having a huge army on standby when rebels are hiding in plain sight among the local population – often for years – is expensive, it's unproductive and it's inefficient." The Defence Minister had privately agreed with him. But although Rove was evidently right, the men in the room at that time were too invested in the status quo to listen to him. Rove continued his tirade.

"The air defence of the future will not require expensive F-35 planes and A.W.A.C.S., but unmanned combat drones. In future wars robots controlled by artificial intelligence will fight our battles, not vulnerable soldiers who require expensive training, care and equipment. I know that for many this is a frightening prospect, but unmanned drones and fighting robots execute more precise and more cost-effective attacks in terms of collateral damage, personnel and money."

That hit home, she thought, and the mood in the auditorium became less smug. Very few people had the guts to say out loud that the emperor in this room had no clothes and Rove's forthright honesty earned respect.

The discussions that followed his speech were thought-provoking. The point was made that current conventions governing the conduct of international war applied only to nation states, not to private individuals. It meant that professional mercenaries, robots and drones could do whatever they liked without being held accountable politically. The Defence Minister was not clear whether Rove regarded this specific point as an advantage.

Now she sat still and looked uneasily at Rove as he politely awaited her decision.

"Given that there are no legal or formal objections, General Rove may stay," she said.

Rove nodded and sat down next to General Bale. The Defence Minister was at a loss: who would chair the meeting, she or the Secretary General? Once N.A.T.O.'s Article 5 was triggered, N.A.T.O. would take charge, and sooner or later, it would go the way the Americans wanted it to. So should General Bale chair the meeting?

The participants settled down, everyone looked up at the big screen on the wall where the Secretary General had now sat down at a conference table.

"What back channels do we have now that official diplomatic channels have broken down?" he said.

The silence among the advisers was ominous. Rove cleared his throat and addressed both the gathering in the room and the Secretary General on the screen.

"Well, the most likely scenario is that the situation will turn into an asymmetrical hybrid conflict where diplomatic efforts will be relatively unpredictable. We must expect a combination of conventional attacks in addition to irregular tactics such as cyber-attacks, sabotage, terrorism and various types of disinformation."

The Secretary General nodded.

"Our biggest problem now is that it's possible for the aggressor to hide who is really behind the attack. Just think about the invasion of the Crimea," Rove said.

"That's exactly what we're worried about. Is this the new Ukraine?"

The voice of the Secretary General seemed calm, but his body language indicated that the pressure was starting to get to him. Rove paused. He was thinking. The Secretary General ran a weary hand across his face and sighed. He would have to ask out loud the question on everyone's lips.

"How can we avoid escalating the conflict? How do we avoid this turning into a war?"

Rove looked from the Secretary General across to the Defence Minister, who sat pale and serious at the end of the table.

"Secretary General, what I'm trying to tell you is that the war has probably already started!"

Rove's words lingered in the air. Could it be true? Had the Russians already declared war on Norway and N.A.T.O. without saying so directly?

"If that were so, what do we do?"

The Secretary General's voice sounded firm still, but they all recognised his alarm at Rove's blunt statement. This was the worst possible scenario for N.A.T.O. and for the world.

"If Russia wants to destabilise the N.A.T.O. alliance, it's pointless to threaten conventional warfare as the Soviet Union would have done. The Russians are militarily inferior, a fact of which they're well aware. We've seen some of the methods they're willing to use. They bombed Syria. This tactic drove tens of thousands of refugees into Europe and created a destabilising migrant crisis, which in turn fuelled neo-fascism and anti-establishment politics which were supported by Russia. To all intents and purposes the migrant crisis brought about Brexit. Their so-called special operation in Ukraine has brought all of Europe to the brink of war."

Rove could sense the unease in the room, but he was used to political leaders wanting simple and encouraging answers rather than hard truths.

"If we hesitate now, we let the Russians have the advantage both in terms of strategy and in terms of battle optics. Our best option is to carry on talking via diplomatic back channels while coordinating our use of cyber tactics, psychological operations and subversive information strategies."

He paused, everyone appeared to follow his reasoning so far and no-one was surprised by any of it.

"At the same time, I recommend the use of paramilitary security companies to carry out physical operations behind enemy lines, this will give us plausible deniability. We don't want to create an open confrontation."

The Defence Minister straightened up. She fundamentally disagreed. They had neither the right nor the mandate to sanction military force beyond that which the member countries had at their disposal.

"General, I repeat, according to the 2001 U.N. Mercenary Convention Resolution 44/34, we cannot authorise the use of private military actors in a conflict."

Rove nodded.

"You are right, but neither Russia, China, the U.K. or the U.S.A. ratified that convention. If we let the U.S.A. take the initiative from now on, Norway is in the clear, even if we have to resort to paramilitary forces to recover supremacy."

"That will not look good in the media," the Defence Minister said.

Rove nodded.

"It's important that a strategy such as this one never reaches the media."

"Do you really think that's possible?"

"It's well known that history is written by the victors, but these days it's the person who writes the history who becomes the victor. War is decided now as much in the press office as it is on the battlefield. In order to regain the upper hand, we need to control the worldwide narrative."

The Defence Minister felt her hands tremble and folded them firmly on her lap under the table.

"And how do you imagine us translating this narrative into action?"

Rove had evidently anticipated the question.

"The worst that could happen now is that press secretaries from different governments and organisations start to shout each other down on behalf of their ministers. When we're under a hybrid attack, it's about which story or version of reality is accepted as true. Our message must be crystal clear and consistent at all levels. Every communication from a N.A.T.O. member state must come from one central source."

"But who would that be?"

Rove turned to Bale. It looked as if they had discussed this in advance and had agreed a strategy.

"We must set up a council consisting of the relevant N.A.T.O. parties. All communication must adhere to the narrative which is developed there."

The Defence Minister felt another objection rear its head.

"And what about the freedom of the press? Freedom of speech?"

"The first casualty of war is usually truth. We have to ensure that our truth wins at all costs. A state of war is an extreme situation, and the battle now is about which narrative the world is willing to embrace."

The Secretary General intervened, he had heard enough. It was time for action.

"Show us the draft for a concrete strategy! We're willing to implement it immediately."

29

Ylva and Evans were making slow but steady progress down the rock face close to the waterfall. The stone was slippery and smooth from running water and ice, their hands were freezing, and they had barely any sensation left in their fingers, but they were making progress.

Ylva looked down, there were only five more metres at most, and she felt a shiver of excitement.

Once safely down, they would have managed what was likely to be the toughest part of their route, and that spurred Ylva on. Evans was climbing right above her, he winced every time he put weight on his injured foot. She looked down. A big, smooth block of ice protruded beneath her, creating an obstacle. She would have to decide whether to climb over the block of ice or go around it. It would be simpler to climb around the block. Then the cold and her impatience got the better of her, she took out her knife, stabbed the ice, got a handhold and started climbing down towards the smooth lump.

Evans had seen what Ylva was doing and took out his own knife to follow suit, but the ice was slippery and when he tried to step onto a narrow ice shelf with his injured foot, he lost his balance. In order to stop himself from falling, he instinctively put his other foot down on the shelf right where Ylva's hand was gripping and she screamed as his boot landed on her blue frozen fingers. She yanked back her hand, the movement upset her balance, and she lost her footing. Evans looked down as in a few short but endless seconds Ylva crashed onto the smooth ice block, then slammed into the rock before she tumbled over the edge.

Then everything went silent.

Ylva lay on the scree on the ground without moving. A wave of fear and rage at his own carelessness surged in Evans, but he quickly regained control of his distracting emotions. He had to continue the descent on his own, calmly and patiently. There was no time to lose. He managed to navigate the ice block and reach Ylva without further problems. She was lying on her stomach – lifeless, it seemed – her shoulder twisted at an unnatural angle.

He squatted next to her and shook her tentatively.

"Nordahl."

Ylva made no reply, she lay facing the ground like a broken rag doll. Slowly he rolled her onto her side. His relief was enormous when she roared from pain.

"You're alive, thank God."

Ylva gave him a dazed look, she tried to get up, but yelped when she put weight on her shoulder. Then she realised she had dislocated it and lay down again.

"Shit! I'm sorry, sir. Shit . . ."

She stayed on her back and looked up. The icy ravine loomed over her, the sunlight was splintered by wet ice crystals which created beautiful little rainbows. They had been so close to making it, she thought.

"You'll have to carry on without me, sir."

"Out of the question, Nordahl."

"I'm sorry I let go."

Ylva fought back her tears. Evans got up and stepped a few

paces away from her, he had problems of his own. His chances of surviving the journey to Norway were small, even with Nordahl as his guide. He was utterly dependent on her, he realised, and he hated that. He turned and looked resolutely at Ylva.

"You idiot."

Then he walked back to her, she was in such agony that she could not respond. He bent down again, carefully opened her jacket and pilot suit and examined her shoulder. Ylva lay very still, breathing slowly while staring grimly into space. Evans saw a dip in her shoulder blade and felt the head of the humerus bone near her armpit. He had seen this type of dislocation before, the shoulder blade had jumped out of the socket and needed to be put back.

"We need to reset it."

Ylva looked up at him.

"Roll onto your stomach."

Ylva ignored her pain and rolled over.

She did not think, she did not feel. In her mind's eye, she saw Lyngsalpene bathed in a magenta dawn light, she felt g-forces, and smiled. There was only her and the sound of her breathing inside the helmet.

Evans let her arm stay in its absurd angle, pressed his knee in between her shoulder blades and gently took hold of her elbow joint. He had been taught how to reset a dislocated joint, but it was years ago, and he had never tried it in real life. He knew that he must pull the arm right out of its socket before bending it back hard. He also knew that the pain would be indescribable.

"Are you ready?"

Ylva made no reply, she stared into the ground. Evans sighed, he had not mastered the art of detachment himself, but he had seen people put themselves into a trance in order to endure excruciating agony. It was a case of mind over matter. Ylva focused on the silence inside her helmet, she felt the joystick in her hand. She was safe. The morning light filled the entire horizon. Nothing in the world was more beautiful. She did not permit herself to feel the pain shooting through her when Evans tugged her arm right out of its socket and, with an audible click, pushed it back into the joint.

She breathed calmly throughout the process. What was she made of?

"Nordahl?"

She looked up at him, distant and disoriented at first, then her gaze grew more lucid.

"Yes, sir."

"Are you able to move your arm?"

Ylva's shoulder was tender, but the insane pain had gone. She hesitated, then tried to bend her arm. It worked, she was able to move it. She produced a pale smile.

"Hallelujah, I am healed."

Evans shook his head, she was making jokes now? Seriously?

Swiftly he made a sling from parachute fabric and helped her to put it on.

"Ready?"

Ylva nodded. With her arm in the sling she rose to her feet and walked a few steps away from the scree and the waterfall to have a look at the wide river. She knew that crossing it would be difficult because it very rarely froze over completely. She would need to find a point where there was plenty of ice or an actual bridge.

"Nordahl?"

Ylva straightened up and pointed along the river.

"We're going this way."

30

Storm sat in front of the computer screen in deep concentration. On the wall behind him was a map of Murmansk and next to it were various photographs from the area along with possible timelines and routes that Ylva might have taken. Storm closed his eyes. Which variables, physical, mental and strategic were at their disposal? He let out a faint sigh. The answer was: far too many.

He had managed to hack the intranet at Monchegorsk Air Base and it had not taken him long to discover who had issued the order to buzz the Norwegian supply helicopter. Now he had gained access to Major Khodrokovska's computer and using the Norwegian army's translation programme, he had just decided that the correspondence in her mailbox was relatively innocuous when suddenly he straightened up in his chair. There was one thing that didn't add up.

Ali was half asleep on an old sofa when Storm nudged him.

"Ali, look at this."

Ali was awake with a start. At first he was groggy, but when he saw the urgent look on Storm's face, he got up and followed him to the computer.

"Major Khodrokovska has been blocked from several email threads."

Ali peered at the screen. It was true. Someone had created an email group for senior officers and Major Khodrokovska must have been a participant, but she had been blocked. This was odd.

"Stonewalling?"

Storm nodded as he clicked his way onto a thread.

"This email from General Svetla was sent to everyone in the group except her."

Ali rubbed his eyes as he sat down in front of the computer.

"It's encrypted."

Storm clicked his way through Major Khodrokovska's emails to General Svetla, emails to which the general had never replied.

"Major Khodrokovska sent off for analysis samples of paint traces she had found on the Fullback that buzzed us. The paint traces are from a General Dynamics F-16 Fighting Falcon – 12 F-16-B, made between 1968 and 1988." Storm straightened up.

"That's ours."

31

A white shower of sparks trailed across the pale tundra. Powder snow whirled up by the wind sparkled like diamonds in the cold daylight. The effect was spectacular for anyone who could appreciate it.

Four young men were standing at the edge of the precipice. They did not take in the surreal beauty that surrounded them, but stared into the wall of an impenetrable snowstorm and cursed it. They had only one goal: to capture the N.A.T.O. pilots. Preferably alive so that they could be interrogated. What happened to them after that was not their concern.

Spetsnaz group A, Russia's most lethal men, were manhunters, trained to find anyone, no matter where they might be hiding. You could try to flee from them, you could go on the run, but you would not be able to escape. The tundra was their habitat of choice.

Only four hours ago they had found the cave where the pilots had most likely sheltered during the night and, unless they were foolhardy enough to climb down the steep mountainside, this route was their only option if they were heading west. Besides, the hunters had noticed that one of the pilots must be injured; they had found traces of blood in the cave.

They were sure that they would catch them by nightfall.

But now they were standing at the edge of the precipice, peering into the shimmering, dense, grey mass. They listened out, but apart from the howling wind and the crashing of the river hurling itself off the rocks nearby, there were no other sounds.

Somewhere down below, behind the snow masses, they knew there was a deep valley, which was the most obvious way out of the mountains. It was only a question of time and stamina.

The Spetsnaz soldiers debated the situation, no-one in their right mind would have climbed down near the icy waterfall, the pilots must have walked around it, they decided.

Having assessed the surrounding terrain, G.P.S. coordinates and digital maps, they decided that the pilots had most probably trekked towards the gentler side of the mountain. It was the only route westwards.

They got back on their snow scooters, nodded briefly to one another, then rode in the same direction as Evans and Ylva had walked a few hours earlier. As they neared the edge of the plateau the hunters made an interesting discovery, they saw deep tracks in the snow. Fresh snow had settled on top of them, but when they stopped and blew away the top layer, they could clearly see boot prints from two people. Based on the depth and the size of the prints, they agreed that one was smaller and lighter than the other. On closer inspection they also found traces of blood in the bigger and deeper prints. The soldiers looked around. It made sense that the tracks led towards the easier route down the mountain and the pilots could not now be far ahead if they were walking in this deep, new snow.

They started their snow scooters and followed the tracks along the slope at great speed.

32

On his way to the Command Centre, Storm had wondered how he should present the information contained in Major Khodrokovska's email. There were loose ends he could not account for, such as why the Russians might want to cover up a collision between the planes. It seemed absurd, surely it was in both sides' interests to assume that the current situation was the result of an accident. In the event of an armed confrontation, Russia would be far worse off than N.A.T.O. This new information could de-escalate the crisis significantly.

He knocked firmly on the door, waited for a response and then entered the Command Centre.

Inside were Generals Rove and Bale, the Defence Minister and her staff. All in deep conversation. The Defence Minister looked up as Storm entered.

"I apologise for the interruption, but I have information that might be of interest."

The Defence Minister took a step forward.

"Yes?"

Storm gave the Minister a printout of Major Khodrokovska's email in which she described the paint traces she had discovered on the left wing of the Fullback. At the bottom of the printout was a translation of the Cyrillic text.

The Defence Minister read it, frowning, and then looked quizzically at Storm.

"The crash could have been an accident?"

Rove and General Bale looked sharply at the Minister, who explained the contents of the email. Rove turned to Storm.

"What source did you get that from?"

"I hacked the encrypted intranet of the Russian Armed Forces Command. This is one of the emails Major Khodrokovska sent to the Command group. Major Khodrokovska is the officer commanding the Monchegorsk Air Base."

Rove took the printout and studied the email.

Storm continued eagerly. "And that's not all," he said. "We've discovered that Major Khodrokovska's superiors have blocked her from an email group." Storm looked at Rove and back at the Defence Minister. "It's the same Major Khodrokovska who gave the Fullback the order to buzz our plane. I've double checked, the paint traces are from our F-16."

Rove looked shocked. He returned the printout to the Defence Minister before giving Storm his full attention.

"Are you saying the Russians are covering up a collision between their plane and ours?"

"Yes, sir."

"And that collision could ultimately have caused our plane to be brought down?"

"I can't prove cause and effect between the collision and our plane crashing, sir, but it's a theory that's worth testing."

The Defence Minister had turned ashen, this entirely changed the picture.

"But if it wasn't an accident—"

Without taking his eyes off Storm, Rove interrupted the Defence Minister:

"—or they might have attacked our plane in order to provoke a military response?"

Storm hesitated. It was one explanation, obviously. Rove's gaze lingered on Storm. It was as if he were searching for more information, as if he thought Storm might be holding something back. Storm did not know what to say, the email thread offered no clear-cut answers, just pieces in a confusing jigsaw puzzle. Rove was by no means convinced that this new information changed the situation. He addressed the Defence Minister: "It looks to me as if they're testing us."

Storm frowned. "Who are they, sir?"

Rove glowered at Storm.

"The Russians, obviously. They could have planted this correspondence to mislead us."

Storm shook his head, that was impossible, he had hacked the Russian servers via a proxy. He was sure it was not a diversion technique. "But that makes no sense, sir. The Russians have everything to lose from a military conflict now, so if only we could—"

Rove interrupted Storm.

"Thank you, Lieutenant."

Then he turned to the Defence Minister and General Bale.

"We must stay focused, disinformation of this kind is something we've seen a lot of from their side. Our priority now is to show predictability and firm resolve. It's the only language the Russians respect."

Storm, aware that he was speaking out of turn, said: "But that's exactly the response they'll be expecting and may have prepared for . . . Given that they initiated this."

The Defence Minister cleared her throat by way of rebuke. Storm held up his hands in acknowledgement: "I'm sorry."

Rove nodded, he wasn't bothered by Storm's interruption, but he didn't have time for it.

"Do you know who Major Khodrokovska was emailing?"

Storm shook his head.

"Her correspondence with the lab is encrypted via another intranet, but we're working on it."

Rove studied the email printout again, then he scratched his short, grey hair.

"We must verify the authenticity of the email first to make sure it wasn't planted as a diversionary tactic."

Rove straightened up and placed a firm, fatherly hand on Storm's shoulder. He smiled warmly.

"Lieutenant Bure, good job. We'll follow it up."

Rove paused to let Storm digest the praise.

"This is important information, and it'll be given high priority, but I think you need a rest now, Lieutenant. Go home, take a shower, get some sleep. We need you bright-eyed and bushy-tailed when you return. We'll get your colleague to verify the authenticity of the email and find out who Major Khodrokovska has been talking to."

Storm hesitated, he did not want to take a break, not now. But with everyone looking at him, he became conscious of his sleep-deprived appearance and realised reluctantly that General Rove might be right. Storm saluted everyone and left the room.

33

Once they were on the floor of the valley, Ylva and Evans made better progress despite Evans' wounded leg and Ylva's throbbing shoulder. They walked in silence along the bank of the Malaja Belaja River which, if Ylva's memory served her right, would lead them to Lake Imandra. The enormous Khibiny mountains were now behind them and in front of them stretched miles of flat, Arctic tundra with no places to hide or seek shelter. The babbling of the partly-frozen river intensified the silence, and Ylva was walking in step with her own breathing when she sensed an ominous rumbling.

The ground trembled under their feet before deep, subsonic thunder-cracks erupted from the mountains. They turned and looked up towards the massif where avalanches of snow were crashing over the precipice on the south side. The white tsunami crushed and dragged with it vegetation, boulders, everything in its path. Evans whistled softly at the impressive sight as tall trees snapped like matches in the path of a wall of ice and snow which mowed them down. At the foot of the precipice, the avalanche exploded in vast, white clouds that rolled across the valley. Evans glanced anxiously towards Ylva.

"How far can an avalanche travel?"

"Approximately three times the length of its height."

Evans breathed a sigh of relief; the drop was five hundred

metres at the most, and by now they were several kilometres away. Huge clouds of snow continued to waft across the landscape long after the rumbling had died down and the avalanche had exhausted itself. Several minutes later the snow masses had settled and their view of the mountains became clear once more. The stripped mountainside looked stoic, as if nothing had happened.

Ylva winked at Evans.

"Amazing, isn't it? I love a loose snow avalanche, it's so fluffy."

Evans rolled his eyes.

"I'd love to surf one of those avalanches," she said.

She wiped her nose on the sleeve of her jacket and walked on.

Evans stopped for a moment and looked after her, then he shook his head wearily and followed her.

"Each to their own."

The snow was not nearly as deep once they started their hike along the riverbed and despite Evans' aching leg, they made good time. The landscape ahead of them seemed limitless, there were no fixed points on which they could rest their eyes or which they could use to navigate. Slowly the river began to turn eastwards, and Ylva began to look for a point where they could cross it. To continue westwards, they would have to get to the other side.

The plan was to cross Lake Imandra, continue until they hit European route E105 and then follow the road northwest to the town of Monchegorsk. From there they could walk across the tundra to the Pasvik Valley which formed the border between Russia and Norway.

As the mountain massif disappeared into the horizon behind them, it wasn't just the topography that changed, they also noticed that the sparkling white snow became increasingly grey, and they could smell faint traces of sulphide. Ylva had heard rumours about the barren, desolate and heavily polluted landscape they were now entering. Monchegorsk was as filthy and contaminated as the Koashva mountains were mythical and spectacular. Her cousins in Lovozero had told her that in Monchegorsk grey snow fell from the sky and if you stuck out your tongue, it would taste of ammonia. Ylva had always thought they were exaggerating about this – as they were apt to do about so many things – but now she was no longer sure. The landscape grew gloomier the further west they travelled.

Evans had also noticed the change in the environment, but he did not have the energy to comment or think a great deal. He just wrinkled up his nose and plodded on with heavy, tired steps through the filthy valley.

Ylva could hear him struggle and stumble behind her. Should she slow down, show consideration and possibly ask him how he was? He was wheezing like a dying whale as he limped through the sludge some distance behind her. No, carrying on at the fastest pace they could manage was better and he would just have to try to keep up, there was nothing to be gained from slowing down now. She knew that Evans had a temperature, possibly because gangrene had started to attack his body. As far as she was concerned they could walk for another ten hours, she was keen just to keep going, but the sound of his agonised breathing and hobbling gait told her that she had to come up with a plan B.

She spotted a small cabin on the other side of the river, and a little further ahead there was a fragile ice bridge they might be able to cross. She studied the cabin as they walked past it, the windows were dark and the place looked deserted.

On the other hand, taking a break now would be madness, she reminded herself. The small advantage they had gained by climbing down the rock face near the waterfall offered them no guarantees. Stopping now would be suicide.

Ylva turned around. The sight that met her was worse than she had feared.

Evans' eyes stared feverishly into nothingness. His face was expressionless and his blue lips were pressed grimly together. Blood trickled from his injured calf.

She was aware of just how much the pain to her shoulder drained her of strength, and could only imagine how Evans' wound was affecting him.

She let out a sigh of irritation.

"Do you need a break, sir?"

Evans said nothing, he carried on walking, his eyes blindly fixed on some point in the distance ahead of him.

He crashed into her like a zombie.

"Sir, if we can get to that cabin on the other side, we might find some food and we could also change your dressing there."

He looked at her vacantly, then staggered on.

"You're bleeding through your dressing."

Evans did not seem fully to take in what she was saying. Beads of sweat had formed along his hairline and his pupils were unnaturally large.

"Sir, we need a short break."

She cursed herself the moment she said it. Why was she trying to make the idea of taking a break sound as if it was something she needed? She wasn't the problem here. But in order to protect his male ego, she was trying to convince him that stopping for a while now was something that would benefit both of them. But she did not need a break. She could carry on for hours, she could handle the cold, she knew the tundra. But no, she suggested that they should stop, so that they could both rest. Ylva knew Evans' type only too well, she knew that he would be too proud and stubborn to accept that to carry on walking would kill him.

She scrunched up her nose in irritation. They called it woman's wiles, but it wasn't cleverness, it was stupidity. She should just carry on and leave him to fend for himself, it was what he would have done if the situation had been reversed, she had no doubt of that. This small act of self-sacrifice reminded her of her mother and her desperate need at all costs to avoid other people feeling uncomfortable or realising that they were a burden. Her chronic people-pleasing was all about everyone else feeling fine the whole time. Surely she could see where that had brought her? Empathetic people were absolutely useless, they floated around with their halos, always feeling too emotional to get anything done. Ylva had spent her whole life trying her hardest to unlearn her mother's self-effacing goodness.

But having pondered the matter, she concluded that no, they were a team, he was her superior officer and he needed to rest.

"Sir, we'll take a short break to gather our strength."

Evans made no reply, he just stumbled along the riverbank like an idiot. Typical.

Ylva led them to the ice bridge, then stopped. She studied the ice, it was thin. The river bubbled under the ice shelf and the water was not deep, but if they were to fall in, they would cool down quickly and it might prove difficult to get back up onto the slippery bank on the other side. Crossing it was risky, but did they have a choice? Ylva examined the uneven ice lump. It was sufficiently thick along its sides, it was the solidity of its surface that was hard to be sure about.

Ylva laid down on her stomach to spread her weight, then she wriggled forwards. There was an ominous crack and she stopped, lay still and stared into the running water beneath her. Gingerly, her movements barely perceptible, she elbowed her way up over the top and slid down on the other side. Evans was motionless on his side of the river, staring into the water, his breathing laboured.

"Sir, are you ready?"

He hardly reacted, he seemed lost in a world of his own.

"Sir?"

Evans looked up, his eyes were dull with fever. Then he nodded. He kneeled and then laid down slowly on the ice and with heavy twisting movements he crawled up the ice shelf. There was a faint crack as the ice broke behind him and a chunk of the bridge fell into the water. Evans stayed stock still. There was no going back now, he would have to make it to the other side. Ylva squatted down and reached out to him.

"Take my hand. You're nearly there."

He looked at her almost as if he did not care. A gust of wind threw a dusting of snow over him and he continued to lie in the middle of the lumpy ice, staring into space.

"Sir, I'm here."

No reaction.

"Pull yourself together, man!"

Ylva yelled at him out of sheer frustration and he turned his vacant gaze towards her.

"I'm coming, Leah," he mumbled.

He made his way laboriously across the shallow hump and slid towards Ylva. She grabbed his sleeve and pulled him close. He murmured softly, mostly to himself, as they collapsed side by side on the river bank.

"Everything will be alright, Leah, you're safe."

Who the hell is Leah? Ylva wondered, but she said nothing.

She got to her feet, brushed off the snow and listened out.

All she could hear was the babbling of the river, gusts of wind lashing the tundra and Evans' feverish panting on the ground.

Ylva took another look at the cabin. It still looked abandoned so she walked up to it. There were no tracks in the snow so it was probably empty, she decided, nor would there appear to be any nearby building. She heard Evans get up and as she turned, he was already heading for the water that flowed underneath the ice. Ylva didn't have time to stop him before he was bent over the stream.

Evans swayed as he stared down at the strangely turquoise water. On the riverbed were the remains of aegirine, eudialyte and other Khibiny minerals that had been washed out with mining sludge from the mines further to the northeast. He cupped his hands and gulped down the alkaline wastewater. Ylva was about to stop him drinking it, but then thought better of it, why bother? Even if she knew that the water was polluted with chemicals from the extraction. He could survive a few mouthfuls, she decided, as Evans coughed and spluttered by the water's edge.

The cabin was derelict, but it was sheltered from the wind. She approached it warily and peered through a window. Apart from a thin couch, a stove, a table and two chairs, there was nothing inside. It would have to do.

She did not have to kick down the door, it was unlocked, so she went in.

It took her eyes a moment to acclimatise to the darkness in the cabin whose tiny windows were covered with snow and barely let in any light. Ylva turned to Evans, who stood swaying in the doorway, confused and delirious from fever. He pushed her aside brusquely as she tried to help him and she let him stagger across the floor before he collapsed just before he reached the couch at the far end of the room.

He did not resist when Ylva pulled him up onto the couch and folded up his trouser leg to examine his injured calf. The stench spoke its own clear language and, as the dressing fell off, she could see that the skin surrounding the wound had turned black with a border of yellow inflammation. Along the swollen edges of the scab, small purple blisters were forming. The stench of rotting flesh and sour infection was acrid and nauseating, and Ylva had to turn away in order not to throw up. Evans had developed gangrene and the infection was spreading.

34

As he drove home from the Norwegian Joint Headquarters, Storm thought of the day he had met Ylva outside the Bodø Arts Centre. He had watched her from a distance and, as she came down the steps, she had undone the tight bun at the back of her neck, letting her blonde hair flow. He had followed her as she crossed the square in front of the town hall on her way to her mother's house, a twenty-minute walk away. Her hair billowed with the wind and she seemed both freer and less self-conscious with it down. Storm smiled at the memory. He found it endearing that she tried so hard to come across as tough and detached, while at the same time she really cared about her sick mother and looked after her conscientiously. He had never heard Ylva utter a single kind word about her mother, but she had not been particularly negative either, she had simply told him that her mother had mental health issues and lived in chaos and clutter. But it spoke volumes that she had made sure to look in on her mother before the start of Exercise Arctic Blizzard. Ylva was ultimately a softie; come to think of it, she could even be kind.

How was her mother now?

Did she have someone to look after her?

Storm became aware that it worried him, why had he not thought about her before?

She must be feeling absolutely awful. He decided to visit Ylva's mother on his way home, he wasn't too tired for that.

His eyes were stinging from lack of sleep as he rang the doorbell. There was no reply, he waited, then tried again, but the house lay silent in the darkness.

He was about to give up and had turned to leave when Mary cautiously opened the door behind him. She peered anxiously out through the narrow crack, then looked at him with hostility.

"Hello, I'm a friend of Ylva's," he said with a smile.

Her expression turned to hope.

"Have you found her?"

Storm shook his head, he was so tired that he felt dizzy. He looked at Ylva's mother whom he had never met before. Mother and daughter were actually quite similar, the same intense eyes and high cheekbones.

"We're working on it," he said. "Can I come in?"

Mary had no time for visitors, she hated people turning up unannounced. She wanted to be left alone. She wasn't presentable, she hadn't been for years, which was one of the many reasons she stayed indoors. But Storm's manner was as friendly as it was insistent. He needed to talk to her, it was obvious.

Mary sighed and stepped aside.

As Storm opened the door fully and entered the hall, he noticed the smell immediately and it was as stale as Ylva had described it.

Mary went to the living room where she stopped, surrounded by a confusion of clothes and books. Storm saw that she was in the process of packing.

"I just wanted to stop by and see how you were."

She turned to him swiftly, her eyes were red and puffy.

"Who are you?"

"I'm a friend of—"

Ylva's mother cut him off impatiently.

"She has never mentioned you."

"We've only known each other for a few weeks. I work for C.Y.F.O.R."

Storm tried to act calm and relaxed, but Ylva's mother was not deceived, she could tell that he was anxious. She glanced uneasily about her as if she thought that someone might be watching her in the dimly lit living room. Then she leaned towards Storm and whispered in a conspiratorial voice.

"They've taken her too."

"They?"

Mary did not reply, but her eyes blazed with fear and she signalled that she could not say any more.

"Have they taken anyone else?"

She whispered, her voice barely audible: "Geir, her father."

Storm frowned. Ylva had told him that her mother's mental health was fragile, but it was not until this point that Storm realised how unwell she was.

"I thought he died from a blood clot to the brain?"

Mary shook her head.

"That's what *they* wanted us to think."

"Who are they?"

Once again Mary gestured to Storm to lower his voice, then she looked about her suspiciously. She waited, listened and made sure that no-one else was present in the otherwise empty living room.

"I don't know," she whispered and continued to stand very still, staring into space.

She seemed caught up in a maelstrom of distress. Storm went on standing helplessly in front of her, not sure what to say. Then, quite abruptly, she turned away from him and with trembling, frantic movements she resumed stuffing clothes, books and medication into a bag.

"Where are you going?"

"I'm going home . . ."

"Where is home?"

"Kautokeino."

"Do you have family there?"

Ylva's mother stopped packing and looked sceptically up at Storm.

"How well do you really know her?"

Storm looked down.

"Not well enough."

Mary nodded wearily.

"No-one does. She keeps people at arm's length."

Storm noticed the pictures on the living room wall of Ylva as a little girl with her mother.

There were also several photographs of Ylva and her parents with her mother's family, all of them wearing colourful Sámi *gákti* jackets. Ylva and her parents looked happy and relaxed. Indeed, Storm had never seen Ylva look so relaxed, nor had he known that she was half Sámi. He would have liked to know such things about his girlfriend.

"I'm going home to my own kind so they don't kill me as well."

Storm watched this petite woman vacillate between the stuffed bag and the clothing strewn across the floor. She seemed desperate and confused, and no wonder, who wouldn't be in her situation? She had probably just lost her daughter.

"Who wants to kill you?"

She scratched the top of her hand in a distracted manner, did she understand his question? Her nails left red welts. Storm felt sorry for her, she seemed to him a terrified, traumatised child who had sought refuge in a fantasy to protect herself against the terrors of the world.

He gently put his hand on hers. She jumped and stared blankly up at him, then she snatched back her hand. Storm looked at her tenderly, but he said nothing. He could sense her fear, her confusion. She did not move, but continued to stare up at the unfamiliar man who was towering over her. He had nice eyes, she thought.

"Who are they, the people who mustn't kill you too?"

She hesitated, she was desperate to tell him, but she did not dare. Her life was in danger. Storm continued to hold her gaze until she turned away.

"No, no, I can't . . ." She shook her head frantically, her long, grey hair dancing around her shoulders. "Or I don't know. His computer disappeared the day before he died."

Storm froze and looked at her closely once more, his instinct telling him that this could be important.

"His computer disappeared?"

She nodded.

"Had he backed up his files?"

Mary stared at Storm, her eyes narrowed yet again. She hesitated, then she returned to her packing with more frenzy. She would snatch garments from the bag, then stuff something else into it. Clearly without any plan.

"Why do you think your husband was killed?"

A jumper was yanked from the bag, a single shoe added, then some books. Which she immediately took out again.

"I'd never seen Geir scared before, never. But he was then. He feared for his life."

"Did he say anything about what or who he was afraid of?"

Mary continued to pack and unpack while she gasped for air, shaking and grunting to herself. *If she carries on like that, she'll* hyperventilate and pass out, Storm thought. He looked at the alarming quantities of prescription medication strewn across the sofa, on the coffee table and in the bag.

"I don't want to get involved," she hissed. "I just want Ylva and me to be left alone. Why can't you just leave her alone?"

Storm could see that there was nothing but emptiness behind Mary's hysterical gaze, her breathing quickened and she grew increasingly crazed.

"They've taken her, they've killed her, they have, they have, nobody believes me, he was killed, they killed him, and now her. They've killed her, she's dead, my daughter's dead. And no-one cares." Her shrill voice rose in panic. "No-one cares!" she screamed.

Storm took a deep breath, he must not allow himself to get caught up in her emotions, instead he needed to comfort and reassure the poor woman before she lost her mind altogether. He proffered a disarming smile.

"May I give you a hug?"

His question penetrated her senseless confusion; she looked up at him, shocked. Storm himself was taken aback by his suggestion, he was not a natural hugger. She said nothing, but fixed him with her wide-open gaze.

Storm waited. Silent tears welled up in her eyes, then with embarrassment bordering on shame she looked down as if she had suddenly become aware of her own wretched state. She did not dare to raise her gaze, but whispered quietly:

"No, or that is . . . If you absolutely insist . . . then I don't mind . . . a hug . . ."

Storm walked slowly up to her with his arms open, she flinched a little and he stopped, still with his arms outstretched. He wanted her to feel that she was in control, that he wasn't trying to trap or restrain her. It was important to let her take that last step towards him. He had realised that was a wise move. Ylva was just the same.

Mary hesitated, then she took a small step forwards and stopped very close to him. She continued to stand like this. Storm wrapped his long, strong arms tenderly around her. She leaned back a little, but allowed herself to be hugged.

Storm held her gently and noticed that she smelled bad. Her skinny body felt frail and yet as tense as a bowstring. He did not know for how long to hug her. He loosened his hold a little so she could make the choice. Mary, however, leaned even closer into him with her arms crossed in front of her chest as if she were freezing. She stood very still, resting her forehead on Storm's chest. He stroked her back, he could feel her ribs through her kimono and she was trembling. She chewed her lip hard and fought it, but eventually she broke. Deep sobs morphed into crying. Storm let the woman cry out her rage. The front of his shirt grew damp as her tears ripped the terrible pain out of her.

"I'm here, we're in this together," he whispered.

His words echoed a despair she had lost the ability to articulate, it was as if this unknown man truly understood.

"You're not alone," he said again softly. "We'll find her."

Eventually her anxiety and her tears ebbed out, and gently he released her.

Mary stared down at her hands, her trembling subsided, her breathing settled and she regained her composure.

"Thank you," she whispered. "All I see these days are doctors and psychiatrists, and none of those geniuses prescribe human compassion."

Storm looked at the pills on the sofa, on the coffee table and in the bag.

"But they give you a lot of great drugs," he smiled.

She looked up at him in surprise, her gaze meeting his smiling eyes and she laughed.

"Yes, and fancy diagnoses. There's no shortage of those."

They both smiled, each a little shy after the intimate moment they had just shared.

"I miss her," Mary whispered.

Storm nodded and felt a pang of desperation he really couldn't afford to indulge right now, he had to think straight. Without saying anything he continued to watch her, there really was a strong family resemblance. Mary's green eyes seemed more alert now as if the tears had washed away some of the madness.

"I miss them both," she murmured.

She looked up at Storm; it was not until now that she really noticed him, he looked miserable.

"So tell me, how are you?"

Storm tried to say something neutral, something that would reassure her. But he could not do it. The pain in his gut, the lumps in his chest and in his throat felt unbearable. He could not allow himself to give way to his own despair and he did not have the strength to talk. Ylva's mother stroked his cheek.

"She was like an aspen leaf when she was little ... but she grew strong, stronger than me and her father."

And Storm could suddenly see the optimism and openness Ylva had told him her mother had once been known for.

"She still is," she smiled to comfort him. "If anyone can survive this, then it's ..."

The words disappeared as the tears welled up once more and she could not finish the sentence. Storm nodded gratefully.

"Is there anything I can do for you?" he said. "Is there anything you need?"

She shook her head.

"It's a long trip for me," she whispered. "I haven't seen Elle, my sister, for five years. And now that I think about it, it's not as if we live so very far from each other, not really . . ."

Storm took a deep breath.

"Are there any backups of the files which were on your husband's computer?"

Mary stared vacantly into space.

"If I could get access to the contents of his computer or his backups, I might be able to find an explanation. Or at least I could see what your husband was working on at the time leading up to his death."

Ylva's mother looked around the chaotic room, defeated, then she shook her head wearily.

"He didn't tell me anything."

There was a pen and some newspapers on the coffee table, Storm scribbled down his name and mobile number.

"You can call me anytime if you need someone to talk to or if I can help you in any way."

She nodded wordlessly and took the paper. Silence descended on the darkened living room.

"I won't keep you any longer," Storm said. "I just wanted to drop by and . . . well, I'll keep you posted."

She nodded. "Thank you."

Storm heard her rummage around the living room as he headed for the front door.

"Wait!"

He was about to step out into the cold when Mary came running after him. He turned and was surprised to see her handing him a beautiful piece of Sámi jewellery.

"Take this."

Storm looked at the pretty necklace with a pendant in the shape of a silver ball. He heard a faint jingle as he took it.

"It's Ylva's Sámi magic ball," her mother said.

Storm looked at her in surprise. He ought to have known what it was, but it meant nothing to him.

"It belonged to my mother and my great-grandmother and I want Ylva to have it."

Storm nodded, still not sure what he was meant to do with the silver pendant.

"Thank you . . ."

"I wore the necklace when I was pregnant and after Ylva was born, the jingling of the ball would calm her. That's our custom. We hang magic balls over the cradle to stop forces from the underworld harming the sleeping child. All Sámi children have one . . ."

Storm gently trailed his fingers over the beautifully decorated silver ball.

"Does the pattern mean anything?"

Mary gulped, her voice quivered. "It provides *šiella* – that means protection."

Storm held the pendant in his big hand.

"I'll look after it and I'll give it to Ylva when I find her. I promise."

Mary nodded anxiously.

"You do that. It has protective powers. It will give you what you need."

Storm placed the necklace in his pocket and looked at Ylva's mother, their eyes met and rested on each other for a moment.

"Find her," she whispered and closed the door firmly.

Storm heard her lock it behind him.

* * *

Storm felt miserable as he got into the car. He slumped against the steering wheel as he thought of the family photographs of Ylva smiling and laughing. He missed her so badly. He took the necklace from his pocket and flung it onto the passenger seat in anger, but the jingling of the ball soothed him; Ylva had listened to that sound since before she was born, it would protect her.

He pulled himself together, started the car and drove home.

Fifteen minutes later Storm parked in his regular spot outside his flat in the centre of Bodø. As he got out of the car, he caught sight of the necklace lying on the passenger seat. He picked it up and studied the craftsmanship. The silver ball was decorated with intricate, interrupted patterns and there was a clasp on the side. He opened the clasp. Inside the ornate ball was another silver ball, which made the gentle jingling sound. Storm took out the silver ball and his heart skipped a beat. It was in fact a small memory stick, disguised as jewellery.

35

Ylva examined the wound on Evans' calf. Fortunately the infection was limited to the flesh for now. Once it reached the bone, that would be the end of him.

"Sir, you need to stay here. I'll walk to Kirovsk to get medication and dressings."

Her suggestion was obviously ridiculous; right now they were Russia's most wanted criminals and they both knew it. If they were discovered, the best-case scenario was that they would be killed, at worst they would end up in a Russian prison. Evans, however, had no energy to quarrel with her proposal. He leaned back and fell asleep.

Ylva would have to be quick, not only so that they wouldn't lose the small advantage they had gained, but also because the infection in Evans' calf was spreading with every passing hour. Without medicine, he would develop septicaemia before nightfall.

Ylva left the cabin and surveyed the landscape. The sun was to the south and if she walked down to the river, followed it to the lake and then headed northeast, she would probably reach Kirovsk in an hour.

She walked along the river where the mounting stench of chemicals told her that she was approaching the mining town.

Having followed a bumpy road with a sign where the letters

"КИРОВСК" could still be made out, she at last reached the dilapidated industrial town.

On the outskirts Ylva sneaked past rows of abandoned buildings that looked like gravestones from the Soviet era. Broken windows yawned at her and she could smell rot and decay. The crumbling houses bore witness to humanity's fleeting passage through this world. Once they had represented the height of modernity, functional and optimistic hopes for the future. They bore witness, as only Soviet architecture could, to its blind faith in state-controlled progress, a planned economy and industry.

Now the broken buildings looked like frail, decrepit old men, abandoned by time and human compassion. The grey blocks were nothing but empty shells with no life to protect. Nature was in the process of reclaiming the grandiose visions that had crumbled into piles of mortar and cement. A ghostly silence drifted through the streets.

Ylva headed east and slowly but surely the town changed character. At one junction there were gloomy ruins on one side, but on the other a motel, some small shops and a café. Ylva stole up to one of the shops, she spotted the newspaper front pages which displayed large pictures of herself and Major Evans. She was not surprised. She looked around nervously, she had to make sure that no-one saw her, people would be on their guard.

In an alleyway an intoxicated man was relieving himself up against a wall, a big bag was lying next to him and his furry ushanka hat had fallen off his head. Perfect.

As nimble as a cat, Ylva moved up behind him. On her way she picked up a rusty iron bar. Flashes of pain shot through her still tender shoulder as she knocked the man unconscious with one blow. He collapsed and red, warm blood trickled from his sparse hair. He'll have one hell of a headache when he wakes up, Ylva thought, and opened his bag. To her relief it contained clothing. She looked about her, two people walked past on the pavement. They braced themselves against the nasty wind, then they were gone. Ylva pulled off her pilot suit and stuffed it into the bag, then she got dressed in the clothes she found in the man's bag. They were men's clothes, too big and scratchy, but they were warm and they would help her blend more easily into the local population of grey, glum people who through the whims of fate had ended up in this town with no future.

She managed to pull the thick duffel coat off the prostrate man and put it on. She snatched the man's wallet which contained a few roubles before she put on his ushanka hat with the ear flaps. Minutes later an apparently skinny little man with a shapeless bag over his shoulder strolled into the street.

Ylva walked along the pavement. At the end of the street she noticed a pale neon sign, a chemist. Keeping her head down and slouching, she entered the shop, there was no staff to be seen and Ylva could see no C.C.T.V. Without hesitation she stuffed dressings, antiseptic products, paracetamol and something she thought was antibiotics into the bag. She heard a door creak behind her and spun around. A fat little babushka came out from the lavatory. She looked at Ylva with a total lack of interest before she sat down on a chair by the till and turned up the volume of an old T.V. on the counter. The room filled with news about the N.A.T.O. plane that had been shot down on its way to the nuclear base in Murmansk. Ylva felt her pulse quicken, she turned up the collar of the coat, slipped out into the cold and was gone.

Food, she had to find food. Shopping for groceries was too risky. She continued warily down the street and could smell goulash and borscht as she passed a tired-looking café. She slipped into the yard behind it, and there, as she had expected, was a row of overflowing bins. Like a vulture she went through the waste looking for food scraps, any meat and vegetables that had been thrown out. She took a few juicy bites of a half-eaten schnitzel and the taste was, if not heavenly, then at least very welcome. She scoffed another two mouthfuls, then she filled the bag with as much food as she could, and darted back into the street.

With her shoulders up, the hat pushed down well over her eyes and the coat collar pulled up over her face, she trudged back through the ghost town towards the tundra.

On the outskirts of Kirovsk, civilisation was completely on its knees. Ylva was slipping in and out between the buildings when she spotted a Black Arctic Cat Z.R. 9000 parked in a courtyard. She looked about her. There was no-one around and, encouraged by the silence, she went into the courtyard and walked up to the snow scooter. This was their salvation, she thought, and set down the bag. With frozen fingers she pulled out a cable to jumpstart the engine.

"Oi, you!"

Ylva froze as a big, fat man came out into the courtyard.

"What do you think you're doing?"

Ylva glanced up at the man and, in the gap between the coat collar and the ushanka hat, she saw him walk towards her. She made no reply, but backed away from the snow scooter. The man came right out into the courtyard and leaned curiously towards her, then he started to laugh.

"You look like a woman. Are you a woman?"

Ylva glanced around, how could she have been so dumb as to wander into a dark courtyard with just the one exit? The man was blocking her only escape route. As if he could read her mind, he took a step forward and grabbed her arm. Ylva cried out as the pain shot from her shoulder and into her back. He was strong and she realised that she would not be able to make a quick getaway, but she sized up her opponent. He was overweight and almost two metres tall. His face was puffy, his eyes bloodshot and his breath reeked of vodka. Ylva scrunched up her nose, she hated drunk people.

Then she smiled, lifted her head coquettishly and looked him right in the eye.

"Yes, I am," she took a deep breath. "Is that your scooter?" Ylva was reasonably pleased with her Russian accent although it had a faint Sámi trace because she had first learned Russian from her family in Lovozero.

The man did not seem to pay any attention to her accent; he just leered at her, revealing a row of rotting teeth.

"Yes, it is."

He glanced around quickly, the courtyard was dark and quiet. They were alone.

"Do you like it?"

Ylva nodded sweetly while she carefully eased her arm from his grip. She attempted to walk past him with an air of innocence and lightness, but without success. As quick as an aggressive bear, he took hold of her again and pulled her close.

"Where have I seen you before?"

Ylva looked away. He tore the ushanka hat off her head and her blonde hair cascaded over her shoulders. The man grinned.

"Oh, right."

She stood still, her heart was pounding. His fat belly and rotten teeth suggested poor health and a low fitness level, but the strength of his grip on her arm told her that he was basically strong. Close combat was not ideal, but she was cornered and had no choice. She listened out carefully, but she could hear no-one else, there were no witnesses to the incident as far as she could gather. She straightened up and met the man's squinting gaze, then she smiled cheekily:

"Right."

"I can make good money out of you," he muttered.

He pulled her even closer.

"But first we're going to have some fun, aren't we?"

Ylva tried to free herself, but he threw her against the courtyard wall. The pain seared through her and she nearly passed out as the back of her head slammed against the concrete and she collapsed. He bent over her, yanked her upright and leaned into her. His breath stank hot against her mouth as he pressed his stomach and thighs against Ylva's body. When she felt his erection, she wanted to throw up. She closed her eyes.

Horny, drunk men don't think straight, they always overestimate their ability and they underestimate the woman's disgust. She looked into his blurred, bloodshot eyes and smiled as she moaned heavily, and whether it was because she had been knocked almost unconscious or she was turned on, she would let him decide for himself, but she could feel that he liked it. He started fondling her breasts and she let him savour the moment and take the power trip that made him careless. With greedy fingers he started tearing at the waistband of the wide trousers she had stolen. She was repulsed as his filthy fingers reached her warm skin, fumbled their way down her stomach and grabbed at her groin. She did not move, she would have to let him grope her. He did not drop his guard until he felt her warm breath settle. He smirked as he continued to pull away her clothing. She tried to wriggle out of his grip, but he was faster and pressed his elbow hard against her throat, blocking out all air. Ylva stared up at him, terrified. She could not breathe. She flailed her arms impotently and he grinned coldly, he liked it when women fought back.

36

Storm and Ali sat hunched over their computers at C.Y.F.O.R. They were absorbed in odysseys through an ever-expanding virtual universe of information and data. It had a meta reality of its own, governed by its own laws. Storm navigated flawlessly through the digital network of zeros and ones in the World Wide Web. All data traffic, every browser search, picture, mundane Facebook update, narcissistic Instagram post, pointless tweet and secret text message from people who loved or hated one another, lay at the end of his fingertips. No-one could hide under their duvet from the Big Brother of the universe. George Orwell's dystopia was a delightful fairy tale compared to today's ever-present spies who, by analysing our meta data and our biometric data, register with terrifying accuracy everything we do and think.

Storm was looking for a lead, a text message, a picture, an algorithm ... anything that could help him find Ylva. At the same time, he was keeping an eye on the simple iPad on his lap. It was a security precaution; he could not be logged on to the Norwegian armed forces' network when he opened the memory stick he had found inside the pendant.

A series of incomprehensible symbols appeared on the screen. "Oh shit, it's all encrypted."

Ali looked over Storm's shoulder at the contents.

"But you can read the file names, it's about Titans Security."

Storm looked at Ali, they had made the same connection, Titans Security was the name of the private security company that General Rove worked for. What did that have to do with Ylva's father?

Storm gave Ali the iPad with the memory stick. "Do you think you can decrypt the files on this?"

Ali smiled. "I thought you'd never ask." And without another word, Ali made himself comfortable and started cracking the encryption.

Storm logged on to all the recordings he had access to from the security cameras on the base. He wanted to see who Rove had been in contact with before the accident. Methodically he scrolled yet again through endless footage of people sitting, standing, coming and going. Played at fast-forwarding speed, human beings looked like swarms of hurtling insects.

The images flickered in front of his eyes.

Suddenly Storm hit the pause button. On some grainy video footage from a security camera in one of the hangars he saw Rove walk alone out of the darkness. The footage was dated the evening that Exercise Arctic Blizzard was launched.

Storm rewound the recording a few minutes and played the footage at normal speed. There, like a blurred shadow against the grey hangar wall, Rove walked past the camera and out onto the tarmac. The timecode showed that it was two hours and forty minutes after he had greeted Ylva and then Major Evans down at Bodø Arts Centre.

Storm continued to speculate: what was Rove doing alone on the runway at that hour? The footage played on and although the resolution became fuzzy when he zoomed in on the picture, he could make out another figure. He was there at the end of the runway, and he seemed to be waiting for someone. Storm leaned forward and narrowed his eyes. But wasn't that . . .? The image was infuriatingly unclear and besides, this person was standing with his back to the camera, but as Rove came up and stopped behind him, the figure turned and Storm could clearly see that it was Major Evans waiting in the dark. Storm had just the video recording, no audio, and he could only guess at the topic of their conversation. But he could see that Evans' body language was tense at the start and became increasingly relaxed as the conversation progressed. Towards the end the mood between the two men seemed amicable and pleasant. What were they talking about?

Storm tried to enlarge the image, but it was so grainy that he could make out nothing at all. He had no hope of reading their lips.

Suddenly the screen image on his computer flickered a few times before glowing cold and clear at him once more.

Ali shot up from his chair.

"What was that?"

Ali came over to Storm's computer.

"A glitch?"

Ali shook his head, then he ran to the mainframe.

"Shit. We're being hacked."

Storm reacted instinctively; he started tracking the intruder straightaway.

"Turn it off, for God's sake!" Ali called out.

Storm typed with lightning speed as Ali started logging off all systems while also alerting the intranet to the security breach.

"It's not Sandworm or S.O.R.M.2, it's . . ."

The processor hummed, Storm had got the bit between his teeth and refused to log off. Ali yanked the plug out of Storm's machine and the screen went black. Storm got up furiously, his chair crashing onto the floor behind him.

"Why the hell did you do that? I could have found out who was hacking us!"

Ali looked at Storm and sighed.

"You need to take a break, man. It's too personal."

Storm glared at the dead computer monitor.

"The person or persons hacking us could have led us to—"

"Storm!"

Ali was more desperate than angry, but he positioned himself firmly between the computer and Storm. He forced Storm to look at him.

"If you go after those hackers, you'll expose all of C.Y.F.O.R. Have you lost your mind?"

Storm glowered angrily past him and at the computer monitor.

"But we have to—" he objected.

Ali cut him off: "As your superior, I need you to stand down. Take some time off."

Storm shook his head, he leaned forward to plug in the machine again, but Ali forced him away.

"Lieutenant Bure, we'll do whatever we can to find Ylva and Major Evans. I promise you that. But right now you're risking the whole operation. You need to take a break and then come back tomorrow. O.K.?"

Storm was about to roar from rage when the whole room was suddenly plunged into darkness. A few seconds later the stand-by generator kicked in and the power returned. One of the other I.T. technicians in the group shouted out into the room:

"All computer centres north of Trondheim have been knocked out. Equinor, Hydro and Avinor all report their systems crashing. The American radar system Globus II in Vardø has jammed the American rocket shield in the north."

Storm looked at Ali.

"That has to be a new type of Sandworm, surely? They're ahead of us, they already know what we're going to do."

Ali looked with incredulity at Storm.

"What do you mean?"

"They feed us contradictory information and red herrings. They're playing with us."

Ali ran a hand across his eyes, what a bloody mess.

"Who is ahead of us, Storm? The Russians?"

Storm hesitated, it made no sense for the Russians to initiate such an attack out of the blue. But if it wasn't the Russians . . .? It seemed as if N.A.T.O. and the Russians were both chasing their own tails, they were continuously on the back foot . . . Someone else had to be running the show, someone who was deep inside the systems on both sides of the border. Storm grabbed his coat and looked at Ali.

"Ali, I've got to go! Can you decrypt the memory stick?"

"Yes, we're working on it now."

Storm lowered his voice so only Ali could hear him.

"Whoever was behind the attack has infiltrated our networks. We need to solve this analogue style without any digital fingerprints."

Ali nodded, but continued to scratch his head as he saw Storm's broad back disappear down the corridor. Storm Bure was suggesting an analogue solution to this?

God help whoever bumped into him.

37

Red and black dots flickered in front of Ylva's eyes, the lack of oxygen was acute and she was about to lose consciousness. Her ears were whistling, and all sound had become muffled and distant as if she were being held under water. She stared into the man's panting, distorted, ruddy face and in short flashes she noticed that the heavy Russian was trying to undo his own trousers, but the zip got stuck and distracted him. It gave her one last chance. He managed to unzip his trousers and fumbled into them. She punched his right ear as hard as she could, he jerked back, easing the pressure on her throat. She gasped and felt cold oxygen rush in. He lunged at her furiously and she felt utterly powerless, but exploited the momentum in his movement by head-butting him across his nose. The pain caused him to lose his focus for a few seconds and, as he leaned forward to raise his hand to his broken nose, she met that movement with a knee kick up towards his face. He groaned as he crashed into the concrete wall behind her. Ylva freed her right arm and plunged her index and middle finger into his eyes. She heard gurgling deep inside his skull as his eyeballs split and were forced out of their sockets. Blinded and disoriented, the man lashed out at her, but she managed to block the blows before she slipped out from under him. She had regained the upper hand and aimed two high side-kicks at his Adam's apple to crush the man's larynx and windpipe. A strange hissing could be heard as he slumped to his knees in front of her. Good, no air could pass his vocal cords now and not a sound would escape from him. Ylva gasped greedily for air, she needed a moment to recover. Blind, breathless and kneeling, her attacker swayed in front of her. Ylva stood watching him for a moment, he looked like a grotesque character in a horror movie.

She put him out of his misery with a kick to his neck vertebrae, crushing them. His neck snapped and the man collapsed like a sack of potatoes. Violent spasms rippled through his heavy body before finally he lay still with his limp penis on display in the snow. Two bloody craters stared blindly up at her while she wiped her bloody hands on his clothing. He was getting off too lightly, she thought, and made sure to pull up her own trousers and tighten them around her waist as best she could. But at least the world had one fewer bastard to worry about.

Just to be sure, she bent down to check that the job was done. Jesus, there was still squeaking coming from his injured airways. He was a tough one. Ylva took her knife and plunged it under his ribs and up into his heart. He jerked – in one final spasm. Ylva was aware that his blood was soaking the sleeve of her jacket, but she waited patiently. She allowed him the time he needed to die. Then it was over.

Now what? His mangled corpse lay at her feet. If she left him where he was, he would be found and that would arouse suspicion. She would have to take him with her when she left the town and then dump him on the way. With superhuman effort – God, he was so fat – she managed to haul the man up onto the scooter. As she lifted him, the pain in her shoulder was agonising, but she managed it in the end. She placed him over the handlebars where his heavy body settled into a stable position.

Ylva sat behind the body, pulled out the ignition switch and broke open the steering lock. Then she placed one hand on the accelerator, connected the cables, stuck the knife into the ignition, and turned it. With a growl the motor revved up, and she accelerated.

Ylva drove the bike as fast as it would go through the town and out across the tundra. She had lost valuable time. But she had made her getaway from Kirovsk and fifteen minutes later she pulled up in front of the small cabin and parked the scooter with the man still draped over the handlebars.

Ylva pulled the man off the scooter and with a gigantic effort she dragged him into the cabin and there she undressed him. He had bled through almost all his clothes, but she could keep them as extra. Fortunately he too had some roubles on him and half a bottle of vodka. They could come in handy.

Evans was lying pale and still on the couch. He had clearly been asleep since she left, but now he woke up and squinted at her.

"Sir, we've got transport."

He didn't seem to understand what she was saying, he was ravaged by fever and he was shaking. Ylva took out the dressing, the vodka, the antiseptic cream, the paracetamol and the knife.

She lifted his trouser leg, revealing the wound.

It stank, if possible, more now, and yellow pus was weeping from the dark purple flesh.

"Sir, I need to remove the infected tissue."

Evans nodded, though Ylva doubted if he had fully taken in what she had said. She gave him some antibiotics and paracetamol and helped him wash them down with vodka. Then she sterilised the knife and the wound thoroughly.

Evans looked at her. His stare was glassy.

"Are you ready, sir?"

He did not respond. She held the knife horizontally along his calf and took a deep breath before she started trimming chunks of dead flesh from the bone. It wasn't until she reached fresh, red flesh that Evans screamed. He arched his back from spasms of pain before he collapsed and lay very still. It's a blessing that people pass out when their pain becomes too great, Ylva thought, it allowed her to work undisturbed.

She knew that she had to remove all the infected tissue and that it was better to remove too much than too little, so she cut generously. Afterwards she cleansed and dressed the wound, then she left him alone. He would wake up when he was ready.

Ylva took out the food she had managed to forage and tipped it out onto the table, she was starving. Once she had lit a fire with old newspapers and some logs that she found in the cabin, she melted snow in a cup and wolfed down a big piece of meat. At this point she finally allowed herself a swig of the vodka and she felt the exhaustion creep up on her. Her muscles were numb and her eyes stung from fatigue.

Ylva glanced at the two men in the room, the Russian had got what he deserved, but she hoped sincerely that Evans would make it. Bizarrely she was starting to warm to the grumpy old man. Exhausted, she slumped down on the table, resting her head on her arm.

She checked her shoulder, it was sore, but she could handle it. As she gave herself permission to relax a little, Storm appeared in her thoughts. She missed him so much. Closing her eyes, she conjured up his face, his clear grey-green eyes, which were smiling most of the time as if he were laughing at a private joke. Even when he was absorbed in algorithms and complex probability calculations, she could sense a smile on him. One moment in particular came back to her; they had been together for a couple of weeks, it was nighttime and they had made love. Spent, she had sunk onto his broad chest, it was like emerging from the deep and out of . . . or rather into a dream. He smiled and looked at her quizzically. She sat up.

"What?"

Storm smoothed her hair tenderly.

"I was wondering about something."

"What?"

"Where are you when you come?"

Ylva laughed. She did not understand the question. She really had got involved with a weirdo, she thought.

"Where am I?"

"Yes . . ."

She smiled and kissed him.

"Here, I guess."

He didn't say anything. He just looked at her, enigmatically.

"I'm here."

"Are you?"

Ylva shook her head wearily, realising she would have to think about it. Where was she really, where are people when they come? Who and what are we in those lost seconds when wild desire is released and we are carried away on a wave of ecstasy?

Nothing and nowhere, she thought. That was what was so wonderful. She disappeared.

La petite mort, the little death . . . wasn't that what they called it, the moment of orgasm? If dying was like that, then she had nothing to fear.

She had not shared these thoughts with Storm, but gone to the kitchen to fetch a 1.5 litre Pepsi Max from the fridge. When she came back, he was asleep. He could fall asleep in seconds. She envied him that.

38

Storm drove to Mary's house right from C.Y.F.O.R. He needed to learn more about the memory stick and what her husband had said about it before he died. But when he got there she had, not surprisingly, left. One Google search later he entered the address of Ylva's family in Kautokeino into his satnav. Storm calculated that the drive along the monotonous roads from Bodø to Kautokeino would take him eleven hours, if he took the fastest route via Sweden. There was just time.

While he drove through the cold north-Norwegian winter landscape, he called Ali, who told him that N.A.T.O., that is the Americans, had taken over the running of the operation. Rove and Bale had laid down strict rules for all external communications, Ali added that he could well understand why. A war of words had already broken out in cyberspace.

"Have you made any progress with the memory stick?"

Ali yawned from exhaustion.

"We're working on it. Tricky business."

To the question from Ali about how Storm was doing, he replied that his taking time off was actually a good idea and that he expected to be back at his desk in a day or two. Ali grew quiet and Storm concluded to his relief that his superior obviously didn't believe a word of what he was saying. Storm continued: "Listen, I wouldn't mind being kept up to speed while I'm off."

Ali was worried about Storm going it alone, but who knew, perhaps it might prove to be to their advantage, in view of the severe restrictions that had been introduced within C.Y.F.O.R.

"Of course, Storm, I'll keep you in the loop should anything major happen."

Storm thought that they would most certainly need each other's help to be able to navigate the grey zone they were about to enter.

Having rung off, Storm stopped at a petrol station and bought some Sim cards for his mobile – they would be difficult to track or link to him. Then he called Ylva's mother's and left a message to say that he was on his way to Kautokeino.

39

Ylva woke up with a start. Shit, she had fallen asleep! A wave of nausea surged in her as she saw the dead man on the floor, Christ, she really had made a mess of him. Somebody, who knows, would miss him.

She shivered. For how long had she been dozing? She looked outside, there were still a few hours of daylight left and they had better make the most of them. She got up and packed the clothing, food and medication. Then she dragged Evans outside and balanced him on the scooter. He surfaced briefly in the cold, but he still seemed out of it.

"Where did you go, Nordahl?"

"Go back to sleep, sir. I've managed to get us a snow scooter, we'll ride for as long as it's light."

Ylva packed the warm clothes she had stolen carefully around Evans, and then started the engine and set off.

The wind lashed tiny ice needles against her face and that revitalised her. They zoomed across the frozen Lake Imandra and when they reached the E105, she followed the road westwards. She enjoyed the wind on her face, the power of the scooter and Evans' body heat. The fever was turning him into a radiator. He had stopped trembling and that boded well. Ylva was so focused on keeping a good speed that she almost failed to register the column of military vehicles on the road.

As the scooter jumped over a snowdrift, Ylva looked up and caught a glimpse of the heavy green vehicles. She took her hand off the accelerator and steered the scooter behind the snowdrift to hide them from view, then she turned off the motor. Had they been spotted? She pressed herself against Evans, stayed very still and listened. Nearby she could hear the drone of the heavy vehicles thundering past, then everything fell quiet. She peered out and saw the column disappear in a westward direction. They must be heading for the Norwegian border and she wondered if that meant that the Russians were mobilising for war.

Ylva looked about her to make sure that no more vehicles were coming. The motorway had grey and white embankments from snow clearing and stretched like a black scar through the white infinity. There were no more vehicles, the coast was clear. She restarted the snow scooter. It was a good idea to ride some distance away from the E511 as there was likely to be more traffic from now on.

The scooter chewed up the miles and despite her exhaustion, Ylva experienced a surge of hope. Evans was slumped forward and sleeping like a baby, it seemed, leaning against her body. She started to hum as the scooter raced across frozen lakes and wide expanses, and eventually her fatigue gave way to a sense of euphoria. It felt as if she were floating across the ice. Floating, as if she were still in the air and the landscape rolled away underneath her, the rhythm of the engine made her whole body quiver as if she were on a shamanic drum journey. To begin with she tensed her muscles to fight it, but eventually they gave in from sheer exhaustion and she relaxed.

It was growing dark, but Ylva did not stop. She rode into the forest and was forced to reduce her speed between the tall trees. She looked around at the unique Arctic taiga of ancient pine trees that grew only in the harsh north. Ylva could feel her pulse slow down and with every breath she took, the strength of the mighty, snow-laden pines seeped into her. They filled her, she was nature, she was the forest and the taiga.

The trees had seen warriors come and go and they had many times shielded people fleeing one another's brutality. They had grown slowly, as does all life so high above the Arctic Circle. Up here time was the most important resource. Some of the trees loomed twenty, thirty metres above the ground; they had stood there for hundreds of years, they had stood there since the ice age, living a stoic and intense life. The trees had time. Time and the will to live. They reached into eternity as far as they could, and there they stayed.

This was what she loved and what she was made for. Nature, only nature and . . . speed. She loved the intoxicating pace which forced her to forget her anxiety and instead go with the flow and be at one with everything.

Ylva was flying, her heart swelled . . . if not from happiness, then from a silent, inner serenity she otherwise only ever found in the cockpit. This was what she always returned to, a place far away from people and their intrigues, their greed and their madness. She flew, she morphed into the landscape. Not bigger, not smaller. The trees were like spiritual guardians, like soldiers frozen in time and clad in mantles of white frost. She had forgotten how beautiful they were as they stood there in their winter cloaks, but now she remembered it. She was free here, no matter what fate had in store for her. The engine growled, wild and ecstatic, she felt its power, she felt alive.

Then it grew silent.

The scooter spluttered helplessly and came to a halt as the fuel ran out. Ylva's serenity was replaced with leaden anti-climax as she was brought down to earth. She muttered curses under her breath.

She dismounted the scooter with a feeling of utter disappointment and looked about her. They were deep inside the forest, but she didn't know exactly where they were. Oddly she had found it easier to navigate the endless plains without any fixed points to aim for than here.

Evans had surfaced and he sat up feeling groggy. In the shrub he saw a wildcat cut twigs and break heavy branches off the trees while singing softly to herself. He listened to the unique voice; it was a strange kind of chanting. He did not recognise it, but Ylva was singing *joik* like her mother had all those nights when young Ylva could not sleep. She had been a restless child who rarely slept, the doctors had wanted to prescribe sleeping pills, but her mother had said no, she sang *joik* for her wild girl instead. Ylva's mother was endlessly patient with her restless child, and *joik* was the only language the girl understood. The soft song was carried forward on a warm breath and a mother's love. And the wolf girl eventually fell asleep once the grey dawn arrived. Such were their nights.

Ylva had improvised a shelter made from branches covered with parachute fabric, and now she spread clothes across the ground, the clothes she had taken from the man who had been pissing in the alleyway and the drunk who had thought she was easy prey. She did not say anything to Evans, who sat slumped on the scooter until she had finished.

"I think we'll get a good night's sleep here tonight, sir."

He almost collapsed as he dismounted – as soon as he put weight on his injured foot. Ylva came running and supported him into the shelter. Heavy clouds hung above the forest and the night was black when she lit a small fire. In the light from the flames she could see Evans' shining eyes and her heart sank. He still had a temperature.

Ylva took out the remaining meat and vegetables. She wrapped them in bark she had cut from the trees. Then she let the food heat up on the fire. Evans was about to get the best dumpster-diving dinner he had ever tasted. Ylva watched him eat ravenously before she gave him vodka and medication. Sated and contented he curled up along the side of the shelter. The embers from the fire, the smell of food and the soft female voice singing to him in a foreign language lulled him to sleep.

Ylva went outside and hid the snow scooter under some heavy branches before returning to the shelter; she was freezing and curled up next to Evans. They lay there, huddled together, like people have lain for millennia to keep each other warm at night. Vulnerable and yearning, people sought company before they were able to relax, turn into themselves and be lost to the world.

Evans' deep, rhythmic breathing made Ylva miss Storm, his warm body and his unshakeable serenity. She pretended that Evans' body exuded the same calm and curled up, hopefully, close to him. It almost worked.

The night settled upon them and Ylva fell asleep at last. Funnily enough, she dreamed of plains and reindeers, of *joik* singing and old, wise eyes. She dreamed of heavy rhythms, breath against warm skin and eyes diving deep into her.

Ylva was fast asleep, but Evans' angry shouting roused her from her slumbers and she realised immediately that he was having a nightmare. She knew how to handle them now and hugged him by way of reassurance. He wriggled free and sat up with a violent jerk, staring at her with unseeing eyes. She moved gently towards him, she tried to stroke his hair, that usually helped.

"John, it's me, you're safe."

Evans reacted instinctively. He grabbed her and pinned her down, locking her head in an iron grip. Ylva fought to free herself, but he tightened his hold as Ylva gasped for air.

"I can't breathe. I can't . . ."

Her voice faded away.

With his eyes wide open, as if in a trance, as if he were a crazed, haunted soul, Evans continued to tighten his grip until Ylva finally stopped fighting him and lay passive and still. It was not until then that he came to and discovered Ylva lifeless in his arms. Startled, he released her and jerked back, who was she?

He looked about him and saw the shelter, the fire and the food. And then he realised where he was.

"Nordahl!"

He shook her, but there was no reaction. He slumped. Had he killed her?

40

The further east Storm drove, the more he thought about Ylva. He had no way of knowing if she was still alive, and his heart ached at the thought that he might never be close to her again. And if she were alive, he dreaded to think of what she was going through now. He muttered curses to himself. His eyes were stinging from lack of sleep and from the tears which kept welling up. But catastrophising helped no-one, he had to find a way to reach her. He was not going to give up. Never. She knew that, he hoped, if she were alive . . . if she was thinking of him.

Having a goal helped, as did concentrating on what he could do to help instead of sitting impotently miles away, reading messages about global disasters and the woman he loved. His gaze cleared, he would find her because he needed her and because he had to cut through the small talk and the game-playing between them. He had been a coward, he realised, because he was scared of being rejected, but also because he did not want to frighten her off. Her being constantly on her guard was deeply frustrating, as was the element of mistrust always present in their interactions.

Storm followed the E10 until he reached the border between Norway and Sweden. So as to attract less notice he chose a side road further north to cross the border, assuming that the principal border crossings would be monitored. The roads through the Swedish forests were eerily deserted but peaceful, it was as if the trees had been there for centuries, as if the noisy world outside would never reach them.

Once in Sweden, he had re-joined the E10 and followed it as far as Kiruna, where he stopped. He took the bag with his laptop and went into Hotel Scandic Ferrum. A group of men were in the lobby discussing the N.A.T.O. plane that had been shot down in Russia. What had the N.A.T.O. plane really been doing there?

Everyone had their opinion about the incident and there were plenty of conspiracy theories. Storm had to smile when he heard one of the men talk about the cretins from QAnon who believed that the story about the N.A.T.O. plane was fake news released by a gang of elitist, paedophile, devil-worshipping cultural Marxists who were secretly running the world. Why these cultural Marxists would lie about something like that, the geniuses from QAnon could not yet explain. The mood was tense and anxious, people were scared. Storm kept himself as inconspicuous as he could.

He took a seat by the large fireplace in the lounge, ordered a Pepsi Max and Spanish tapas with a taste of Norrland. He made sure that his laptop could not be hacked before he logged on to the hotel's Wi-Fi network. Then he dived into cyberspace.

It did not take him long to discover who were listed as the main investors in Titans Security, they came from the U.S.A., Europe, China, Russia and the Middle East. He also discovered that several of Titans' shareholders had invested in Yvas Group, a Russian security firm. The ownership structure was well hidden behind a series of shell companies with "headquarters" in tax shelters in many parts of the world. *Cui bono* was always the question. Once you find out who profits from an evil deed, you will soon discover the guilty party. Storm was used to tracking money in cyberspace and he should have worked out a long time ago who stood to profit the most from conflict in the Arctic. A familiar name appeared among the Russian owners, General Svetla. Through several straw companies, he held shares in both Titans and Yvas. That explained a lot, the Russian general was Rove's counterpart.

Storm had considered asking Ali to show the memory stick Ylva's mother had given him to the Norwegian Defence Minister, but one look at the ownership structure of the different security companies convinced him that he was wiser to have kept quiet. The Defence Minister would undoubtedly feel obliged to involve Rove, and Storm had a hunch that Rove would not be grateful to know about the information on the memory stick.

The irony was that it was Rove himself who had pointed out that of the fifty conflicts registered across the world in 2017, only one of them had been a conventional war. The others were asymmetric, hybrid conflicts where private actors played just as big a part as national armies. That same year Rove had gone from being a three-star general in the American armed forces to becoming a full-time C.E.O. of the private security company, Titans Security. Storm had also discovered that Rove was a shareholder in Titans Security since as early as 2003, weeks before the invasion of Iraq.

In strictly commercial terms, the Iraq war was a huge success ... for a handful of war profiteers. Vice President Dick Cheney, who headed the oil company Haliburton from 1995 to 2000, was receiving a pension from the company when he argued in favour of the U.S.A.'s invasion of Iraq. The Iraqi war – or Operation Enduring Freedom, as it was rebranded – turned out to be very profitable indeed for Haliburton. The company managed to secure for itself around $226 billion of the roughly $800 billion which poured out of the American Treasury and into the pockets of various war profiteers. Storm thought it improbable that Rove had done a Cheney in this instance. He was too smart for that.

Storm scrunched up his nose as he came across an article about one of the sickest examples of the Bush administration's media manipulation. The article described how the U.N. had allowed itself to be pressured into covering up Picasso's anti-war painting *Guernica* behind the U.N.'s pale blue flag when Defence Secretary Colin Powell presented at the U.N.'s headquarters his fabricated evidence of Iraq's weapons of mass destruction. The famous depiction of the horrors of war was not regarded as an appropriate backdrop for Powell's warmongering speech. But Storm did not think that Rove would be that vulgar. He looked at the press photographs of General Rove. He was a handsome man with an appearance that encouraged trust. And he looked good in a uniform. His career was an example of a trend in the modern world in which power and resources are transferred from state ownership into the private sector. The moral and power vacuum, which arose in the wake of nation states crumbling under the deregulation of neoliberalism, had bred a new elite with its own ideals reflecting the new orthodoxy. Multinational companies immune to national legislation, drug barons and super-rich warlords: the new overlords.

Storm wondered if Ylva's father could have found evidence that compromised Titans Security and whether he was planning to go public with it. In the hotel bar the discussion about the N.A.T.O. plane had become very vocal indeed, it seemed to suck everyone into its vortex no matter where they were on the political spectrum.

So far Storm had only circumstantial evidence, nothing concrete to connect Rove to the fate of the F-16. Perhaps he was himself turning into one of those conspiracy theorists who saw the devil in broad daylight? Rove might simply be an honest war hero who served N.A.T.O., and Titans Security an entirely law-abiding security company. Maybe, then again ... maybe not.

Storm packed up his laptop, paid for his food and went out into the biting cold. Four hours later he parked his car outside the house of Elle May Hætta.

41

The seconds Ylva was unconscious were among the longest in Evans' life, not only because he needed her for his own survival, but also because, to his amazement, he had started to care about her. He liked her.

Shaking all over, he had begun to resuscitate her and when she came to, he felt a thrill of joy. He wanted to hug her and hold her tight, but given what had just happened, he knew that would be a very bad idea indeed.

The moment she regained consciousness, she had exploded with rage. She had pushed him away and tried desperately to escape the shelter. He was utterly insane. And evil. She had to get out of there and carry on without him.

Evans got up to stop her, but that proved to be a mistake because Ylva aimed all her fury at him. She punched and kicked him and he let her do it. It was only fair that she vent her rage and he did not blame her. He took his beating without complaint even though she hit very hard. Not until he saw a kick aimed at his groin did he move to get out of her way. That was his limit. She almost lost her balance by Evans' manoeuvre, and stood for a moment glaring at him. She was as angry as she was scared, and then she went for him again.

"You could have killed me! Was that what you were trying to do, eh? Was it?"

Evans made no reply, he stood still and let Ylva pound him. Eventually her blows became slower, more of a token assault.

"You are a crazy bastard!" she panted.

As her adrenaline and rage subsided she felt the sharp cold and the night and her despondency cling to her. She was exhausted and it required too much effort to hit him. Besides, her shoulder hurt like hell. Ylva knew she was trapped, she was painfully aware that she was alone in a shelter in the middle of the tundra with a volatile killer. How many people had he killed? How many during peace time? Ylva had no idea. But he was damaged, that much she did know for certain.

As if he could read her mind, Evans grunted harshly:

"If I'd wanted you dead five minutes ago, you'd have been dead five minutes ago."

Ylva believed him.

She lingered inside the small shelter, not knowing what to do. She did not want to be anywhere near the man, but she had nowhere to go. She was unable to breathe deeply, she simply did not dare. It felt as if he were still constricting her throat and chest, she gasped desperately for air and touched her neck. Two attempts at strangulation in twenty-four hours was absolutely her limit. Her mind was spinning: now what? Which strategy would work best on Evans? Like so many others caught in a similar dilemma, fearing for their lives, deprived of the chance to fight, flee or play dead, she opted for the only rational approach available: she flashed a disarming, almost obsequious smile.

"Sir, the next time you decide to flip out, would you please let go before I black out?"

Evans looked at her quizzically.

"Seriously, sir, I'm open to a lot of kinky stuff, but strangulation is not my thing."

Evans stared at her and it took a few seconds before he caught on; she was trying to make light of his attack on her. Ylva continued to smile, but her smile did not extend as far as her guarded eyes. He watched her with a growing sense of unease. She really isn't mentally stable, he thought, as Ylva sat down.

She nodded to indicate for Evans to sit too, for him to relax. He sat down, but he was anything but relaxed. So there they stayed in silence.

Ylva wanted to find out why he had attacked her, but she was already sensing the answer. Sadly she knew only too well the intrusive demons and the war that never ended. It explained the man's clenched jaw.

"You shouldn't have woken me," he mumbled. "You came at me too suddenly."

Ylva did not reply. She had calmed him down and comforted him through several nightmares already, so she did not take the remark personally.

"It was a reflex action," he continued in a low voice.

Ylva smiled. She was still both scared and angry, but made a great effort not to show it.

"A reflex action? Strangling your co-pilot?"

The question was confrontational, but her voice was light. Evans stared vacantly into space and had to make an effort to suppress his fear and self-loathing.

"We're trained to attack anyone who takes us by surprise, you know that."

Ylva felt her fear be slowly replaced by exasperation. Dear God, the man did not know it himself, but he was broken. She had seen it before; war veterans who finally came home to safety, happy to be as full-bodied as when they left. But time and time again they turned out to be anything but safe because a war was still being fought inside them. In less than a decade, almost sixty thousand American veterans had killed themselves, more than twenty people a day. Many more soldiers die by suicide than in battles, her fact-fixated mother had told her that when Ylva had announced that she wanted to be a pilot. The most dangerous time in a soldier's life was when the fighting was over; many had said that this was when hell really broke loose. Ylva knew it to be true. She had scarcely been able to recognise her father after his last deployment in Afghanistan in 2001.

Evans lived in two worlds and though fragments of the person he had once been survived, the darkness and the emptiness were encroaching on him. Soon they would strangle him the way he had almost strangled her.

Ylva coughed and touched her neck, her body had not forgotten the sensation of his arm squeezing and blocking her air supply. Fortunately she was able to restrain herself or Evans would have ended up like the fat guy in Kirovsk.

"Sir, I'm surprised that the army lets you work in the field."

Evans made no reply. The light was faint inside the shelter and he became aware of the rustling of the trees outside as they bent stiffly in the icy wind; the sound brought him back to reality. He shuddered. How the hell had he got himself into this mess?

Ylva could tell that he was still rattled and spoke to him in a soothing voice.

"When did it start? Was it Libya?"

Evans stared into the dying embers of the fire.

"Do you know why we bombed Libya?"

Obviously Ylva knew why N.A.T.O. had bombed Libya.

"Of course, Operation Unified Protector was about protecting Libyan civilians against Gaddafi's terror regime," she said.

Evans laughed bitterly.

"Exactly. Which was why Norway, such a peaceful country, dropped five hundred and eighty-eight merciful bombs on them."

Ylva baulked.

"As a member of N.A.T.O., Norway had an obligation to contribute."

"To protect civilians?"

Ylva sat up warily, Evans' hardly concealed fury worried her, where was he going with this?

"Gaddafi was planning the mass murder of rebels who wanted to oust him, that's why N.A.T.O. intervened."

Evans shook his head. That particular claim had been disproved and yet the young Lieutenant Nordahl still believed it. He had no idea she could be so stupid.

"Gaddafi had already agreed a truce with the rebels," he said. "There were hardly any of Gaddafi's forces in Benghazi when we attacked."

Ylva said nothing, she genuinely could not see where Evans was going with this argument. He carried on talking, mostly to himself.

"The rebels we so heroically protected turned out to be bloodthirsty gangs who have gone on to slaughter hundreds of thousands of civilians and earned billions smuggling Arab and African refugees into Europe using Tripoli as their departure point. Unified Protector ... who were they protecting?"

Ylva was aware of the debate about the legitimacy of the Libya attacks, of course she was, and yes, sure, the conflict could have been solved differently. But couldn't all conflicts? Evans refused to back down, he was trying to provoke some kind of reaction from Ylva.

"Who do you think profited most from the N.A.T.O. bombings?"

Ylva had heard this argument from pacifists and wise-after-the-event lefties, but never from people in the military. She was tired and what was there to say? It was idiotic listening to Major Evans, of all people, insinuating that N.A.T.O. was used to promote Western economic interests. He was a war hero, for God's sake, had he forgotten?

"But Gaddafi was killed by the Libyans themselves," she said.

Evans sighed, he was weary of this discussion and he knew the kind of truth she needed to believe in order to do the job she did.

"We unleashed hell on earth. That was what we did. After eight months of bombing Libya, we left the country to its own devices."

Ylva could feel her exhaustion drag her down, her eyes were leaden. She knew that Evans had a point, but she was a pilot not a politician, and soldiers could rarely know all of the variables in a conflict. Soldiers executed orders, plain and simple. And right now she was a tired soldier who needed rest in order to gather strength for tomorrow's long walk to the west.

"Sir, we need to get some sleep."

Evans was yawning too. He had nothing more to say. He had already said too much.

"We'll take turns sleeping," he said. "You rest first."

While Ylva slept fitfully, Evans kept watch. He ate the rest of the food and wondered whether he could trust Rove and what would happen to Ylva if they made it across the border to Norway. In reality he knew the answer to the second question. Once they did not need her anymore, they would erase every trace of her.

That was a shame because as irritating and painfully naive as she was, he had grown fond of her.

With shaking fingers, he untied the dressing she had applied to his leg. He saw the scarlet wound where the gangrene had been cut away, but the tissue was still swollen and warm, the infection was slumbering.

He cleaned the surface of the wound with disinfectant, put on a new dressing and chucked the old, blood-soaked dressing outside the shelter. As he leaned out into the clear night air, he had a sense that the forest was unnaturally still, as if it were holding its breath and getting ready to pounce.

The night was at its darkest, but a merciless new day would soon seep through the treetops. Ylva had said that she thought they were only one day's march from the border and they should get going before it grew light, he thought with a yawn. He could manage one day more, then the mission would be complete. He would be free.

42

Feeble dawn light filled the small flat, but the noise from the city did not reach up here, not yet. Serkin sat at the breakfast table with a cup of cold coffee, looking out over the gloomy concrete desert that was the outskirts of Murmansk. He was suffering from yet another sleepless night. Other people were sleeping. How could they? Did they not understand what was at stake? The President's speech to the nation had made him physically unwell. The President had given the world three days, and now, two days and fifteen hours of Babel-like confusion later, the world was teetering on the brink. A surreal feeling had replaced his initial confusion. The numbing fog had lifted and the world appeared unnaturally sharp, defenceless and naked. The light was brighter, the darkness darker, he experienced all sounds and colours more vividly.

On the previous night he had really noticed his children as they sat doing their homework at the kitchen table. He saw young Sergey's frown of concentration, the chewed pencil, the chubby hand impatiently picking at the corner of the maths book, the woolly jumper scratching his soft neck, the chipped cup on the table, the chair where his father had sat for years and whose upholstery bore his shape. Serkin was consumed by a crazy despair and a grief he could not articulate.

The poetry of everyday life and human warmth heightened the madness that was about to be unleashed.

He left the flat to run off his frustration.

In the stairwell he met a neighbour who shuffled along, red-faced and tipsy, bottles clattering in his bag. The man greeted Lieutenant Serkin solemnly.

Outside the apartment block he passed a group of youngsters who were flirting and smoking furtively behind the corner. They were giddy, excited and faking their air of cool. Serkin had been like them once.

In the street Mrs Chekova was walking her dog. She had been old since the dawn of time and was as always walking alone while babbling baby talk to the scruffy dog. She, too, greeted him with politeness bordering on reverence.

He looked away.

This was the animated backdrop for the life he had lived in accordance with his plan. It had pretty much gone as expected until three days ago. He stopped between the concrete blocks and looked up at the glum sky. It would be the end of everything. Images of the charred bodies of children scattered along the road outside Apatity flitted in front of his eyes. Burned beyond recognition by his lie and betrayal of duty. It was his job to cope with this and his lot to bear the consequences.

The news was inundating them with features on the N.A.T.O. pilots who had survived being shot down and were now on the run. They would inevitably be captured. These pilots knew the truth and Serkin wanted them dead. The many mass graves in Russia were a sobering testament to the fact that the truth is rarely anyone's friend if it contradicts the official narrative. How did it help an honest man to be declared a hero when he himself knew that he was a coward? Serkin did not have the energy for a run, it would not make him feel any better. The exhilaration and the endorphin rush were gone, and he walked home.

Serkin noticed that his father was settling down in front of his computer. He immediately started his running commentary on world events. Normally Serkin found it entertaining, but not today. Soon the children were running around the flat like wild animals. They really did not have enough room, he thought, he could hardly breathe. Natasha came in and stopped at the kitchen counter, still bleary-eyed, and took one look at him.

"Aren't you going to work today?" she said.

Serkin did not have time to reply before the doorbell rang. He stared down at the table as she went to answer it. His heart was pounding.

Major Khodrokovska was standing at the door.

"I need to speak to your husband."

Before Natasha could say anything, Major Khodrokovska had marched into the kitchen. Natasha followed right behind her, clearly taken aback by the major's behaviour. Serkin stood up the moment he saw his superior, she didn't fit in here. She belonged to another world.

Major Khodrokovska was obviously upset. At first they glared at one another with hostility. Serkin blinked first.

"Let's go out on the balcony, I need a cigarette."

Major Khodrokovska nodded and followed Serkin out onto the narrow balcony. Natasha, the children and his father were watching them. They could not hear what was being said out there, but they could tell that Serkin felt under pressure. Major Khodrokovska went straight to the point.

"Lieutenant Serkin, you need to tell the truth about what happened!"

Serkin lit a cigarette, the smoke felt acrid as he inhaled it deep into his lungs.

"That is what I have done."

"If that N.A.T.O. plane flew into Russian airspace due to an accident, then we're about to start World War Three on the basis of your lie!"

Serkin felt her words like blows to his solar plexus, he took another drag on his cigarette, but it made him feel sick.

"I have said all I have to say."

Major Khodrokovska looked hard at her younger colleague, she knew that he was a bright and fundamentally honest man, but she also knew that he was lying to her, his superior, to her face.

"Why?" she wanted to know.

Serkin made no reply, he felt sick.

"Is this about honour? About loyalty to Moscow?"

Serkin was aware that his family were all looking at him from the living room and he stubbed out the cigarette.

"Major, you ordered me to buzz the plane. I acted on your order."

Major Khodrokovska nodded, she had thought about it all night. That was indeed her fault, she should not have followed the order without knowing who had issued it. She had played a part in this and was willing to accept the consequences.

"Yes, I'm responsible, I accept that. And if you tell the truth about what happened, I'll take the fall. You acted on my orders at all times."

Serkin glanced at his family, who were trying to pretend that they were not watching him.

"It'll put Russia in an awkward situation," he muttered.

"Quite possibly, but anything is better than war, wouldn't you agree?"

Serkin looked down. His orders had come from the highest level and he had had to obey them.

"I've said all I have to say and I must ask you to leave."

There was no question that Serkin was conflicted … and exhausted.

"Come to work today and give a full account of what happened. You'll thank yourself for it. We all will."

Serkin stared at her, but she did not blink.

Little Sergey had walked right up to the windowpane where he stood with tousled hair and wide, puzzled eyes. Was his daddy sad? Major Khodrokovska smiled and waved awkwardly to the child. Serkin had never seen her smile before, suddenly she seemed almost human, he thought. When she turned to him, he was even more torn.

"I understand your dilemma, Lieutenant Serkin, I really do."

Major Khodrokovska's gaze rested gently on him, she placed her hand on his shoulder, maternal and empathetic. Serkin took a step back as if she had branded him with her kindness.

"And yet I ask you to do this. Tell the truth, Igor, I'll support you and take full responsibility for the consequences."

He could see Major Khodrokovska more clearly now. She was honourable and brave even though she seemed just as worn out, uncertain and frightened as he was. She's doing the only right thing she can, he thought. Ivana Khodrokovska, the middle-aged grey mouse, was the real heroine in this story. Serkin felt – if that were possible – even more like a miserable cockroach.

He remained silent in the winter cold. Now he could hear it, the noise from Murmansk, the ugly city he loved so much. Khodrokovska kept her attention fixed on him, she could see that he was still struggling. Serkin turned away and she realised that she had done all she could, now it was up to him. He's an honourable person, she thought, deep down he's a good man.

Then she opened the balcony door and went into the living

room. She said goodbye politely to Serkin's family before leaving. He was left behind on the narrow balcony in the bitter cold.

One hour and forty-five minutes later Major Khodrokovska parked in the car park behind Monchegorsk Air Base. She was ready to say what needed to be said at the morning briefing. This had gone way too far. Her blood felt fizzing and warm, she had butterflies in her stomach, she was ready to fight. She knew what she had to do and though she feared that the price for going up against her superiors would be high, she was willing to pay it. It was her duty. It wasn't until she had locked her car and started walking that she became aware of a vehicle moving some distance behind her. Major Khodrokovska stopped and without turning around she sensed that the car too stopped. She walked a little further, then stopped again. The same thing happened. Major Khodrokovska turned around, but she could not make out who was behind the wheel of the car which was following her. Her fears felt like cold lead and she started running to cover the last three hundred metres to the entrance to the base. The car came up behind her, Major Khodrokovska ran faster. Seconds later she was knocked down from behind and then dragged into the car by two men.

43

It was still dark when they dismantled their shelter and set out on what would, they both hoped, be the last stretch of their journey. Walking through the deep snow in the forest was hard work. Ylva soon found herself out of breath and slowed down in order not to sweat excessively. Evans was walking right behind her and she could hear that he, too, was wheezing. Her chest stung and burned with every breath, and she made a conscious effort to lower her rate of breathing to give her body a chance to compensate for the loss of heat.

She continued to keep a watchful eye on Evans. Last night's incident had made her see him in a new light; the man was not well and she felt both pity and fear. She was also puzzled as to why Major Evans, the hero with the Distinguished Flying Cross and many meritorious distinctions, had agreed to train N.A.T.O. pilots when he so ardently distrusted the legitimacy of N.A.T.O.'s interventions.

Leaving the claustrophobic forest and setting out into the open tundra was like entering a different universe. It had been dark when they had set out and the forest did not let much moonlight through the snow-laden branches. On the tundra, however, the moon lit up the landscape like a gigantic spotlight. The dawn light was smouldering in the horizon and Ylva could now see the landscape in front of them. She glanced sideways at Evans, his expression was as grim as ever and his gaze was introverted. Nothing saps a human being of strength like constant cold and pain.

They both had frostbite on their face and hands, but it was bearable for now. Ylva was more concerned about the pain in Evans' leg and his agonised mind. It was as well that they would be in Norway in less than twenty-four hours, she thought, because she doubted that he could last much longer than that.

They were vigilant and walked in tense silence. Although the light was still faint, they knew that they were totally exposed here. It was all about staying focused now because on this final leg through the godforsaken Arctic desert, they were at their most vulnerable. They would both have to keep a constant look-out to make sure that Spetsnaz soldiers, drones or surveillance planes did not catch sight of them.

Ylva stopped. Apart from Evans' wheezing breath, it was perfectly silent. She looked up, a glassy halo shimmered around the moon. Ylva cursed softly under her breath.

"Sir, the weather is about to change."

Evans turned to her with a frown. There wasn't a cloud in the sky, the night had been cold and clear and there was scarcely even a mild breeze.

"Looks alright to me," he mumbled.

"Look up, there's a halo around the moon."

He followed Ylva's gaze, the moon glowed barren against the dark blue firmament. He had to smile as the sight of the moon transported him back in time. He felt the heat and the last rays of sunlight on his forehead. He was sitting with his grandfather in a battered old Cadillac watching "E.T. the Extra-Terrestrial", it was a high point in the little boy's life. Movies were best when you got to sit in the open air as you watched wondrous worlds unfold. He must have seen that movie at least twenty times since that first evening, but he still looked forward to the iconic scene when the boy on his bicycle with E.T. in the basket races towards the police cordon. The audience gasps, certain that the film's two little heroes are now lost. Then suddenly, as if by magic, the bicycle takes off from the ground, and the boy and E.T. fly high, high above all obstacles. Young Evans had known that it must be a special effect, but he couldn't work out how they had done it. So he was both moved and impressed every time the boy on the bicycle and the little alien soared in front of the moon as if the Earth's gravitational pull could not reach them.

"Sir, did you hear what I said?"

Evans looked at her, confused. "What?"

Ylva shook her head in despair. The guy had lost the plot, he seemed not to take in anything at all.

"Sir, look!"

She pointed to the moon.

Now he could see it, the moon was surrounded by a glassy halo. So?

Out in the furthest layer of the atmosphere tiny ice particles had gathered, creating a veil of feather-light clouds so thin that they were scarcely visible to the naked eye. The microscopic crystals were reflected in the bright moonlight and shimmered like a gossamer nimbus around the light source. Ylva pointed and Evans peered in the same direction.

"They're cirrus clouds."

And then he grasped the implication of what Ylva was saying. Cirrus clouds are the front runners of low pressure and the magical moonlight instantly became menacing. A storm was the very last thing they needed now.

In the dark forest they had left behind, a small pack of wolves was hunting. The alpha wolf ran with her muzzle along the ground. She had caught the scent of fresh blood, stopped where Ylva and Evans' shelter had been and started digging in the powder snow. The wolf carried on digging until she found the blood-soaked dressing. Greedily she snapped at the rags and started licking them, but found only slim pickings. The wolf looked up, her pack was hungry, the winter had been severe. She sniffed the air; she, too, noticed the change in the weather. But that was not all the wolf noticed. Once she had caught the scent of blood, she never let it go. The she-wolf and her pack needed no tracks in the snow or surveillance planes to detect where Evans and Ylva were.

44

Storm looked out at the village of Kautokeino as gradually it emerged from the deep night-time darkness. The silhouettes of small houses huddled along the broad Kautokeino River were outlined against the dawning light.

The horizon seemed endless in the flat landscape that stretched far and wide, and he felt incredibly small and separated far from the world he knew. Then again, no matter where he was, he had always felt like an outsider. After all, how many cyberneticists frequented the toughest bodybuilding environments? How many guys who could leg press 170 kilos turned up for Mensa's annual get-togethers? And how many long-haired, bearded nonconformists did you find in the army's officer corps? It had been like that his whole life: no matter where he was Storm was an odd one out. But, oddly enough, up here, five hundred metres above sea level, surrounded by an apparently limitless Arctic wasteland, he felt a little bit at home. It was weird because he generally preferred big cities. It was counterintuitive for him to find serenity in this flat expanse of ice.

The landscape around the village consisted of far-reaching plains with low mountain ridges arching their backs every now and then, providing welcome fixed points for your gaze. The region was monotonous and the rules for survival clear, something that instilled calm. You could lose yourself here, Storm thought, you could disappear altogether.

Though the village of Kautokeino was only three hundred years old, the region and the plains had been home to the Sámi people since time immemorial. Storm had never been to this part of Norway before, nor had he been terribly interested in learning either about the Sámi people or about Finnmark. Like most Norwegians, he had assumed that the Sámi were busy herding reindeer and practising *joik* singing, and that they lived in a part of the world where no-one else would want to live. But now that he was here, he could sense their strong presence.

Storm was sitting at the kitchen table in Mary's sister's house after yet another sleepless night. Had it not been for the noise from the radio spewing news into the room, you might have thought that this was a day like any other in Kautokeino, but you would have been wrong. Today would turn out to be a fateful day, N.A.T.O. had failed to prove its lack of involvement in the plane crash, and Russia intended to respond to what they had resolved was an attack.

Storm jumped when he heard a violent roar right outside the window. He looked out and, to his relief, the noise was coming from a snow scooter leaving the next-door house and heading down the slope towards the Kautokeino River. On the scooter sat a father dressed in a snowsuit with his young daughter seated snugly in front of him. They were both wrapped in thick scarves and wearing furry hats and reindeer fur boots. Storm checked the thermometer: it was −21°C, and he was impressed. No-one from southern Norway would have done that. The neighbour's three tame reindeers were standing outside his house. Stoically they stared at each other as the day began.

In the living room he could hear Elle and her husband argue, the noise from the news had woken the whole house, but her husband was refusing to turn it off. Storm heard a monotonous female voice on the radio announce that skirmishes had been reported between Russian and N.A.T.O. forces, both in the international zone in the Barents Sea and on the border between Norway and Russia in the Pasvik Valley. Norwegians living in regions bordering Russia were fleeing to the south and west, and Russians living in Norway had begun to travel back to their home country. A family man from Kirkenes was interviewed. He had heard shooting and fighting the whole night, he said.

"We never thought this could happen in Norway," the man said in tears.

There had been disturbances at a few border crossings. People feared that the border to Russia would be closed and that Russians living in Norway would not be able to cross to their own country.

The West was in shock. Was this really happening? Would Russia go to war with N.A.T.O.? The Russian President's speech three days earlier had seemed to suggest so.

Storm knew that Rove had been tasked with leading a hybrid attack on Russia to be carried out by Titans Security personnel. The attacks consisted of hacking central digital infrastructure and trolling Russian media to provoke internal fighting and to undermine the President. However, when Storm followed the money trail to the security company, he soon discovered that it had also funded various nationalistic organisations in Norway, including one in Kirkenes. The three men who killed Aleksey Galba, the Russian composer, were on the payroll of a Titans-financed organisation. The murder had been staged.

Storm understood to his dismay that given how the situation was unfolding, Ylva would soon find herself trapped behind the closed borders of a country which, at best, would want to kill her. He could not bear to listen to any more and put on his headset to distract himself with music, but he could not block out images of her, her blonde hair dancing over her naked back and the way she snuggled up to him like a cat. He knew that she was playing with him while her blue-green gaze scrutinised his reactions. And then there was her raucous laughter. Storm had to smile, she went all in – especially when she laughed . . . At first he had thought that she was too good to be true, and he was soon proved right. She was wild and as tough as she was honourable; the moment he tried to pin her down, she pushed him away. With force, if she had to. It was not that she was playing hard to get, rather it was as if she were testing him, as if deep down she needed convincing that she had not been wrong about him. Arrghh, why couldn't she have been a clerk, a nurse or a nursery school teacher? Why did the woman he fell for have to fly an F-16, crash outside Murmansk and start World War Three?

With his gaze fixed on the laptop screen he tried to follow the Russian internal reports about where they believed the pilots to be. It was exasperating how good they had become at frustrating hackers. The Internet, a starting point for the liberal West's idea of openness and the free flow of information, had turned into the most powerful weapon for the enemies of the Western world. The colour revolutions in the Ukraine and Georgia, not to mention the Arab Spring, merely strengthened Russia's belief that her best defence was extensive surveillance and control of digital communication. And even as the world's superpowers used assassins and mercenaries to carry out their shadow wars, self-employed hackers were hired to attack one another in cyberspace.

The market for power and chaos was huge – especially in the virtual world.

A communications thread recorded that a hunting cabin had been found with blood-soaked dressings and the body of a near-naked and very dead miner. This was believed to be connected to the N.A.T.O. pilots. That was all Storm could find. Apparently the Russians did not know where the pilots were now or which one of them was injured. They were not even sure if it was the pilots who had been in the cabin.

Ylva's mother, Mary, was standing by the cooker.

"We have family in Russia," she said.

Storm nodded, he knew that.

"My niece is married to a Russian Sámi from Lovozero."

Storm hardly had the energy now to listen to Mary's neurotic ramblings, but he managed a smile.

She sat down opposite Storm, evidently intent on talking to him.

"They herd reindeer."

Then she smiled, but her eyes were neither cheerful nor demented.

"Right?"

It took a few seconds before Storm realised where she was going with this and then the thought presented itself to him like a sunrise. Of course. They were Sámi. He thought he could see the outline of a chance, a desperate hope. He realised that he would not actually find Ylva by hacking Russian computers; if the Russians found the pilots, they would make prisoners of them on the spot. They had to get there ahead of them.

"Can you call them?"

Mary gave him a conspiratorial look.

"Of course."

Mobile coverage across the tundra was patchy and Mary had to try several times, but eventually she got through. Despite her speaking Sámi with her niece, Storm could intuit what she said from the context.

"Hello, Inga Marja, it's Aunt Mary. Are you out with the herd at the moment?"

She listened impatiently to the response.

"Listen, I need your help!"

Inga Marja had stopped as a stream of thousands of reindeer moved around her. A thundering of hooves drummed on the tundra, snorting reindeer sent out clouds of steam and their bells jingled merrily. She could barely hear what her aunt said and she stuck a finger in one ear to block out the noise of the animals being driven to the feeding grounds.

"Tell me again what you said, Auntie."

"I don't know if you've heard, Inga Marja," Mary said, "but one of the pilots shot down over Murmansk is Ylva."

Inga Marja thought she must have misheard.

"Who?"

Mary was about to explain, but Storm snatched her phone and introduced himself briefly before getting directly to the point.

"We think that Ylva and the other N.A.T.O. pilot might be near Nyavkyul or Ymos. Are you far from there?"

"No, we're near Ymos now."

Storm's face lit up.

"Please would you look for them?"

Inga Marja shook her head at this. Southerners had absolutely no idea of life up here.

"This is an enormous area and—"

Storm interrupted her.

"I can give you information as I get it from listening to Russian reports about where they think the pilots are. It may be our only hope."

"But how. . .?"

Inga Marja said no more. She understood that time was of the essence and she neither needed nor wanted to know everything.

"What do you want us to do if we find them?"

Storm could feel his pulse quicken. He had someone on the ground in the area where Ylva and Major Evans might be.

"If you find them, we need you to take them to the Norwegian border by Rayakoski. Not Pasvik. The Russians believe they will try to cross the border in the Pasvik Valley."

Inga Marja said, "Where do we begin? What do you know?"

Storm gave her all that he had managed to gather, and Inga Marja confirmed yet again that yes, they were in the same area as the Russians thought the pilots were in and they would immediately begin searching. For the first time since Ylva's plane was brought down, Storm felt a dawning, impatient hope.

"I'll drive to the border at Rayakoski now and I'll be there in about six hours. We'll keep in touch by telephone."

Inga Marja agreed.

When she had ended the call, her husband, Issàht, looked at her quizzically. He could tell that something was up. Inga Marja gathered her family and the young herdsmen and rapidly explained that one of the pilots who had been shot down over Russia was her cousin Ylva, the daughter of Mary. The pilots might be in the area and they had to find them.

Inga Marja's husband looked incredulous. "That's impossible . . ."

Inga Marja cut him off. "No, it's not, because I've been told where Spetsnaz think they might be."

"You want us to help Spetsnaz find them?"

"No, we'll track Spetsnaz."

The whole group turned to her in shock.

"She's one of us!"

A young herdsmen interrupted her. "And what happens if Spetsnaz see what we are doing?"

Inga Marja snorted with impatience.

"If we stop talking and start searching, no-one will catch us."

45

A squally wind had started blowing from the northwest. It was heavy going on the tundra. Evans felt the pain in his leg and foot as a constant, burning torment. The infection had flared up again. The wind was biting cold and tiny ice crystals, beautiful individually but diabolical in a cluster, stung his face like needle pricks.

Ylva doubled up against the strong gusts of wind. Freezing snow penetrated every crevice, it slipped down her neck, up her sleeves, into her boots. Her lips were blue and her face had stiffened. Icicles stuck to her hair, eyebrows and eyelashes. The cold was sucking all hope out of her.

Her body battled against being so mercilessly cooled down, her muscles shook uncontrollably to generate heat, the blood vessels in her skin contracted, leaving the skin pale and numb. Her pulse and blood pressure had rocketed and she was panting like a dog. So far, so predictable. What she dreaded but knew was coming, was the stage when the trembling would subside, her pulse would grow weak and she would inexorably begin to lose consciousness.

She monitored herself for signs of the time when her shivering would be replaced first by indifference, then by delirium. In this final stage the cold would feel like burning heat. Victims would often undress and fall asleep naked, sweaty and exhausted in the snow while their blood froze to ice.

One step, two steps ... Ylva shivered and panted and begged for mercy although she knew that no-one would hear her prayers out here on this godforsaken tundra. She was alone, everyone was alone, and her only option was to bow her head and keep going.

Three steps, four steps ... towards the West. She staggered on in a daze. Five steps, six steps ... she no longer heard the wild howling and moaning of the wind. Nor did she feel how frostbite ate its way into the thin skin on her face and carved out open sores. Ylva walked on, seven steps, eight steps. She did not notice that Evans had stopped, that he could not breathe, that the wind and the cold had finally broken his resistance, that the infection in his wound caused his leg to buckle, that he had collapsed and the snowstorm had pounced on him like a hungry demon.

He tried to cry out, but yelling against the storm was futile. The wind filled his mouth and chest with hailstones and icy rain.

The cold made his body burning hot. The pain in his calf was driving him mad. He had to do something, anything, to stop this nightmare. Shaking, he pulled up his trouser leg and while the snowstorm wrapped him in a white sheet, in desperation he tore off the bandage. The skin on his leg was pale grey, but almost black around the wound. Yellow pus foamed along the edge. Gangrene was eating him up from the inside. Skin, flesh and muscles were poisoned, he was fighting with strength he did not have against forces no man could resist. Death spread from cell to cell ... and it was happening quickly. The fever raged, the wind raged and Evans gave up. He collapsed, bitter, lonely and frightened. It was enough now, he wanted to go home, but home did not want him. That was the truth. He had no home to go to.

Ylva soldiered on, putting one foot in front of another. She was numb and she walked as if in a trance, fuelled by defiance.

She was going westward, that was all she could think of, she had no other thoughts.

None.

That was a lie.

She had many thoughts, thoughts she kept returning to like mantras. In quick glimpses she saw him, in the moonlight, between white sheets, his eyes closed, turned into himself, his chest rising and falling. The memories and her longing for him gave her strength. She returned over and over again to the space which he filled. She could feel him close to her body, warm and sleeping. He was smiling in his sleep. Who the hell smiles in their sleep?

He smiled, wrapped his long arms around her and pulled her close. They were spooning. He was asleep and she was awake, but she let herself be held. She was so tired, she wanted to go to sleep so she could wake up to the dream of sleeping next to him.

The wind moaned, she walked on. Nine steps, ten steps . . .

It was not until then that she noticed.

Evans was not there.

She looked about her.

All she could see was a white tsunami coming at her from all sides, it knocked her over, it flung her against the ground. She tumbled head first into the hard snow crust which scraped the skin off her forehead and it stung. Ylva did not get up.

She could just stay there, lie still, close her eyes, think about something else, think about him. It was an option, she could block out all pain, she could endure more than any man because she had learned to shut down her feelings. But not now, she could not shut down her senses now. Focus on the pain, she thought, it's good that you can feel your body, suffering is your friend. The pain triggered a surge of adrenaline and with that came rage which kept her alive. With her head lowered against the wind, she struggled to see clearly.

"Major Evans!"

There was no reply, only the sound of hissing, wailing wind and sleet filled the tundra.

"Evans, I'm here!"

He was lying in a foetal position, the cold had paralysed him and taken control. His spasms subsided. It was almost wonderful to encounter the limits of his endurance. He had nothing to fight for, no-one was waiting for him, he was no-one's hero. It was time for him to embrace the end.

Evans was ready, he could let go now, he had done his bit.

The howling around him changed character.

"Major Evans!"

He opened his eyes with a start and listened out. It was a woman's voice, was it her? What was she doing here?

He could make out her silhouette. It seemed to tower above the horizon. Sparks were flying around her, he felt a swell of happiness. The relief, the tenderness was intoxicating, his joy complete. God, how he had missed her.

"Major Evans!"

Did she want him back?

Would he be able to come home after all?

Was his penance over? Every painful step he had taken to earn her forgiveness. Would he finally get to kneel at her feet?

Loved, absolved, safe.

He would die and be resurrected, born again in her arms. He would erase everything he had been, forget all the betrayals and brutalities, they no longer mattered in the greater scheme of things. He had to die as a cancerous tumour must be cut from its dying host. The past must be expunged so that he could live through the two of them, mother and child.

He had stood on the outside, naked, looking in at them as they lived their lives without him. He would be there and believe as they believed, love as they loved. He would start over, he would be cleansed of the person they had turned him into. Hardened by every savage moment he had endured, he would, like an alchemist, turn cruelty into pure love, aimed at her, at them. Only that and only them.

Look, I am fighting for you.

Look, I am dying for you.

Look, I have been resurrected for you.

Over and over again.

Together they had experienced closeness, but they had also been far apart from one another – even when they were together; he had found himself in these two, mother and child. He would not rage and mourn that he had lost them, rather he would find meaning in the knowledge that they were still alive somewhere out there. Only not with him.

Evans stood up, the pain became his hallmark. It was the only thing that mattered, everything and everyone became irrelevant. All the people he had trusted and sacrificed himself for – and sacrificed others for – were like poison in his blood, they must be eradicated. The world order of greed, money and sick power ate its way into every innocent soul like a disease. It must be destroyed so that pure, new dreams could grow. He was bigger than the sum of his darkest moments and he was no longer scared of them because he had nothing and no-one to lose.

"Major Evans!"

He was not going to betray her now, not after everything he

had subjected her to, everything he had cost her. He heard her cry out and thanked the universe, finally she opened herself up to him, finally she let him in.

"Kathryn," he sobbed, "I'm here . . . can you see me?"

"Major Evans!"

He lifted his head and listened. What was it about that voice? It was not as singing and pure as he remembered it.

"Major Evans!"

He heard her call out to him over and over. It did not matter now, she could be whoever she was. He did not need her youth, innocence or naivety. There was no growth and development in a woman who didn't allow herself to be touched or affected by life. He loathed those infantile women who prided themselves on their cowardly ignorance while greedily marrying into money and social status that men had fought for. But rich and powerful men were even worse. He despised everyone who was able to remain ignorant in comfortable self-righteousness, while lacking the ability to empathise with the suffering of others. He hated people who would coldly judge anyone who actually had to fight – be it in mines, in battlefields, in brothels, in filthy streets – those who fought . . . without any hope of dignity. While others, the stockbrokers, the bureaucrats and Gucci angels . . . they never sacrificed anything for anyone, they only ever took. They danced over dead bodies in their quest for security, money, sex and luxury. Evans thought of these men and women as the embodiment of cowardice.

Had he fought and died for these parasites? Why should these decadent reptiles enjoy the freedom and security that men like him provided them with? Had he committed the worst atrocities on behalf of people like that? Had he turned into a sadistic monster in order to coddle spoiled brats the world over? He could feel his rage devour him. Did he kill and die so that these ignorant bloodsuckers could take for granted the continuation of their fairy-tale life?

Kathryn was nothing like that, he thought. She was not an underperforming, self-infantilising woman with Botox and a baby voice. She was mature, a real woman. She represented life and she looked at him with tenderness. She could contain him, he was safe with her. She did not judge him, she understood. Didn't she?

"Major Evans!"

The hope which had briefly surged in him when he thought of his wife and his daughter, ebbed out of him.

"Major Evans! I'm here!"

With his last strength he looked around, the hollow howling of the snowstorm surrounded him, sometimes rising and wild, then sinking and ominous. He concentrated on following the sound.

"Major Evans!"

He looked up and into the dense, grey snow. At times the sunlight pierced it and like a mirage or a dream he could make out fleeting silhouettes, zombies, spectres and demons dancing in front of him. They seemed diaphanous. He had never seen such beautiful creatures, he saw eternity reflected in every snowflake, the strange, undulating shapes were creatures of light. He wanted to taste them and stuck out his tongue, cool kisses from transparent ice crystals met him. He could not help laughing as he stood there enveloped in a cloud of whirling stardust. It was as if a membrane between him and eternity was dissolving.

The pain and the cold camouflaged the beauty. He had to suffer to deserve this blissful moment where he could sink into her again. For that reason, and only for that, did he get up again and again.

"Major Evans!"

With every step, with every movement, he sensed nuances in the snow. What had been a monotonous entity, had suddenly come alive to him. Filled with wonder he felt the thin, frozen crust of ice crack open and let him sink into a pillow of soft powder snow beneath. With every step he pierced the virginal surface, there was a crisp crunch as the crust gave way and his foot went through it. It was almost like when you tap your spoon against the layer of burned sugar on the top of a crème brûlée, he thought and laughed.

"Major Evans!"

There she was again, waves of expectation flooded through him.

"Kathryn, here I am!"

"Major Evans!"

He collapsed again. Sad but relieved, he realised that the rasping, cracked voice shouting out to him belonged to Lieutenant Nordahl. Of course it did, no-one else would be calling out to him here.

He crawled towards her voice, every movement an act of contrition and each one more painful than the last.

"Where are you? Major Evans!"

He spotted her through the drifting snow. Surrounded by the white chaos, she looked like a tired child, pale and defeated.

"Where are you, sir?"

He crawled towards her voice.

"Nordahl! I'm here."

The moment she saw him, Ylva threw herself at him and he opened his arms to her.

They hugged.

The wind lashed them with snow, but they continued to cling to each other.

"You found me! You found me!"

Clutching one another, they sought refuge in the other's warmth.

Layer upon layer of snow settled on top of them until they were covered.

46

Inga Marja and her family had put up their *lavvu* to shelter from the storm. The wind was battering the sides of the tent, but inside it was warm and comfortable. They had spread birch twigs over the ground and covered them with reindeer fur. This insulated them against the frozen earth and made the tent feel cosy. Hearth stones in the centre circled a crackling fire, the heart of the *lavvu*.

Over the stones hung a long chain supporting a large pot of *biđos* simmering promisingly. Inga Marja stirred the food while she looked at her family. The steam from the nutritious reindeer stew mixed with smoke from the fire and the sound of contented bubbling. The comfort of the tent, a hot meal and good company was always most welcome when winter storms raged outside.

Inga Marja remembered Ylva as a badly behaved little brat. She really loved that girl. During the period that Ylva and her mother had lived with them, she had spent a lot of time with her cousin. Everyone thought there was something exotic about her and her mother, they had lived abroad and were more cosmopolitan and experienced than the others. But they did not prove to be terribly useful, city girls that they were. Inga Marja felt troubled and conflicted. She would search for Ylva to the extent that was possible, but the area was immense. And if Spetsnaz did not find them first, then the merciless Arctic wind would probably do for them.

She had told the herdsmen and her children about Ylva, her cousin who flew F-16 planes, and they had been star-struck at once. Her youngest daughter had looked up at her mother with a dreamy expression and declared that she too wanted to be a pilot when she grew up. Then you need to clear your plate and do your homework, Inga Marja had smiled. That's what you have to do, if you want to fly a plane. The girl had nodded gravely and polished off her food.

The storm that had been raging and roaring for hours, dropped eventually and turned into a thin whistle ...

Then there was silence.

They listened intently. Yes, that would appear to be the end of this particular snowstorm.

Issàht left the tent to keep a look out.

The break from the constant howling was welcome, you did not realise what an infernal noise the storm made until it subsided.

Issàht stood by the entrance to the tent. He could hear a rumbling sound in the distance. The sound came ever closer and became unmistakable, snow scooters were approaching. Spetsnaz soldiers had been riding around in the storm, searching for the pilots. Now they were under pressure and impatient.

Soon the tent was surrounded by bulky snow scooters and there was no escape. Issàht feared what might happen next and positioned himself protectively between the soldiers and the entrance to the tent.

"*Bores bouton*, can I help you?" he greeted them.

He looked at the men coming towards him, but his friendly smile concealed a lifetime of mistrust of this type of visitor. The leader – he was the youngest, but he had a burning contempt in his eyes, which meant that no-one doubted his authority – looked at Issàht.

"Have you seen these two?"

He showed Issàht pictures on his mobile of Ylva and a man in uniform. Issàht shook his head. At that moment Inga Marja emerged behind him. She squinted against the sharp daylight and stood by his side. She too looked at the photographs, she and Issàht exchanged glances, and she took another look at them. Then she smiled innocently and shrugged.

"No. We haven't seen them. We haven't seen anyone here. Not in this weather."

The Spetsnaz leader pinned his gaze on Inga Marja. He detected some unease and he was not a man easily deceived.

"Could I offer you gentlemen some *biđos*? We've just heated some up," she said.

The leader gestured to his men and Inga Marja's face hardened when the soldiers shoved her aside and flung open the entrance to the tent.

They dragged the herdsmen and the children out and forced them, with Issàht and Inga Marja, down on the ground before pointing machineguns at them. Inga Marja lay still, she could hear one of the herdsmen sob from fear. He was a young lad, this was his first winter on the tundra. He hated school and he loved reindeer, this was his dream. Now he was lying with his face pushed into the snow and the muzzle of a gun against the back of his head.

The soldiers turned everything the Sámi owned upside down. They shouted at each other and screamed at the Sámi lying on the ground.

The sound travelled far across the plains.

Inga Marja hoped that if Ylva was nearby, then she would hear the commotion and keep well away.

When the soldiers failed to find what they were looking for, they started discussing among themselves. The Sámi might have seen something they didn't want to tell them, you could never trust those people. They decided to carry out a body search.

Issàht coughed to attract the soldiers' attention and in that same moment Inga Marja fished the mobile out of her pocket, dug a hole in the snow and dropped the mobile into it. She rolled over, spreading snow across the mobile as she did so. Then she lay still again. She glanced up warily at the men with their machineguns. One of the soldiers had noticed that she had moved and that she seemed nervous.

He came over to her and kicked her ribs hard. She groaned. She was seething with rage, but she managed to stay silent and compliant. He started to search her. Pressing his knee against her neck, he tore off her clothes. Inga Marja lay still, it was hard to breathe and she was scared. One of the young herdsmen jumped up and ran over to help her, but the butt of a gun crunched against the boy's temple and he collapsed unconscious. His blood dyed the snow red.

The Spetsnaz soldiers were thorough as always, but they found nothing.

They disappeared as rapidly as they had arrived.

A little further to the west, three mercenaries from Titans Security crossed the border from Norway into Russia, having picked up a signal. It was faint but unmistakable, and now they were heading across the Russian tundra towards Ymos. The leader of the group had a screen linked to a G.P.S. receiver. He saw a red flashing dot grow ever stronger. They were very close.

47

Ylva and Evans were huddled up in a small cave they had managed to dig out of the snow. Evans had curled up into a foetal position. He was shaking. His voice was thick and he was hallucinating again.

Ylva was holding him and trying to keep him awake, his falling asleep now would be fatal. In a soothing voice she told him stories of the Hyperboreans, the mythical people from the land where the sun never rose in the winter or set in the summer.

"Do you remember Kuiva, the stone giant, the one we saw on the other side of the mountains?"

Evans looked up at her vacantly. He struggled to follow her. What did she want from him? Why couldn't she just leave him alone, let him sleep?

"Do you remember Seydozero, the lake we crossed before we reached the mountains?"

Evans nodded, he could remember the mountains.

"Kuiva was a giant who lived in the mountains by Lake Seydozero. He was supposed to protect the people of the north, but when he robbed and killed one of them, the local gods intervened and burned him with flashes of lightning which came from the water in the lake. It is said that the stone giant in the mountains is Kuiva's charred body." Evans listened to the sound of Ylva's voice, it was as if he was a child again and could relax.

No-one had done that for Evans before, no-one had told him a fairy tale.

"Why did he kill a human being if he was supposed to protect them?" he said, his voice barely audible.

Ylva thought about it, she hesitated, then she laughed.

"I don't remember, it was ... something or other ... no, I don't remember."

Evans was grateful that Ylva was making the effort to distract him because he knew that she knew that he would never now reach the border. His thoughts and the connection between his thoughts were starting to fail. His thoughts took off like herons on broad wings as the morning mist lifts. They bounced around between muddled images of moments he did not know if he had actually experienced or only dreamed.

"Major Evans, you'll make it. We haven't got far to go, we'll get to the border."

He nodded, he was thinking of a sandstorm in Libya, a girl he had kissed at a school prom and a village he had bombed. He thought about burning cities, burning people, burning hatred. He did not feel the cold anymore, he felt warm. He sensed a fluid heat wash over his body. Ylva's voice had stopped and he looked up at her.

"Tell me more, what happened next?"

She did not reply, the expression in her eyes was watchful.

"You're a good pilot, technically you fly well and ... Intuition, you're good ..." Evans lost his train of thought, but Ylva was no longer listening to him.

"I'm sorry that I—"

"Shh!"

Ylva looked hard at Evans and gestured for him to shut up,

then she slid towards the opening of the cave which was now covered with snow. He reached out to her.

"I should have let the plane crash."

Ylva made a sign again for him to shut up and strained to listen.

Outside the cave there was a crunching of light steps on the crisp snow. Someone was out there. Then everything went quiet.

They listened with bated breath, the silence continued and that was, if possible, even more disturbing. Surely they had heard something or someone?

They waited, but the stillness lingered. Sick with fear Ylva scooped out the snow that had filled the opening and soon the bright daylight poured in. She peered at the white landscape where the silent tundra stretched towards the horizon and took a deep breath of clear winter air. There was no-one there.

Just as she felt sure that they were alone, a huge creature appeared, filling the opening. Ylva recoiled, but she had nowhere to flee. She stared stiffly into two shiny yellow predator eyes and a blood-red muzzle. The wolf pushed its head into the opening, and Ylva pressed herself against the furthest wall of the cave.

Right above their heads they could now hear the sound of many paws as the pack of wolves surrounded them. Their leader forced its head further inside the cave and with one paw scraped at the cave wall, scattering snow. Ylva could feel the heat from its breath as the wolf's muzzle swung towards her. She saw glistening as the predator snarled and bared its teeth. Then it snapped at her. Ylva screamed and pulled her legs up underneath her.

Evans tried to focus, he had to think clearly, he had to react. The wolf growled ominously . . .

Ylva kicked out in desperation and the animal retreated. Evans and Ylva each held their breath, but seconds later, the monster returned, snapping at them again.

Evans did not need to think anymore, what use was thinking now? His reflexes took over.

With a roar, he pulled out his knife and threw himself at the opening. The wolf jerked backwards and Evans crawled out of the cave in pursuit of the beast.

Blinded by the white light, he sensed at first only the silhouettes that surrounded him. They crept up on him just like the dark shadows of the men who had dragged him from the wreckage of his plane in Libya. He raised his knife.

"Stand still. Don't provoke them."

Inside the cave Ylva was whispering to Evans as calmly as she could, telling him to stop moving.

But he did not hear her, he did not hear anyone any longer. With a furious scream he lashed out at the wolf.

"Die!"

But the animal dodged his knife and stopped a short distance away, watching him without moving. Evans flailed desperately at the wolves and yelled hoarsely at them, but they refused to let themselves be intimidated. They could smell the adrenaline, the powerlessness and the fear he was exuding. Menacingly they lowered their heads and crept towards him, their yellow-green eyes looking right through him. They lapped up his fear, his desperation and helplessness, it excited their hunting instinct.

Evans stood with both arms hanging limply by his side, he could not reach them, they were too quick.

The leader of the pack lowered her head, the time to kill had come, the prey was ready. She gave a loud growl, and with a single bound she pounced on Evans and sank her teeth into his arm. He stabbed at her in fury and managed a deep cut to her left shoulder. Yelping, she let go of him and retreated, but another wolf soon took her place, a young wolf ready to find its place in the pack. It lunged at Evans, knocking him over, and tore a gash in his neck.

Ylva had crawled out of the snow cave and saw him lying bleeding on the ground, surrounded by the wolves.

"Stay very still," she whispered, "let them sniff you and they might go away."

Evans tried to get up as he stared at the attackers that were circling him ever closer.

"Stay calm. If you move, you'll encourage their instinct to attack."

Evans fought to get up onto his knees.

"Wolves don't usually attack people, unless . . ."

"Die!"

With a demented scream he hurled himself at the nearest wolf, lashing out with his knife. The wolf easily escaped him.

He stumbled, he could hear light steps as the wolves crept closer. He tried to get up one final time, but his injured leg betrayed him and he fell. He lay still and looked up at the jaws snapping at him, rows of teeth snatching slivers of red flesh.

In panic Ylva took the emergency flare from her combat vest and fired it at the wolves. Once, twice, three times. The blood-red balls of fire whizzed into the pack and the wolves retreated. Yelping, they stuck their tails between their legs and ran off.

Evans continued to lie motionless between the balls of fire. Feeling dizzy, he watched the strange sky that now arched over the tundra, it was raining fire.

The Spetsnaz agents and the Titans Security mercenaries also watched the emergency flares as they fanned out across the horizon. Locating the source of the lights was an easy job.

* * *

Inga Marja, Issàht and the herdsmen saw the light. It sparked a hope in them and they jumped on their snow scooters immediately and rode towards the flares.

Ylva crawled forwards and got up on her knees, she trembled as she held Evans. His body was perforated by wolves' teeth and he was bleeding heavily. In the distance she heard a humming sound that grew louder. Ylva looked up, it was a surveillance plane. The Russians must have received reports about a light on the tundra and dispatched a plane with a heat-seeking camera.

Evans opened his eyes and looked beseechingly at Ylva:

"Get back in the cave!"

Ylva started dragging Evans to get them both to safety. Evans screamed from pain and rage.

"Leave me. You get into the cave!"

Ylva refused to listen, she tried to help him stand up.

"We have to . . ."

He cut her off immediately, his gaze was calm.

"That's an order, Nordahl, get into the cave."

The determination in Evans' voice got Ylva's attention, she let go of him and managed to slip into the cave just as the surveillance plane flew over them and caught only an image of Evans lying in the snow.

The Russians reported back to their H.Q.

Only one person had been captured by the heat-seeking camera and the image was surprisingly clear.

"We have identified one of the two N.A.T.O. pilots."

The moment the Russian surveillance plane had passed, Ylva crawled back out to Evans. He was breathing painfully.

"Sir, we need to get going!"

Her voice was shrill and desperate, but Evans barely reacted. Trembling, he took off his wristwatch and gave it to Ylva. She looked blankly at the bloodstained watch that Evans was pressing into the palm of her hand.

"Give it to Kathryn," he whispered.

"Sir, why are you going on about a stupid old watch now?"

Ylva tried to help him to his feet, to make him fight on. They would be there soon, they were so close. Evans clasped Ylva's hand in his.

"Promise me you'll give Kathryn the watch . . ."

Ylva looked down at him, confused.

"Get up, sir! We need to get going!"

Evans made no effort to get up, instead he pulled Ylva close and turned over the watch in her hand to show her the back. Ylva saw that a number had been engraved into the metal.

"Make sure that my girls can access this account. I opened it in Kathryn's name."

Ylva stared down at him, tears were streaming down her face. She had understood, but was not ready to accept what Evans meant, what he wanted. She tugged at him desperately.

"Come on, man, get up!"

But a sense of resolve and serenity had descended on Evans and he let himself sink back into the snow.

"Nordahl, you didn't lose control of the plane," he said.

"What?"

"I took control and I reduced our speed because I could see that the Fullback was accelerating. I knew we would crash. I did it on purpose."

"But . . .?"

"We were supposed to collide and crash into the sea, that was the mission."

Ylva looked at Evans in disbelief.

"What mission?"

"My mission."

"But we didn't crash, we kept flying for almost ten minutes before we were shot down?"

Evans nodded grimly.

"That was my fault, my survival instinct kicked in. I shouldn't have . . ."

Ylva let go of him. She had wondered about this. She had countless times relived the moment before the crash, but no matter how hard she thought, no matter how accurately she had tried to reconstruct the incident, she could not see how she could have caused the crash.

"Why?"

Evans' voice was barely audible.

"*Cui bono?*"

"What?"

"Who profits from war?"

Ylva stared at him with incredulity, he looked twenty years older now than when she met him less than a week ago. She was too tired to respond.

"I'm bought and paid for by George Rove. They needed a war in the Arctic . . . and I gave it to them . . ."

Ylva shook her head, but she did not ask any more questions. It made sense, it explained everything.

"I've completed my mission," Evans said again.

Ylva looked down at him as the shaking and his laboured breathing ceased. Major Evans had surrendered and he felt no more pain or fear.

"Wake up, sir!"

Ylva shook the lifeless body.

"Major Evans. Wake up, damn it!"

He could no longer hear her, he wasn't there. His exhausted body lay still in the snow, the grimace of pain was gone from his face and his lifeless gaze stared past her. His expression was almost relieved. Ylva closed his eyes, let go of him and left him where he was. Then she slipped the wristwatch onto her own wrist. It was up to her now.

The sighting of emergency flares on the tundra was top secret, everyone knew that, including Storm, who learned about it from Ali.

He had reached Rayakoski and was on his way to the border when the encrypted message arrived. Storm rang his superior immediately.

"Ali, tell the Defence Secretary to send a rescue team to the border by Rayakoski."

Ali was taken aback.

"Rayakoski?"

"The Russian intelligence that we've got says the pilots are trying to get to the Pasvik Valley. That's wrong!"

Ali protested, but Storm had no time to explain.

"You have to trust me, send a rescue team to Rayakoski now. Immediately."

He heard Ali rummaging for some papers. He would be making notes.

"I need to get this approved by a senior officer."

Storm said: "No, go directly to the Minister. Above all, make sure that she does not tell General Rove or anyone connected to him that we have located Ylva. Speak to the Defence Minister only."

Ali asked no further questions.

48

On his way into the hangar, Serkin was still thinking about his conversation with Major Khodrokovska. Her words had etched their way into his consciousness.

"Tell the truth, Igor, for our country, for your children and for your own sake."

The words consumed him like bitter poison, they made him feel ill. To his relief, he saw that she was not yet in her office.

But why was he so relieved? Was she talking to someone? What had she decided to do? Now that he thought about it, he could not remember a single day when Major Khodrokovska had not come to work.

She was part of the furniture. Serkin felt a growing unease. Something must have happened for her not to turn up and he had every reason to be worried.

As he walked in, he greeted the flight mechanics as usual, and he noticed that their way of looking at him had changed. Fighter pilots always commanded respect, but this was different, he saw admiration and gratitude in their eyes and he looked away in shame. He could not bear the thought of being mistaken for anyone's hero, it only added to his anguish.

Inspecting the plane was always the day's most important and enjoyable activity, it was like seeing a dear old friend. He knew every nut, every screw and his hand trailed the metal with reverence. He absorbed the strength smouldering in its body.

The first time he sat in a fighter plane, he had realised how its raw strength made him feel almost almighty. But today he felt nothing, the plane was but a pile of heavy, dead metal. He did not know if he would ever experience the intoxication of flying again, and that filled him with sadness.

The Fullback was in tiptop condition, he had no reason to doubt it, yet he felt uneasy as he peered into the cockpit. In brief flashes he relived the moment when his plane had collided with the F-16, the seconds when he had shot down the plane and the grotesque images of children and innocent people being burned alive outside Apatity. Serkin accepted that human suffering was an inescapable collateral damage of war. It was a tragedy, of course, and he was not unaffected by the misery, but that sacrifice would sometimes have to be made in order to prevent a greater tragedy. He also understood that fighter pilots might be given the wrong orders or might themselves make operational errors. That was what happened when you were at war. The suffering and the responsibility that that entailed was something he had taken on with great earnestness. He found serenity in the knowledge that he did what he had to do for a cause greater than himself; he was fighting for his country and his people.

But this was different, they had not been at war, and he knew that the justification for the order to shoot down the N.A.T.O. plane relied on him never telling the truth of what had really happened.

He knew what he had done, and now he saw the consequences for the whole world. The fact that Major Khodrokovska had declared herself willing to assume the blame if he told the truth had made a deep impression on him. She had acted honourably. It was he, Serkin, who was in the wrong.

After Major Khodrokovska had left, he had stayed outside on the balcony, by himself and bitterly cold. The nausea refused to budge, he could not bear to go inside and confront his family's innocent gazes. Their unwavering trust in him made his shame heavier to bear. Finally Natasha had come out on the balcony with a coat.

"Do you want to talk about it?" she had said, handing him the coat. Serkin shook his head, lost and helpless. He continued to stand there, shivering without feeling the cold. Natasha hesitated, should she go back inside and leave him alone? Or should she stay and give him a chance to tell her what was going on?

Because, what was really going on?

In the last few days she had barely recognised him, her husband had become a shadow of himself. They had known each other since childhood and had married after high school. He was the most stable and least capricious person she had ever met. No matter what happened, no matter what he might be worried about, he never showed any sign of anxiety or sadness to her. He had had tears in his eyes when their children were born, but apart from that she had never seen him so emotional, but now he displayed a bewilderment and a despondency which broke her heart.

Serkin was unable to look her in the eye.

Natasha sighed from despair and leaned towards him.

"Talk to me, darling, I'm here for you."

At that very second he was close, so very close to telling her what had happened.

She seemed to sense it and stayed where she was. Their eyes met and Serkin whispered:

"I know."

That was as much as he was able to say.

He knew that he could trust Natasha, she was the rock in his life. Yes, she might be fiery and absent-minded, indeed she was quite chaotic, but above all she was loyal. She looked tenderly at him and waited, but he was unable to return the warmth she was showing him. She realised that she was not going to get through to him now. Whatever it was, he would have to endure it and go through it alone.

"I know that you'll do the right thing, Igor. We love you and we trust you. Always."

She kissed him lightly and went back inside.

As she closed the door, Serkin could feel the cold, it was coming from inside himself. Carrying a secret like this was the loneliest experience a human being could have and he was doomed to suffer it for the rest of his life. He would have to take it like a man and endure this too, it was his duty.

Inside the hangar the alarm went off, the loud ringing snatched Serkin from his melancholy. Soon afterwards the order was issued, and he prepared to get airborne.

49

Soon after the glow from the emergency flares faded on the tundra, three scooters from Titans Security reached the scene. They had followed the light from the emergency flares and the G.P.S. signal, both of which had taken them to this point. Safe in the knowledge that Spetsnaz had been fed the wrong coordinates by Titans' man within the F.S.B., the mercenaries might have an advantage of several minutes. It was enough. They were trained for this and as former Spetsnaz soldiers themselves, they knew both the tundra and the methods of the Russian forces. Titans Security was a global company and it worked with mercenaries from across the world. At times it could be tricky, but being out here on the tundra required a particular skill set which very few people had and which was why, on this occasion, the security company had sent out only former Spetsnaz officers. The men had absolutely nothing on them which could identify who they were, where they came from or who had put them on this mission. If anything went wrong, their presence could not be traced to their employer. They must be invisible, do their job and get out. That was their mission. And if they failed, they knew they were on their own, no-one would miss them or claim responsibility. This was reflected in their generous wages.

* * *

The operation to retrieve the pilots appeared straightforward, given that Titans' own man had a G.P.S. tracker. The fact that his signal had been picked up so close to the border convinced them that the extraction would happen quickly and according to plan. They could get in, carry out the mission and get out in a matter of hours. Whatever happened to Major Evans thereafter was not their business, but they assumed that Titans' "asset management team" would take over and fly him to a secret location where he would be given a new identity and a new job. He was one of them now.

Lieutenant Nordahl was to be executed on the spot and her body left behind. She had served her purpose, which was to guide Evans to the border. The job was clear-cut and the mercenaries felt confident of success; now that they had located the pilots, they could take control of the situation.

But they found no Nordahl and no Evans. The wind had blown away all superficial traces, yet they could still see smears of blood in the ice and snow. One of the mercenaries found a bundle of clothing, it was a U.S. flight suit size 44. The label on the chest read "Major John Evans, U.S. Air Force", and as they cut up the collar of the suit, they found the G.P.S. chip that had been stitched into it.

The mercenaries straightened up, had he taken off his clothes? People dying from hypothermia were known to do this. In which case he must be dead, a naked human being could survive the biting cold on the tundra for a maximum of four to five minutes. They searched the radius Evans would have been able to walk in five minutes, convinced that they would find him frozen to death in the snow. But they found no John Evans. He was gone.

50

The golden eagle flew above the tundra in descending circles. The wind caressed its smooth feathers as it glided through the air.

Ylva looked up and smiled, the mighty bird carried the tundra on its wings. She wanted to fly like that, settle on the wind and circle her prey silently. All ties connecting her to the Earth must be severed because down here everyone died, everything that lived would eventually be eaten or rot. Ylva felt a heaviness and a darkness seep into her. She could not take any more, she wanted only to fly away.

Inga Marja and Issàht had stopped not far away, they could not ride too close to where they had seen the emergency flares because they could see that someone had already beaten them to the location. Spetsnaz could not be far away.

Inga Marja slumped, they were too late, there was nothing more she could do for Ylva. She was filled with horror at the fate awaiting the wolf girl; nothing could save her once she was caught in the claws of human predators.

Issàht scouted across the plain, the light was fading. Soon it would be dark. On the horizon he saw a bird of prey circle ever lower.

It carried a silent message of death and the law of nature.

He straightened up.

* * *

Ylva watched the golden eagle float above her. Its wild, amber eyes were hypnotic and, as if in a trance, she saw herself through the eyes of the predator. She floated above the helpless figure on the ground as she realised that her life was ebbing out of her. She closed her eyes.

Ylva, the eagle can fly higher than any other bird, it looks across the world with eyes that can see in the dark, eyes that can stare right into the sun. It does not yield, it notices everything and everyone. That is why it is the shaman's helper. If you look the eagle in the eye, it will give your soul strength, courage and clarity.

So her mother would have described it. The golden eagle symbolised happiness, at least for some.

When the eagle finally attacked, Ylva reacted on instinct but without strength or purpose. Once when she was a little girl, she had seen an eagle snatch a reindeer, it had been a young one, a calf. With controlled savagery the eagle had pecked away at its prey with its long, curved beak, it kept on stabbing until the reindeer calf stopped wriggling. Then the bird of prey spread its mighty wings. They unfurled like a giant fan and with a jerk the eagle lifted its prey in its talons and flew off with it.

51

For some strange reason Major Khodrokovska felt no fear. It was as if she were watching everything from outside herself, as if she were floating above it all. She had done everything she could, what happened now had nothing to do with her. Her body felt numb, alien almost, the sounds were coming from far, far away. The car door was pulled open and a man dressed in black dragged her out into the snow. In the car she had heard one of the men say that they had found the pilots. Major Khodrokovska felt sorry for them, none of this was their fault.

Passively she let herself be led into the snow, like a lamb to the slaughter. She did not beg for mercy, she did not try to explain what was at stake, men like them would never understand. They followed orders and got their reward. It was nothing personal. She slumped to her knees and as the muzzle of the pistol was pressed against the back of her head, she started to wonder: why did they always shoot people from the back? Weren't they men enough to look their victims in the eye? Did that make them too human? Did that make it too personal?

She knew this type only too well, they wore their coldness and their barbarity like a carapace, like a shield, to guard their quaking, broken little boys' hearts. Who had broken their hearts? Who had hurt them so severely that they had lost their humanity? Deep down, the whole spectrum of violence and weapons were surely just props and rituals used by terrified, disillusioned children pleading for attention. If I can't have your love, if I can't earn your respect or arouse your pity . . . then you must fear me! Look at me, look at me! If you don't want to look at me, then you must feel me, I'm your fear and you must acknowledge me. If your life depends on my will, if you really fear me . . . then you must listen to me, see me, feel me, and I'll be inside you for ever. It's not until then that I exist. Because when you suffer, I have all the power, that's my substitute for all the love I do not have the capacity to earn. Do you see me now?

Major Khodrokovska closed her eyes, there was nothing she could do. The shot echoed across the landscape and her body toppled over as she departed this life. The woman who seconds earlier had been Major Ivana Khodrokovska lay on the ground. But it was as if she were lifted up towards the universe. She knew the way.

52

Ylva was still fighting even though she did not stand a chance. The eagle went on stabbing at her. She instinctively protected her face, but its beak sliced open the skin on her hand and she snatched it away. Ylva looked up and managed just then to catch its wild, demonic gaze one last time. The eagle lifted its head, it scented the air, its pupils narrowed. Then suddenly it released its hold of her and flew up and away.

Ylva could not understand why the eagle had stopped attacking her. Predators like the eagle could not afford too many attacks out here on the tundra, the cold meant that every calorie counted.

What had happened?

Then a loud noise enveloped her like thundering drums of war. Ylva closed her eyes. She was tired. Closer, closer, now there was thumping, the earth was shaking, the air was quivering, finally she was surrounded by chaos and she was carried along with it.

Ylva had lost consciousness when the herd of reindeer came running, the herd split like a river and undulated past on either side of her. She was surrounded by warm, snorting animals, they ran in synchronicity as if they were a flock of birds or a shoal of herring, organised intuitively by unknown forces. Inga Marja and Issàht were driving their sledge in the middle of the herd, the herdsmen were riding snow scooters on the outside to keep the animals together.

The eagle had guided them to the location. When a predator circles ever nearer the ground, it is a sure sign that it has a prey in its sight, it is a sign that all indigenous people recognise. The world is ultimately comprehensible, even if people are not. If you pay attention and understand the signs, you can always trust nature.

Ylva lay still, she lay like a sleeping wolf cub as Issàht lifted her up and laid her on the sledge. He covered her with reindeer fur before he drove the sledge on. The reindeer continued their wild gallop through the icy landscape, just as they had carried souls home since the dawn of time.

Storm had warned them and they had been prepared for the Russian surveillance plane which flew across the herd with its cyclops eye. The heat-seeking camera saw no Ylva, only the heat from more than three thousand reindeer appeared on its monitor. It was not an unusual sight up here in the north at this time of the year. The Sámi tended to round up their herds in order to brand and separate the reindeer. Some would be taken to summer pastures, others would be slaughtered.

The surveillance plane flew on, still hunting the second pilot; the Russians were sure that she must be in this area.

On the other side of the border Storm was peering eastwards; the darkness grew as his hope faded. Finding Ylva out there on the plains would be virtually impossible at night. Exhausted, he leaned back in his car seat and closed his eyes. The silence was total.

When his mobile rang, the noise shook him from his slumber.

"We have her!"

Storm's heart skipped a beat.

"What?"

"We have her."

They were the three most joyful words Storm had heard in all his life. He sat up, he must stay focused, they were not safe yet. The most dangerous stretch was still to come.

53

There was no expression on the Defence Minister's face when Ali passed to her Storm's request.

She listened without interruption while he pleaded with her to send a team to the border at Rayakoski, *without* informing General Rove or N.A.T.O. When she asked him why she should not tell them, he brought up the memory stick they were still trying to decode.

"What memory stick?"

Ali hesitated, he could sense the Defence Minister's resistance and doubt, but he ploughed on regardless.

"We haven't managed to open all the documents yet, but there's already sufficient material to suggest that Major Nordahl, Ylva's father, was offered a job with Titans Security."

The Defence Minister challenged Ali:

"And when did it become a crime for military personnel to seek civilian jobs?"

Ali chewed his lip, then he continued with all manner of prevarications: "As I said, we haven't managed to open everything, but it does look as if Major Nordahl carried out his own private investigation of Titans' activities."

The Defence Minister was impatient. "It is common sense to me to check out a potential employer before . . . "

"Yes, but . . . well, it looks as if he discovered a link between Titans Security and certain terrorist organisations."

The Defence Minister frowned at Ali. She did not like the sound of that.

"When?"

Ali noted her reaction and paused. Then he said:

"In 2001."

The Minister could not hide her exasperation.

"If I had a krone for every fanciful conspiracy theory I've heard about the year 2001, I'd be a rich woman."

The Defence Minister glanced at her watch. She had a meeting shortly and was keen to wrap this up.

"Did he find any damning evidence?"

Ali shook his head.

"I don't know yet. We have one of our best hackers on the case, but so far we've only managed to access some of the files."

"Don't they have more important things to do?"

"Yes, or . . . whoever stored these documents clearly believed their life was in danger should the contents be known."

The Defence Minister heaved an eloquent sigh, and then she stood up to signal that the meeting was over.

"You'll have to ask Major Nordahl to contact me and we can have a talk."

Ali's eyes widened as he looked at the Defence Minister. *Did she not know?*

"That's going to be tricky."

"Why is that?"

"Major Nordahl died, it was said from a blood clot to the brain, the day before he was due to hand his evidence to the Norwegian Defence Command."

The Defence Secretary looked at Ali with disbelief. The story sounded far-fetched, but the man appeared to be utterly sincere.

"How long will it take you to decode this memory stick?"

"Impossible to say, ma'am, but we're working on it."

"Well, right now I'm sure your people have other priorities. We'll have to discuss this later."

Ali got up to leave.

"Thank you, Minister."

He stopped, then looked at her hopefully.

"And Rayakoski? Will you be sending a search and rescue team there?"

The Defence Minister smiled stiffly.

"I will give it serious consideration."

The Defence Minister mulled over her dilemma. A week ago it would never have crossed her mind to take Ali's fantasies seriously, let alone follow his advice, but much had changed since then and now she was having doubts.

What were the possible consequences for Norway?

If she sent in a team without informing their allies and something went wrong with the mission, it would weaken the U.S.A.'s and N.A.T.O.'s trust in and commitment to protecting Norway. She personally would be on the political naughty step for an indefinite period of time, and that could prove awkward. If she dispatched troops without briefing their allies and the mission was a success, it would still be a slap in the face as far as the reputation of the alliance was concerned, and the enemies of the West would have won a victory in the unceasing game of divide and conquer. But if she shared the information with N.A.T.O. and Ali's fantasies turned out to be true and that there were in fact forces in the Allied command group that were willing to sabotage the mission out of self-interest, she would have squandered the only chance they had to prevent a global war at the twelfth hour. The doomsday clock was seconds away from midnight and she had a choice to make.

Ideally troops would be deployed under N.A.T.O. leadership in order to save the alliance, the missing pilots, the truth and the world. This option was indeed the most advantageous, but ... The Defence Minister had a bad feeling about the ways in which events were unfolding, decisions were being taken at a furious pace, important safeguards were being ignored or overridden, and she was sure that something did not add up. However, she regarded it as unthinkable that General Rove might be involved. After all, he was the one who had displayed the greatest composure and willingness to send Russia a moderate response. He had even offered for Titans Security to dispatch anonymous, former Russian elite soldiers to look for the pilots, soldiers who could in no way be traced back to Norway or to N.A.T.O. Norway and N.A.T.O. could not authorise such missions. What he was really offering them was plausible deniability, one of the most cunning weapons of modern warfare.

The situation reminded her of 2011, when the traditionally peace-loving Norway decided by text message to bomb Libya. The rationale for this hasty and slipshod decision was that it was taken on a Friday afternoon and there had not been time to discuss alternative solutions before everyone went off to the pub! She had been working for the U.N. in New York at the time and watched developments at home with horror. How could Norway reconcile its reputation as a peaceful nation with going to war on such grounds? A frustrated African human rights activist she had met during a meeting about aid versus trade, had said that Norway's foreign policy was a bit like helping the bullies beat up the weakest boy in the class, then giving him some money to buy sweets as a consolation. Then again, the Defence Minister thought to herself, it's easy to be wise after the event. Ultimately you had to act on the information available to you. Or, worse, on the information you knew you did not have.

Whether it had been down to wilful blindness or pure ignorance, she had no way of knowing, but what was done could not be undone.

Back then she had been both indignant and outraged, but now she was facing a similar dilemma. She had to unravel the Gordian knot, and time was of the essence.

The priority is to keep the Western defence alliance united, she thought, *we must stand together, nationally and internationally.* The command centre for the operation had been transferred to N.A.T.O. in Brussels, but she was still a part of the team and she was a good team player. Always. So why was she having doubts now? Suddenly she understood bloodlust, the fury that consumes you as you are sucked into the self-perpetuating maelstrom of a conflict. But she stayed calm. She knew what she had to do.

54

"Mines" – the sign was clearly visible behind the electrified barbed-wire fence on the Russian side of the border. It did not surprise Storm that the area between the two borders was mined. It was exceptionally difficult to cross the one hundred and ninety-six kilometre long boundary between Norway and Russia illegally, the Jakob River and the Pasvik Valley providing two natural obstacles, while the land border consisted of a broad security zone, reinforced with electric fencing. Mines had been laid in the security zone between the border fences southwest of the Pasvik Valley.

Storm and Ali had used all their hacking skills to get an estimate of how many mines there were and whether they had been laid in a predictable pattern. Unfortunately, apart from learning that the whole area was peppered with explosives, there was no more specific information to be found. They did not even know whether the minefield was a remnant of the Second World War, at which time the Russians mined the border area as a final farewell to the German forces as they drove them out of the Cola peninsula and East Finnmark in 1945, or if the area had been mined more recently. All they knew for certain was that Ylva would have to cross a minefield in order to reach Norway in safety.

Another challenge was that the fences on both sides of the

border were fitted with sensors which, if touched, would trigger an alarm and attract guards on each side of the border. Which meant that from the moment they cut open the fence so that Ylva could enter the security zone, she had a maximum of three minutes to cover the six- to seven-hundred-metre distance between the fences. She would not have time to think or to make a single mistake. Any error would be fatal.

Storm knew that defending the Russian border was the responsibility of its security service, the F.S.B., and that they patrolled the area regularly. He had managed to get hold of a timetable showing which guards patrolled which sections and when; the only help he could give Ylva was the optimum time for crossing the minefield.

But it was never going to be enough. The women's six-hundred-metre world record was just over one minute and twenty seconds, and that was in rather more favourable conditions. Ylva would have at most three minutes, if she was lucky, but she might be badly injured; the conditions were the worst possible; and she would be crossing a minefield. There was no way they could pull it off. Storm was not sure that Ylva should even attempt it. After almost five days in an Arctic ice hell, not many people would be able to move at all, let alone run six hundred metres through a minefield.

Despondency settled on him like a cloak. It was hopeless. He must not allow Ylva to run the distance between the fences, it would be tantamount to suicide.

But so was staying on the Russian side since it was only a matter of time before she was caught. On his iPad Storm constantly received updates from the Spetsnaz soldiers whose communication exchanges he had hacked. They were heading for the border area south of the Pasvik Valley, they had put two and two together and realised where Ylva was most likely to attempt to cross. The time for hesitation had run out. He had to act.

Six hundred metres, six hundred measly metres lay between him and Ylva, and there was nothing he could do about it. All he could do was watch as she was either captured by Spetsnaz or stepped on a mine.

On the other side of the border Inga Marja had revived Ylva. Now she was wrapped in a warm reindeer jacket and was wolfing down biđos as if it were her last meal. Which it probably was, Inga Marja thought. They had dressed her in Sámi clothing – if they were stopped, they might be able to convince the Russians that she was one of them. Because she was, and she spoke fluent Russian and Sámi. However, Ylva's face was certain to be recognised and Inga Marja knew that Ylva would not survive for very long if she stayed with them.

She was warm again and the food was doing her good. She had to fight back her tears when Inga Marja passed her her mobile and she heard Storm's voice on the other end. It was difficult for both of them, there was no time for them to say what they wanted to say to each other and they grew awkward and formal. Storm had spoken to her plainly as he set out her options.

"Ylva, you'll have to get from the Russian side of the border to the Norwegian side on your own."

She could manage that.

"We're at the security zone, I'm ready," she said.

Storm remained silent. Ylva hesitated, she was sure that he was holding something back.

"Will you be there?"

Storm's eyes filled with tears.

"Yes, Ylva, I'm here."

He was there, he was waiting for her. She could do it, six hundred metres was nothing, she was up for that. There was still an odd silence at the other end.

"But . . .?"

Storm was struggling with himself, how do you tell your beloved that she is doomed?

"Ylva, there's one thing you need to know."

"O.K.?"

"The zone between the border fences is mined."

"Mined!"

How would she cope with that? Shock, rage and fear washed over her, but she kept her voice neutral.

"Do you know where the mines are?"

Storm coughed to clear his voice. "No, we don't."

Ylva slumped, she could not run straight into a minefield. It was madness, like everything else in life.

"O.K.," she said, "I'm good to go."

Storm could not handle her despondency and rang off reluctantly.

Ylva stood in silence, the ground felt unsteady under her feet, her muscles seemed leaden and feeble . . . and her heart was pounding. She was so close that she could see him . . .

Storm rang Ylva's mother. He felt he owed it to her to tell her that they had found her child.

"How are you going to get her across the border?" she demanded to know.

Storm said nothing, but Mary refused to back down:

"You know that the border is mined."

"Yes, I know."

Mary had to sit down for a moment, she had been out with Elle tending to the herd every day to get her mind off everything that was going on around her. Her thoughts had become clear as she rediscovered an ancient calm in nature. She was able to master her feelings and be present in them.

"They used reindeer during the war," she then said.

"What?"

"When people had to cross the minefield during the war, they made reindeer run in front of them to detonate the mines."

Storm looked up, his heart seemed to start pounding like crazy.

He barely had time to thank her for her suggestion before he rang off. This could work – if Inga Marja and Issàht agreed to it. He rang Inga Marja.

She answered his call and as she listened, her heart sank. The reindeer? Would they have to send the reindeer into a minefield only for them to die in terror and pain? Storm explained that it was their only hope.

While she listened, Inga Marja looked across the herd. Every animal was a part of her and her instinct was to protect each one of them. Even though the herd belonged to them, they also belonged to the herd, they were all a part of the circle of life, you only killed a reindeer to end unbearable suffering or for food. People were meant to protect the reindeer and give them a good life, and in return the reindeer gave them their lives. To send these shy, soulful creatures into a hellish war zone was out of the question. They could not do that.

She looked at Ylva, staring ashen-faced at the border fence. A darkness had settled upon her, she was on the verge of giving up.

Issàht walked up to her, put his arm around her shoulder and Ylva slumped heavily against him. Inga Marja knew that this would break her husband's heart, but she also knew that he would understand that it had to happen.

* * *

Minutes later Ylva was ready with her Sámi family on one side of the border and looking towards Storm, who was waiting on the other. He had not heard anything from Ali, which suggested that he had not managed to persuade the Defence Minister to send troops. Ylva walked up to the fence, her gaze fixed on the minefield that separated them. Thick snow covered the ground, the landscape lay apparently virginal at her feet. She looked towards Storm. Six hundred metres, that was all. Inga Marja handed her her mobile, she had Storm on the line.

"Ready?"

Ylva nodded, she did not have a choice.

Without hesitating Storm cut open the fence on the Norwegian side, while Issàht cut open the fence on the Russian side. Inga Marja and the herdsmen started driving reindeer into the minefield. The animals ran into the zone between the fences with Ylva following behind them.

She was in the border zone. At first it was quiet, she could hear nothing apart from light hooves on snow.

Then the first explosion.

A reindeer had stepped on a mine and it detonated with a boom. Ylva was thrown to the ground. Smoke, blood and snow mingled in the air before falling slowly to the ground, covering the snow and her. There was an infernal ringing in her ears and her eyes stung from smoke. Several of the other reindeer panicked and ran back. Ylva curled up and shielded her head as the animals triggered more mines. The ground was shaken by explosions, more blood, soot and smoke poured over Ylva. She got up, disoriented. The ringing in her ears refused to go away, it grew worse and turned into howling.

She saw where the first reindeer had run, and followed its tracks in the snow until she reached the crater.

The first fifteen metres were behind her.

Inga Marja herded more reindeer in between the fences.

Another mine exploded right next to Ylva who had just enough time to throw herself to the ground to avoid the violent pressure wave. Smoke billowed and bloody strips of flesh were scattered before they settled on her like a blanket and an eerie silence wafted towards her. The mines exploded right next to her without making any noise, she felt only the vibrations on the ground, but could hear nothing except an intense whistling inside her head.

In furious glimpses, she saw the reindeer flee as they panicked, as disoriented as she was. It was impossible for her to get her bearings in the chaos, flames from the explosions were lighting up the dense fog of black smoke, but she had lost her sense of direction. Which way should she run?

This is what it's like, she thought, this is war.

After her father's death, her mother and she had gone through his things and, at the bottom of a locked drawer, they had found folders with eyewitness accounts from Kosovo. He had evidently collected reports and video recordings from the Bosnian War which he himself had helped to win. Ylva could not remember him ever talking about that war, he had not really said very much at all after Kosovo, and she had realised that it had been a turning point for him. Up until then everything had made sense, but something had happened in 1999.

Ylva had looked at the photographs and read the horrific descriptions of war. They were appalling, but they had nothing to do with her or her father, it had happened in another world, in someone else's reality. She did not know what he had experienced, it was just something on the news and it was like any other news story of war and misery.

Another mine exploded. Ylva screamed.

Yet again she had this sense of shock. She could cope with the pain, but not the randomness and the not knowing what her next step might lead to. With every breath she was one step closer to her last. This was her worst nightmare, she had always hated being at the mercy of people's twisted whims, their fickleness. She wanted to avoid helplessness and unpredictability more than anything in the world.

Dying would be easier, Ylva thought, because then the struggle would be over. It could stop here. She could choose it now, if she wanted to.

What difference would it ultimately make if she got up and walked through the minefield and just kept walking until the ground exploded and it was her blood raining down over the snow?

Storm was standing on the other side, watching the inferno in the border zone. He saw Ylva slump to her knees in the middle of the chaos. Feeling desperate, he forced his eyes away from her and started to study the configuration of exploding mines. He also noticed places where there were no explosions. A pattern was emerging, surely?

Not far away a fighter plane flew low across the ground. It was Serkin's Fullback approaching the border zone from the Russian side. He felt his pulse rise, the N.A.T.O. pilots were on the border by Rayakoski and his order was to shoot to kill. They must not get out to Norway.

Storm heard the plane before he saw it, but even so he still turned his attention back to the mines exploding between him and Ylva. He could not be sure if the pattern went all the way to the Norwegian side because no reindeer had survived the stampede this far, so he would have to trust his calculations.

He took his first step forwards. No explosion. He took another step. Nothing.

Serkin could see Ylva and Storm in the minefield as he flew over them. His heart sank when he saw her, so that was her, the pilot who had taken part in the dogfight, she was the one who had triggered his bloodlust. A tall man was walking towards her, was he the other pilot? Had he walked out here with her? Igor reported his observation and was given orders to fire immediately.

Serkin flew over their heads. Storm tried to signal to Ylva where to walk, but she could not hear him. However, she was able to see the mine craters in the churned up ground that lay between them. She looked up as Storm continued to walk across the minefield towards her, and got to her feet. Desperately she started throwing herself from one crater to the next.

Serkin turned the plane around. This was his chance, he could put an end to the nightmare now. Adrenaline made him totally calm, the target was in sight and he was locked on target.

He got ready to fire.

Ylva was swaying from exhaustion. In short, flickering glimpses as if she were bathed in manic strobe lighting, she saw Storm shout and point towards the Norwegian border as he ran towards her.

He came, she thought, he came.

A mine exploded and covered the area between them in smoke. Everything turned black.

Serkin swore, he couldn't see a thing. He would have to turn again and make another approach. He flew back. The target would still be within reach once the smoke had cleared.

Storm took a chance and ran the last few metres towards Ylva.

He found her standing in the middle of the smoke, she stared up into the air, stunned, had she heard a plane?

He grabbed Ylva's hand and despite the thick smoke, he was able to make out his own tracks in the snow, tracks that would guide them back to the Norwegian fence.

Ylva was trapped in a hell of indecision. She did not want to go on. Storm fixed her with his gaze.

"Trust me."

She felt her reluctance, she did not want to.

"Trust me," he said again.

She nodded.

Without further hesitation they clung to one another as they ran back in the tracks that Storm had made in the snow on his way into the minefield towards her.

Serkin kept his finger on the trigger, he saw Ylva and Storm run like shadows in the smoke that covered the minefield, they were now on the Norwegian side of the border zone, but so far no reindeer had survived long enough to detonate mines there.

He let his finger glide along the trigger . . . now he had them in his sights, this was the one chance he had to save his honour and bury the lie once and for all.

A new serenity filled him, a certainty, a crystal-clear certainty. But it was more than that, he felt joy, a profound sense of joy. He took a deep breath. How wonderful. For the first time since the nightmare started, he was able to take a deep breath and let it fill him.

Mines were still detonating on the ground, but he could make out the outline of Ylva, now he had her. Waves of relief turned into focused calm.

"I know you'll do the right thing, Igor. We love you and we trust you. Always."

Major Khodrokovska's voice from earlier that morning filled him, he could feel her presence now.

He knew that she meant it. They trusted him as he trusted them. The thought was endlessly clarifying; of course. This was what it was all about. Trust. That was why this nightmare had hit him so hard, he had broken their trust.

But they could trust him now, he was trustworthy, that was all he needed to know. Serkin firmly drew his finger ... away from the trigger and let the plane pass over Ylva and Storm as they ran in panic through the minefield.

Storm and Ylva heard the deep roar of the Russian fighter jet flying low above them one last time before it disappeared into the smoke and headed away across the Russian tundra.

Serkin flew from the chaos and into the blue darkness of night. He was no longer scared because he had nothing to hide, nothing to fear. He was on his way home.

55

It had been a close call, but General Rove could finally breathe a sigh of relief; the crisis had been averted and the world had started to settle down. He had had some extremely tough days after the return of Lieutenant Nordahl, her report had been highly ... how could he put it ... unhelpful. It did no-one any favours for Major Evans' confused ramblings to be made public, and it had cost Rove considerable resources and political capital to put a lid on the accusations, specifically about Titans Security and his own role in the F-16 incident.

It was also unfortunate that Titans' somewhat unconventional customer base had been made public. The public refused to understand that the world was not a fair place and that in his line of work you could not simply do business with the good guys. In the real world, everything was about domination and access to resources, everyone was fighting for their place in the food chain, people were predators and like everywhere else in the animal kingdom, you had to choose between eating or being eaten. It was too late to be a bleeding heart liberal now. That ship had sailed as far back as 1961 when Dwight D. Eisenhower warned against the unjustified influence of the military-industrial complex. A very young, idealistic George Rove had listened to the outgoing president's warning, but as he had watched people plunder and slaughter each other while depleting the earth's resources, he had come to the conclusion that life was a zero-sum game. There were only winners and losers. He chose even at that early age to be a winner.

Power follows money and money follows power, it was a closed system with room for a decreasing number of people. General Rove did not make the rules, but he was damned good at playing the game. Information about the flow of money from various tax havens to Titans Security and to him personally had been made public. Thousands of documents linking the company and again him personally to terrorist groups and criminal networks had been leaked online. It did not look good. They had to undertake a full damage limitation exercise, obviously. He had faced the media and heads of state like a shameful schoolboy and undertook that the company's internal routines for background checks of potential clients would be reviewed; Titans Security must come across as if they were in favour of full transparency. Today's political climate demanded this.

Whenever the moral outcry and clamouring voices demanded proof that the big boys took the situation seriously, someone had to be sacrificed. Heads would have to roll at every level, and the hunt for scapegoats was already in progress.

"Kill them with confusion" – the only strategy that worked was information dominance. So staff had been sacked and information leaked about who had made errors and when. The media bought it and their spotlight was diverted away from him, from his shareholders and clients, to systemic errors and a few incompetent middle managers who would appear to have been asleep at the controls.

Now he was seated in the front row at the press conference, watching N.A.T.O.'s Secretary General step onto the podium. He registered that the man had beads of sweat along his upper lip and was clearly affected by the situation as he stiffly read out a statement Rove had helped to word. War had been avoided and the peace was won, the relief in the room was tangible and palpable.

56

Ylva had watched the press conference and subsequent media coverage from her hospital bed with a growing sense of disbelief. After the press conference, the story of Major John Evans was broadcast on a loop on every channel. N.A.T.O.'s F-16 and the Russian Fullback had clipped one another during a buzzing incident and the villain was Major Evans, an unstable N.A.T.O. pilot who had made a mistake.

How could they spin the story in that direction?

Cui bono? Who stood to benefit?

No-one seemed to care about the truth. Storm had found evidence that the F-16 incident as well as the cyber-attack on Norway and the murder of Galba had all been carried out by Titans Security's subcontractors. The strategy was as brilliant as it was tried and tested. Stage a horrific spectacle of violence to make the public demand that the state demonstrates its power and willingness to act.

People demanded security. At the same time all political leaders knew that no-one could hope to win a third world war. The ability to annihilate your opponent was total on both sides. Outsourcing war was the new trend.

The problem was that when Storm tried to prove Rove's and Titans' part in this, the cover-up was already in progress. Norway's Defence Minister had given Rove access to all the information she had got from Ali and, hey presto, the files on the memory stick, which Ylva's mother had given Storm, were gone. What did not disappear, but was instead exaggerated, was the story of the tragic Major Evans and his mental breakdown. The crash and his captivity in Libya, his P.T.S.D. diagnosis, his serious addiction issues and the violent attack on his wife were dissected in full public view. The strain of his experiences in Libya had become too much for him, it was said, N.A.T.O. should not have allowed him to work as an instructor. Allegations that "someone" had paid him to bring about the incident with the Russians were too absurd to be publicised. They collapsed under their own implausibility.

Both the Russian president and N.A.T.O.'s Secretary General appeared satisfied with this ending of the crisis. They had each emerged stronger from the episode. They had maintained calm and contributed an astonishing and not unsatisfactory outcome given how close to Armageddon the world had come. The world would keep on spinning on its axis – for now.

Epilogue

The air was quivering with heat when Ylva and Storm climbed out of their rental car in Texas. Mother and daughter were expecting them and were waiting outside as they drove up in front of the small house in the middle of nowhere.

John Evans' daughter recognised Ylva immediately as she got out of the car together with a tall man. She had seen her on T.V. and on the Internet. Everyone knew who Ylva Nordahl was, just like everyone, sadly, also knew who her father was. He was a memory they would have to live with.

Minutes later the broken old wristwatch lay in the girl's delicate palm, its hands frozen in time. Ylva watched the child as she carefully closed her fingers around the old watch and pressed it to her chest. Her lips trembled and her eyes welled up with tears of bravery.

The girl's broken heart pounded, but she said nothing, she could not get a word out, they all stuck in her throat. She swallowed her grief in silence, she did not want to cry in front of her mother and the strangers. The hands had stopped at 09.13 and Leah did the maths. She would have been fast asleep when her dad's plane crashed in Russia, there was a time difference of seven hours between Norway and Texas, not that it mattered. The watch told the truth, it told her clearly what she already knew. Her dad was gone for ever, he was never coming home. Time had stopped at that point. Life would never be the same again, although everything carried on as before.

Leah and Kathryn listened as Ylva told the story of how John Evans had fought to get back to Norway to be able to return to them. Her mother wept, but Leah continued to sit immobile.

It felt like such a long time since she last knew the man Ylva was describing, she had struggled to remember her dad and now he was gone. Ylva asked her mother to make a note of the number engraved on the back of the wristwatch, she believed it to be a bank account. The money in it would apparently take care of them, she said, Evans had seen to that. He had looked out for them at the very end.

Ylva stared at Leah as if she knew her, as if the two of them shared an unmentionable secret.

"My dad died when I was your age," Ylva said. "They died for the same reason, but in different ways."

Leah could feel a cold emptiness take over. She refused to believe it, it wasn't true, her dad was not dead, she could feel it, he would come home to them soon. He would walk through the door, laugh out loud, and swing her round until her body tingled right down to her toes.

"I'm so sorry for your loss," Ylva said.

What else could she say?

Leah could not bear to listen any longer. The smile and the kind words were meant to be comforting, she understood that, but they only made her angry. She clutched the old wristwatch even harder to her chest, it felt cold and alien in her hand. In brief flashes she remembered her dad: he ran through the forest, he chopped wood and carried logs inside for the fire, he stirred food on the cooker, he massaged her mum's feet when they watched television, he fixed the sink, he ran her bath, he put together the fishing rod. She remembered his hands, his eyes, and his voice.

But his warm smile when he tucked the duvet around her at night and those big bear hugs of his, she would have to forget. If she didn't, she would never be happy again.

Kathryn collected herself, then she fetched a big jug of lemonade and four glasses. And so they sat on the porch while the air quivered hot above the lifeless desert that crawled towards the house to which John Evans would never return.

Ylva's story of how he had talked about them and yearned for them until the very end, warmed them long after the sun had gone down. They stayed on the porch after the words had dried up and there was nothing more to say. Silently the dark sky above the house was speckled with tiny dots of light.

The desert sand shimmered white in the pale moonlight and Ylva's thoughts returned to the tundra. I'll take care of it, John, she thought, and I won't ever forget. This isn't the end, it's just the beginning.

Confessions of an Author

Having written and directed films and TV programmes for more than twenty years, the transition to literature has proved quite refreshing. I believe it was Hemingway who said that if a movie is a stock cube, then a book is an ox. I would agree with that because a book can contain so many more levels of fiction than a film script.

Mayday takes as its starting point the growing risk that a geopolitical conflict between Russia and N.A.T.O. could start in the Arctic. The idea came to me during the filming of the movie "Operation Arctic". We were standing on the runway at Bodø airport where we were filming during a N.A.T.O. exercise and nearby a group of F-16 planes were taking off, one behind the other. Bodø was full of fighter pilots taking part in the exercise and I ended up chatting to some of them. They talked about tense buzzing incidents with Russian fighter planes on the border with Russia, and I thought . . . what if there was a crash?

While writing this book I have received invaluable help from several people and it has been an adventure in itself to listen to and learn from some of Norway's foremost experts in their respective fields.

First of all I would like to say a big thank you to my editor, Knut Gørvell, who with stoic patience has followed the script from its tender beginning to the book you now hold in your hands.

After my brief conversations with N.A.T.O. pilots in Bodø, whose names I sadly don't remember, the eminent brothers, Ulf and Bjørn Sverdrup, entered the scene. Both are wise and experienced in precisely those areas where I had the most to learn, and they gave me inspiration and suggestions that put the book on the right track. Former head of the helicopter section at Norway's air traffic control and helicopter pilot in the Norwegian Armed Forces, Geir Hamre, also contributed as a sparring partner early on in the process. Geir had just made a major contribution to the movie "Operation Arctic" and has been generous with good advice in connection with *Mayday*.

When Knut Gørvell introduced me to one of my great heroes among authors, Torkil Damhaug, to be my literary consultant, I must admit that I was humbled and nervous. But Torkil's goodwill and wise guidance, both at the book's tender start and also now that it is finished, has raised the quality of the final result considerably. I am a literary novice and I could have had no better mentor. Thank you also to my editor-in-chief Mariann Fugelsø Nilssen, the editor of Krimklubben Anja Rålm, head of design Miriam Edmunds, and everyone at Cappelen Damm Publishing for their heartfelt support, confidence and trust.

Furthermore, I want to thank one of Norway's greatest Russia and Putin experts, Bernhard Mohr. His thorough reading of the script and his constructive comments have been an invaluable help. At the twelfth hour I also benefited from insightful contributions from Hans-Wilhelm Steinfeld, no less, who inspired me to highlight the risk of a simple misunderstanding potentially leading to a nuclear war. A striking example of this was the incident which was so wisely averted by Stanislav Petrov in 1983, described in Steinfeld's book *Putin*, and which I refer to in *Mayday*.

I have enjoyed enormously filming in the Sámi village of

Kautokeino over the years, both for N.R.K. and for foreign production companies. The landscape, the culture and the people of Sápmi have made an indelible impression on me, and I believe that we need to protect and listen to the wisdom that the world's indigenous people preserve. I would like to thank my dear friend Mary Sarre, who has shared her own experiences of Sámi life and invited me to a series of inspiring performances by Beaivváš, the Sámi National Theatre. A big thank you also to one of Sápmi's and Norway's most prominent *joik* singers and cultural ambassadors, Sara Marielle Gau Beaska for the insights she has given me.

My heroine, Ylva Nordahl, is something as rare as a female F-16 pilot, and as part of my research I had great fun talking to one of Norway's two female F-16 pilots, Major Marianne Mjelde Knutsen. I must admit to being a little starstruck because she is a legend. I have also received additional help with F-16 planes from the Norwegian Armed Forces, but if any technical errors have crept in nevertheless, that is entirely my fault.

Although my intention was for the book's plot to reflect today's reality, I have also taken artistic licence where I believed it to be necessary. In the art of storytelling the relationship between fact and fiction is constantly debated, but I align myself with the poetic licence of fiction, which gives the author room for manoeuvre beyond the purely documentary. Last but not least, I want to thank my boyfriend, Torben Snekkestad, who has read countless versions of the script. With eagle-eyes, he has commented and corrected like a boss! Torben has lived with Ylva, John, the ferocious Arctic conditions ... and me ... for quite a long time now. I admire his patience and attention to detail, and I am infinitely grateful for his wholehearted support. Hopefully he won't get rid of us for quite a while yet.

I am delighted and honoured that you have all given me your

time and knowledge. Thanks to your help, as well as support from family and friends, *Mayday* will now finally see the light of day. It is said that "writing a film script is like swimming in a bathtub and writing a novel is like swimming in the sea". With *Mayday* I now declare myself officially launched!

Grethe Bøe, 6 December 2020